OPPORTU... FUTUR...

"On an exceptionally hot eve...   ...uly a young man came out of the garret in whic... ...ged in S. Place and walked slowly, as though in hesi... ...on, towards K. bridge. That might be the subject of a new story, but our present story is ended."

— F. DOSTOYEVSKY, *CRIME AND PUNISHMENT*

"I have never begun a novel with more misgiving. And however superciliously the highbrows carp, we the public in our heart of hearts all like a success story; so perhaps my ending is not so unsatisfactory after all."

— W. S. MAUGHAM, *THE RAZOR'S EDGE*

"In my younger and more vulnerable years my father gave me some advice that I've been turning over in my mind ever since. So we beat on, boats against the current, borne back ceaselessly into the past."

— F. S. FITZGERALD, *THE GREAT GATSBY*

"This is the saddest story I have ever heard. She was quite pleased with it."

— F. MADOX, THE GOOD SOLDIER

"All this happened, more or less. One bird said to Billy Pilgrim, '*Poo-tee-weet?*'"

— K. VONNEGUT, *SLAUGHTERHOUSE-FIVE*

"The past is a foreign country; they do things differently there. But I didn't, and hardly had I turned in at the lodge gates, wondering how I should say what I had come to say, when the south-west prospect of the Hall, long hidden from my memory, sprang into view.

— L. P. HARTLEY, *THE GO-BETWEEN*

"All children, except one, grow up. When Margaret grows up she will have a daughter, who is to be Peter's mother in turn; and thus it will go on, so long as children are gay and innocent and heartless."

— J.M. BARRIE, *PETER PAN*

"It was a pleasure to burn. When we reach the city."

— RAY BRADBURY, *FAHRENHEIT 451*

"A story has no beginning or end; arbitrarily one chooses that moment of experience from which to look back or from which to look ahead. I'm too tired and old to learn to love, leave me alone for ever."

— GRAHAM GREENE, *THE END OF THE AFFAIR*

"I have never seen anything like it: two little discs of glass suspended in front of his eyes in loops of wire. This is not the scene I dreamed of."

— J. M. COETZEE, *WAITING FOR THE BARBARIANS*

WE SLEPT IN WHAT HAD ONCE BEEN

THE GYMNASIUM

ARE THERE ANY QUESTIONS?

Exercises in Literary Taxidermy

SHORT STORIES

MARK MALAMUD

for Ann and Dan

.

THE GYMNASIUM

First Regulus Press printing January 2018
Signal Library 00-7102-72-21

Regulus Press, Seattle WA
www.regulus.press

ISBN: 0999446207
ISBN-13: 978-0999446201 (Regulus Press)

Sometimes just one time can be enough.

— Marion Crane, *Psycho*

CONTENTS

Introduction

"We slept in what had once been the gymnasium," she said.

"Uh-huh," I replied. It was early Sunday morning. Like, before noon. So cut me some slack. I wasn't feeling particularly articulate.

"No, really. It's perfect."

I rolled over. Cracked open an eye. "What are you talking about?"

"For the collection. It's perfect. The perfect title. The first line is both meta and metaphoric. And the last line demands a search for context and meaning."

I sat up. I mused (as best as I could — it was early).

"Hmm," I answered. "It's a bit long, isn't it?"

"Pffft," she said.

So, welcome to *The Gymnasium*, nineteen stories built around a common theme — theft. They were written (mostly) between 2003 and 2006, and each began with an act of plagiarism: grabbing the first and last sentences from someone else's work (often a novel, sometimes a short story), and then using those lines as an explicit frame; that is, as the first and last sentences of a new and original story. The idea was to forget the source material (as much as possible), and to treat these first and last lines as my own.

So the unifying theme of these fictions isn't love, or death, or (given the title) weight-lifting or spinning. And, ok, it's not really plagiarism, either. The theme is the process — the process of taking ownership of someone else's words, of interpreting (or re-interpreting) them, of finding one's own narrative within their boundaries. The resulting stories are eclectic, to say the least.

I used to call these my Frankenstein fictions — since they were stitched together quickly from previously-existing work. But really it's more an effort of literary taxidermy than artificial reanimation. These stories may be contained by their first and last lines, but it's the stuffing that counts. It's like moving into someone else's space. It's like sleeping in what *used to be* the gymnasium.

After each story, you'll find a short note that includes the source of the story's first and last lines, the approximate date of composition, and a few random thoughts concerning the work — at least as well as I can remember, ten or more years on. (Middle-aged memory is a *bitch*.)

For example, here's the note for this introduction:

INTRODUCTION
First and last lines from
The Handmaid's Tale by Margaret Atwood.

When I sat down to write this introduction, I thought, "Wouldn't it be cool to write the introduction the same way I wrote all the stories?" Well, *that* was a stupid idea. Really, did I need to make this any more difficult to pull together?

Written on 30 September 2017

OK, that should be enough before we get started. Are there any questions?

Mark Malamud
30 September 2017

Beatrice Dalle

THE SCENT AND SMOKE AND SWEAT of a casino
are nauseating at three in the morning. Take my word for it.
It's worse than the geriatric tourists that roll in every
morning at eight in their polyester pantsuits, covered in
croissant crumbs and dappled with grapefruit juice; worse
than the noon-time businessmen with their rumbling
stomachs who regularly skip their lunch for a few desperate
turns of the wheel before racing back to their routine
occupations; worse than the late-afternoon delinquents and
swindlers and cheats in their cheap Italian shades and ten-
year-old suits; worse even than the after-dinner crowd, who
arrive during the so-called "prime-time" of the casino, when
every table has its share of dabblers and dilettantes, when
you can close your eyes and smell the shampoo and talc-y
make-up, the musky aftershave and "fruity" perfume, not to
mention the inevitable volley of after-dinner burps and farts
that pop and splatter from the baccarat tables in the *Salles
Brizet* to the slot machines in the *Salon de l'Europe*.

(When I first started here four years ago I was so naïve
and wide-eyed and enthusiastic that I thought those burps
and farts must be some sort of secret communication *sous-
table,* from player to player, a gambler's Morse code used to
cheat the house. What a dopey girl I was then!)

No, the best time of day for a Monte-Carlo casino is
from ten p.m. to sometime before two, when the elderly
have long gone to bed, the struggling businessmen and
women have returned to their unhappy families, the thugs
are off strong-arming their neighbors, and the dilettantes

have moved on to the parties farther up the coast in *Villefranche sur Mer* or Nice. This is the time of day when the truly adventurous players arrive, the sanguine men in their mid-thirties, well-tailored with cold grey-blue eyes, their bodies snapping with electricity, and the women, usually a bit younger, physically-fit, with an exciting feral scent and dressed to kill. These are the high-stake players, the *very* high stake players, who often have as much at risk on the table as off. They are serious, aggressive, successful, and in love with the sport. They come in after ten, but are out the door by two, win or lose. This is the time I most enjoy, this is the time when I like to hear the roulette ball whiz around the rim, when I listen for each gasp or short breath, when I can smell the pure animal sex on every man and woman, when the special language of the casino comes to life, each "*banco*!" or "*carte*!" spoken with authority and aplomb. The time of day when there is no distinguishing risk and reward.

But at three a.m., when the carpets are stained with alcohol and nicotine, and when the casino is littered with these hollow-eyed gamblers, drifting from table to table like nomads, falling deeper and deeper into debt, lonely and forlorn, who stay because there is simply nowhere else to go — all those whom Michelin calls "the leftovers" — that's when the casino's aroma becomes intolerably sad. It makes me sick.

Luckily I don't have to stay here for long. Michelin's gone home with that French girl Marissa again (second time this week!) and he's left me here on my own, and when he's away, I can hang out as I please, roam the floor, sniff out trouble if I want, or — as is my wont tonight — just turn my back on the scam artists and cheats and take a break. And truthfully, at this hour, the scam artists and cheats are so pathetically obvious, I feel comfortable leaving that job to the Security night shift, two young Frenchmen named Barthes and Honoré.

(It wasn't always that way, of course. I used to be as stupid as they come. My first two years in Monaco I had no job, no home. I was living on the streets. Eating things you couldn't imagine. And too wild for my own good. I don't know what would've become of me if I hadn't run into Michelin that night on the beach. I needed rescuing and he took me in. He fed me, housed me. Straightened me out. Turned a wild animal into a team player. I'll never forget that. He's the best friend I've ever had.)

Anyway, it's been a strange day. I need some time to relax, to collect my thoughts, and to make some sense of the past eighteen hours.

I head out through the Atrium — a magnificent vestibule featuring columns supporting a gallery with balustrades — and move across the casino to the southern veranda. Out here, there's a cool breeze blowing, which is nice, considering how hot and humid it's been the past week, and there's a clear view over the dark blue water of the Mediterranean, about a half-kilometer away.

The *Casino de Monaco* is no *Casino Royale*, but it's still one of the top-ten casinos along the coast, with forty roulette tables, twenty baccarat and *punto banco* tables, as well as areas for blackjack, craps, slot machines, and even video poker. The casino clears something like twelve million French francs a day — that's about 1.8 million Euros, still less than one-third of what *Casino Royale* pulls in, but it's respectable.

Personally, I don't understand gambling. It seems like a waste of time and energy, and it seldom produces happiness. I'm a pretty simple girl when it comes down to it. I'm more than content with two meals a day, a steady job, and the company of friends. I don't understand the driving need for risk. And I'm never greedy, except maybe certain times a year when it comes to sex. But even then, I'm not picky, and I'm as happy with one horndog as the next, so my stress level is low; and after a rousing screw (on a bed, on a floor, on a carpet, on the grass — I'm not picky about location either), I've pretty much got a smile glued to my face for the rest of the day.

But enough about me. A couple has just come down the curving marble steps that connect the veranda to the *Salle Blanche* upstairs. I look up briefly — they're a middle-aged pair, and well-groomed — but I'm happy to ignore them if they'll ignore me.

"Ah, Honoré's just found you," the gentleman says, stepping up to me. His wife leans forward and whispers, as if it's a secret, "I think he's trying to decide whether to call Michelin, or wait until he returns."

I'm confused. Do I know these people? I look more closely, but nothing rings a bell. He is in a cheap tuxedo, she is in a knock-off gown. They both have these funny scars across their faces, like spider-webs, which would be memorable, I suppose, if I had ever seen them before. They look like your average "prime-time" couple, which is a little odd only because it's three in the morning. But, then, it's been that sort of day.

"Who's trying to call Michelin?" I ask.

"Honoré," the husband says, as if it's obvious.

"Why?"

"I suspect he's been out in the bushes. Near the side entrance."

I shake my head. It's a conversation, and admittedly I'm not very good at conversation, especially with anonymous patrons, but this *tête-a-tête* seems particularly inscrutable, so I just try to be polite. "Well, you can tell Honoré I'm here, if you'd like."

That seems to satisfy them, and they both nod and drift back into the casino. — And that's exactly what I'm talking about. Weird shit like that. It's been going on all day, practically from the moment I showed up for work....

I'd arrived at the casino early that morning, just behind Michelin. The rent-a-cops were already in place of course

— they're on duty 24/7 — but the other members of the morning Security team — Leon Färber and Nik "The Fist" Koch — both tall, German, and angry — wouldn't turn up for another hour or so, at nine. The first busloads of geriatrics had already arrived, bussed in from the Monaco Hilton. I went off on my own and started sniffing the tables, looking for trouble. I didn't expect much — the mornings are usually quiet — but today turned out to be different.

I noticed something was wrong right away. Michelin always said I had a nose for crime, and he was right — my nostrils started twitching as soon as I approached the second craps table in the *Salle Benetin*. I could smell something sour, literally sour, and in my book, that meant someone was nervous, maybe *too* nervous, and that could mean trouble. I approached the table from the far side, away from the croupier, and made my way around slowly. There were seven people playing.

The first two players were your typical "greys" — that's Michelin-speak for the seriously elderly, the threshold-of-death types, who frequented the casino with surprising regularity and almost always traveled in pairs. Practically somnambulant, these two were typical, a man and a woman, probably husband and wife, sitting close together, leaning on one another for support, while in-between them, under the table, was a small oxygen tank on a dolly with two feeder lines leading up to plastic masks strapped to their sad and sagging faces. And although their breathing sounded like Darth Vader, I didn't think they'd cause the casino any trouble. (Unless they actually dropped dead — although even then, it's not the kind of trouble I worry about.)

The third player was solo. She looked slightly younger than the greys, and in much better health. She was dressed in white pants and a sweater with blue and white stripes — some sort of nautical theme. She also had her dog with her, a female Chihuahua, yapping away at the end of a rhinestone-studded leash. I did my best to ignore the pet, which, to be honest, wasn't hard. I can't stand lapdogs, especially on a tether. Of course, that didn't mean she was going to ignore *me*, and she didn't, sniffing and growling — doing her best to jump up and smell my butt, I guess. But I didn't get any suspicious vibes off either of them, so I continued my way around the table.

The fourth, fifth, and sixth players formed their own troika. Three women, comfortably middle-aged, obviously close friends, probably old friends. They couldn't stop giggling. I suppose it was possible they could be planning something — some middle-aged players were into simple cons — but I was willing to bet that whatever they may have gained in wisdom over the years they had lost in ability.

Then I got to number seven. He stood out from the others like a blackjack draw on eighteen. He was young, dressed in jeans and a denim button-down shirt, over which he wore a black windbreaker. He was thin, probably under 150 pounds, and he kept shifting uncomfortably on his stool. I was willing to give him the benefit of the doubt, but the guy was a veritable sweat factory of fear. I saw right away how he used only his right hand to move his chips on and off the table, but kept his left fixed in the pocket of his windbreaker. I could see his fingers working something in that pocket. He might have looked straight from the croupier's point of view, but he looked perfectly crooked from where I stood.

The croupier passed the dice to him and he pulled his left hand out of his pocket so that he could cup the dice in both hands. As he did this, his right elbow nudged his drink — not enough to topple it, but enough to make even his senescent neighbors start. Then, taking the dice in his right hand, he brought his fist up to his mouth and blew for good luck.

I grinned — he didn't know how badly he'd need that luck in a few minutes.

His move was smooth, I'll give him that, with a well-played misdirection, and as I watched his left hand return to his left pocket *with our dice*, I marveled at the ease of the switch, and the daring. We don't often get cheats bringing in loaded dice; it's just not an easy scam. The switch can be difficult enough, but the real challenge is getting hold of a good pair of loaded dice in the first place. Casino dice are manufactured to 1/5000th of a centimeter and changing their load — the weight of the fill used to plug the small dimples drilled out for the spots — is more art than science; plus, in our casino, each die has its own fingerprint, a serial number hidden underneath one of its spots.

The cheat threw his first roll, and I left the table to look for Michelin. I found him near the bar, busy chatting up that young waitress, the French girl named Marissa. It was easy enough to get his attention, though; he could tell that I was agitated and business came before pleasure. Michelin notified the rest of Security that something was up, then he followed me straight to the craps table in the *Salle Benetin.*

When Michelin strode into the room, the crowd parted, like leaves blown out of the path of an oncoming truck. At over six feet and two-hundred-sixty pounds, I guess that's not surprising. I led him to the craps table and he stood back a second, getting a fix on the situation. He spotted the trickster right away. When the two rent-a-cops appeared, Michelin leaned right into the guy's personal space, signaled the croupier to halt play, and examined the dice. What followed was controlled, violent, and over quickly.

Understand: Michelin's a dangerous guy. Born and raised just outside Dabou in the *Cote d'Ivoire*, he learned to survive on the streets of a city slowly deteriorating into a police state. He was fifteen when he fled to Paris, settling in Pigalle, and earning his keep first by petty theft, then robbery, then extortion. He broke plenty of arms and legs. He broke a guy's neck when he was seventeen, but he got lucky: some cop took an interest, and after just four years in prison in Vézelay, he was back in Paris at the American University, studying casino management, and making honest money boxing and bouncing. His first real job was

working security at the *Casino Biarritz*, a small casino in the
south-west of France, and he quickly made a name for
himself as being smart and tough. Three years later, and
about five years ago, he got the position of Head of Security
here at the *Casino de Monaco*. Now he makes good money,
leads a staff of six (not including the two-dozen or so rent-
a-cops), speaks three languages without an accent, wears
these light cream suits which accentuate his dark black skin,
smokes a lot, drinks a lot, fucks a lot, and is still more than
happy to get his hands dirty taking care of scum like this guy
with the loaded dice.

   Michelin's large hand dropped on the cheat's shoulder.
Then, before the cheat realized what was happening,
Michelin got him in a choke hold and pulled him right off
the stool, the guy's feet kicking the empty air. Michelin
dragged him out of the *Salle Benetin* as calmly as if he were
lugging groceries. The two rent-a-cops stayed at his side,
and I followed close on his heels. Michelin apparently knew
the guy; he called him "Dureur" twice, and half-way to the
exit Michelin whispered in his ear that if he didn't stop
kicking, he would break his fucking neck in two and then
piss down his throat. Dureur stopped kicking.

   At the side entrance just beyond the *Salle Médecin*, one of
the rent-a-cops went through Dureur's pockets while
Michelin kept him in a choke hold. The cops kept his wallet,
several dice, and a handful of casino chips, but passed a valet
parking ticket to the doorman, who had stepped outside to
join us. The doorman just looked at the ticket, not doing
anything, but before Michelin could curse him out I barked
the obvious. The doorman ran off to the garage to get the
cheat's car.

   While the doorman was gone, Michelin released Dureur
and gave him the usual lecture: a mixture of veiled warnings,
blatant threats, imprecations, and brass knuckles. After a
few minutes the guy's face looked like a loaf of broken
bread, but that's the way Michelin liked to work. Dureur
sank to the ground, blood spilling from his right eye and his

nose. His car came about two minutes later, a small blue Volvo, maybe ten years old. Michelin hauled Dureur up and as the cops opened the front door, he heaved him inside. Michelin slammed the door once on his foot and the guy screamed and cursed, but he was smart enough to get his foot out of the way the second time. Then Michelin and the two cops just turned around and walked calmly back into the casino, not even giving the guy the respect of waiting to make sure he'd leave. Truth was, everyone knew the guy was beat.

The doorman raced inside behind Michelin, and I stayed outside for another moment. Michelin hadn't called me, so I guess I was supposed to add insult to injury: leaving a girl behind to send him off.

Dureur wiped his jacket sleeve across his face, trying to clear his eyes, and smearing himself with blood and snot. He revved his engine hard several times, either because he couldn't see to get his car in gear, or because he was hoping at last to vent some rage. When he finally released the brake, I needed to jump out of the way to avoid being hit.

The next few hours were pretty much a blur. I suppose the adrenalin rush of the morning wiped the more mundane memories that immediately followed. But shortly after noon, I was back in the casino, patrolling the floor.

I noticed some odd things right away. For example, the casino was unusually crowded. Yes, there's a swell of players that start coming in just before the ornate clock in the Atrium strikes noon, gamblers rushing in from all the local shops and businesses for a quick hand of cards (despite a law prohibiting the citizens of Monaco from entering the establishment); but today the casino was not just crowded, but packed full to bursting. It was as if the busses that usually take the geriatrics home had gone on strike, as if the debutantes and dilettantes had all decided to start their gaming early. Everyone was here.

I walked past the front door of the Atrium and noticed that not only were there more gamblers present, but also a lot more rent-a-cops. The fat guard at the front entrance, for example, now had two partners loitering behind him. One of them was a tub o' lard with pale skin and a huge, ugly gash over his right eye. I felt sorry for him. When Michelin saw this guy, I knew he'd be out on the street in a second. Michelin didn't tolerate scraping the bottom of any barrel.

There was something else, and this may sound strange, but all of a sudden people started *talking* to me. Sure, the rent-a-cops would say "hi" to me on occasion, in passing, and the other members of the Security team would occasionally invite me out on the veranda or the front steps while they had a drink or a smoke, but that was the extent of it. (I usually attributed this lack of interest on their part to the fact that I was a girl pushing my way into a boy's world. Woman had made big advances in the casino front lines — manning the tables, for example, or serving drinks — but the back office work, particularly Security, was still pretty much an exclusive club.)

Now, however, as I entered the *Salon de l'Europe*, a rent-a-cop tried to engage me in actual *conversation*.

It started simply: "Hey, BD!" he said.

(My full name's Beatrice Dalle — yes, just like the sexy French movie star, how sharp of you to notice — but everyone — thankfully — just calls me BD, for short.)

I looked up at the cop and smiled. I didn't think I knew him — the rent-a-cops come and go, but I would have remembered this one: not only was he in an old-fashioned uniform, but he had a large bruise that ran from his right ear down inside his buttoned-up shirt — so I continued on my way, pretty much assuming our interaction had finished. But he held up his hand to stop me.

"I saw you out there this morning, BD. Catching that charlatan. That was good work. Really good work."

I was taken aback. "Thanks," I said. I'd helped stop plenty of guys before and no one ever bothered to say so much as thanks.

"It's good to have you around," he said.

I left the *Salon de l'Europe* and headed farther back into the casino, feeling a little stunned; but over the next hour, I was stopped by six more people, all wanting to talk about the good work I had done that morning. And not just cops. There was a teenage girl who was missing an arm, an old man whose skin was the color of snow, and two middle-aged men in bathing suits who smelled *awful*. Actually, they *all* smelled bad. If this kept up, I'd have trouble finishing my rounds. I was starting to feel a little creeped out.

By six the set-up for prime-time was in full swing. This meant my job was mostly to stay out of the way of everyone who was spiffing up the joint for the evening's big money. That was fine with me, of course; I was happy to stay out of the way of all the weirdoes who suddenly wanted me as their best friend.

As the evening wore on, I ran into Honoré once and, thinking perhaps my position in the exclusive boy's club of Security had changed, I tried to talk to him, but he totally ignored me. So not everyone wanted to be my friend. In fact, the tap was running either hot or cold. I had somehow lost the middle ground of friendly acknowledgment. I was now either part of some new secret club (whose members included both cops and one-armed teen-age girls) or I just didn't exist. Either way, I didn't like it.

I didn't bother looking for Barthes, suspecting he'd give me the cold shoulder like Honoré, and it turned out I didn't see Michelin until much later that night when I saw him darting out that side door exit with Marissa, the French girl from the bar. I tried to catch his eye, but he was obviously distracted by the bet he was hoping to lay.

And that pretty much brings us to where we started, with me here, out on the veranda by myself at three a.m., tired, hot, and *confused*.

I gaze across the Mediterranean and watch a group of shadowy birds trailing a sailboat that's motoring through the nighttime water, and I sigh; then I finally curl up under one of the tables on the far end of the veranda and sleep.

When I open my eyes again, the sun is already up, shining down on the sparkling turquoise of the Mediterranean, absolutely stunning.

I wonder whether Michelin's returned and/or recovered from his evening's tryst, so I head back into the casino. I nod at the overweight pale cop near the *Salon de l'Europe* (still on duty — and I thought I was the only one who pulled crazy hours!) and head back through the Atrium towards the Security offices.

Almost immediately I sense something is wrong. My nose starts twitching and I wonder if that thug Dureur is back. But, no, it's a different scent today. Someone's in trouble, and I race through the *Salon Médecin* towards its source. I hear crying, but not little girl tears. I turn the corner and there's Michelin, hanging on the public phone in the foyer just outside the hallway to our office, and he's bawling, his enormous body shaking. He's in his cream-colored suit, but it's crumpled and creased, and he's bent over, leaning against the wall for support. I've never seen him like this before, and it doesn't seem right.

At first I think something must have happened between him and Marissa, because I hear that distant tremble of her French accent through the receiver. But he's not arguing with her, he's seeking consolation. He's almost incoherent, and I can hear Marissa on the other end of the line, and she sounds as confused as I am. Then Michelin starts to curse into the phone, and I'm getting worried. Some of the casino's patrons gather around — mostly the ones that have been there all day and all night — the ones that have been talking to me — yes, the slightly weird ones.

The extra rent-a-cop with the ugly infected gash over his eye pats me on the back, and I flinch in surprise.

"It's alright, BD, you'll see," he says, and as politely as possible I move away from him.

Michelin starts shouting: "Dureur! I'll fucking kill that *connard!*" And I'm immediately reminded of the previous morning, the blood pouring down Dureur's face as he started his car. I remember the acrid smell of burnt rubber as he floored the accelerator, I remember meeting his eyes just before he released the brake and the car hurtled forward, I remember trying to jump out of the car's path....

"*Je suis fou!* That stupid bitch. That *stupid* bitch. Four years — we've been together four years. She was huge, she was *huge* — "

I remember Dureur. I remember meeting his eyes just before the wheels caught the road and the car hurtled forward, I remember trying to jump out of the car's path, I remember the driveway, the air, the light....

I hear Marissa say something on the other end of the line and my ears stand straight up. My name. She says my name.

Then I remember meeting Dureur's eyes, sensing his fury and hatred and rage, I remember trying to jump out of the car's path... *but not quickly enough.*

I remember the impact, the loud crack, the sad sound from my belly, and I remember sailing through the air....

I bark several times at Michelin and rub up against his leg. I bark again, louder, but he ignores me. I look up into his face, tears rolling down his cheeks. I feel his love, his intense love, and I want to cry, too, but I can't. I bark and bark until I fill up the entire casino I bark and bark and bark.

Michelin's fingers grip the phone, his knuckles turning white. "Yes, dammit, I said 'was.' The bitch is dead now."

"Beatrice Dalle"

First and last lines from
Casino Royale by Ian Fleming.

I guess the idea here was to write an all-too-literal "shaggy dog" story. Sorry about that. But the first and last line together screamed, "dog!" so I knew right away I had a canine protagonist. The setting is pure Fleming, something I'd prefer to have avoided — but the explicit mention of a casino in the first line felt like a pass. Why a ghost story? I suspect I'm going to say this more than once in the pages that follow: I've got no idea. But I ended up liking BD a lot, and was sad to see her go.

Written between 12 and 24 February 2003

Rum Alley

A VERY LITTLE BOY stood upon a heap of gravel for the honor of Rum Alley. Other boys, ranging in age from six to twelve, equally ragged, jostle one another as they try to take their place at the top of the imaginary mountain. Dust billows around the boys, and in the light and shadow of the early morning the scene is both chaotic and contrived, like a painting by Bruegel, rich and attentive to detail, Arcadian and realist, the little boy above, bathed in a halo of gritty luminescence, proud and taunting, and the dark horde below, reaching upward, all fists and fingers, struggling to displace him. The little boy shifts his weight and shouts something that's more absurdity than obscenity, but it's enough to unify the aggressors. The muddy grimaces and bloody noses advance, and the little boy raises his chin against the aggressive tilt of many shoulders. His small fist shoots skyward in triumph, however temporal, while high above, a chord of angels, nearly invisible, circle in silence. These are not Botticelli angels, of course, nor Fiorentino blonde-haired cherubim playing lutes, but sharp-eyed vultures of victory, who, sensing their moment, swoop down out of the blue sky and into the abandoned lot, and the little boy loses his footing to the sound of fast running gravel. He is struck in the face then by several of the weaker boys, while the others, sensing possibility, strike one another on their way to the top. The little boy crawls away from the tussle, bruised but satisfied; and the angels depart, a tiny flutter of wings. He brushes himself off, surveys the battle from a distance, and when the next boy falls, he dives back into the fray.

I remain in the car, observing the fracas from across the alley, watch as it mutates into a game of freeze tag, then kick the can. I smile. The little boy looks war-torn, I suppose, in dirty t-shirt and shorts, but also happy. It suits him. When the last game ends, I still stay in the car, and watch the boys leave, pouring noisily out of the abandoned lot through a gap in the chain-link fence that separates their improvised play area from the street. They rush past me, but no one notices a middle-aged man in an ordinary car. I stay in the car as the last boy disappears around the far corner of the alley. I stay as their enthusiastic discord fades to silence.

I wait a few minutes, then I roll down the window and lean my head outside. The air is cool and clear — unusual for a summer in the city. In fact, everything here is remarkably fresh and clean. I twist my neck and gaze up into the bright blue sky. It's empty except for a distant white contrail, moving slowly and silently across the heavens....

It's seven a.m. when Alison Rummi awakes from the dream. The first thing she sees when she opens her eyes is her ceiling where she's just noticed an ashen smudge, like a dirty chalk mark, running from one side of the room halfway to the other. It looks like the kind of trail a jet leaves as it moves across the sky. She immediately starts to cry.

Outside her bedroom window are birds. Maybe even songbirds. There is green grass, probably. Most mornings there is warm and vibrant light. Somewhere someone is making French toast on a griddle, or pouring a bowl of Frosted Flakes and setting it beside a tall wet glass of orange juice. There are blown kisses. There are handshakes and hugs. And on some mornings Alison Rummi has about one-half second during which she feels all of this, feels buoyant and happy. Then she remembers who she is and where she is and what she is and she wants to die. And today, staring up at the ceiling over her bed, pulled right into the jet stream of memory, even that half-second is stolen.

Time passes, minutes or hours, and she's *still* flat on her back in bed. She thinks about sitting up, but instead just raises her arms. She thinks this is a reasonable compromise, creditable. She raises both arms together, straight up, so that they are at right angles to her body and the bed. She has to wonder whether these bony appendages are really the arms of a forty-two year old woman. They're more like those fragile limbs you see on trees in the dead of winter.

One arm falls back to bed, but she keeps the other straight up, determined to demonstrate some sort of will power, some sort of self-control. She twists the raised arm and bends her wrist so her palm faces the ceiling, imagining she's striking some new sort of yoga pose, yoga for the terminally depressed, yoga for the bed-ridden, yoga you can make up as you go along, yoga that you don't even have to do. There's a ring up there, she notices, on her crooked finger high above her, a thin gold band, but what she remembers is *his* hand, so delicate, an artist's hand. She remembers his signing for the ring, long ago, scribbling his illegible signature like something off the Richter scale, signing the top of the carbon copy Visa receipt at the jewelers. She thought the ring was too expensive then, but how little she knew about the cost of anything; and now the memory alone is like a knife in her chest.

She drops her left arm back to bed and turns her head to the side. She starts to sob as she pulls the sheet up, burying her face in its suffocating whiteness. Perhaps, she thinks, I can just lie here, in my underwear, thinking about dead trees and winter, until I expire. Perhaps, she thinks, I can just stay here forever.

She rolls over. She looks around. It's a very pleasant room she's got, or it should be. The walls are painted powder blue, sensual and serene, and the wood floor is painted white with a floral trim of tiny flowers lavender and green. There's a white wicker chair next to a small white dresser, opposite the door, more comfortable than it looks, and of course there's the king-sized bed, made from dark walnut by a famous designer in Sausalito whose name she can never remember. But then there are the vases, several times too many vases filled with murky water and phantom floral displays, lifeless, desiccated, surrounding her on every side, shedding dark-colored buds and shriveled, brittle flowers. They're like fossilized fireworks, she thinks, marking time, and fading. Except for those, over there. They look freshly cut, those flowers in the tiny pink vase on her dresser, next to her mirror, and their reflection makes it look like she's got twice as many. Or perhaps it's a magic mirror and she's seeing into another room, through the looking-glass, wouldn't that be nice, if she were peering into someone else's room — there, you can see its door, painted white like mine, and the dressers, all the same, I think. It's Cape Cod style, all of this, though maybe it's called Cod Cape on the other side of the mirror, I don't know, that's stupid, but the door in that other room is ajar, just like mine, and maybe someone will….

Oh, fuck it. Who is Alison Rummi? Alison Rummi is a *widow*. All lower-case, wanting to vanish. Webster defines "widow" as a woman who has lost her husband; but she can think of far better definitions, more apt, more cruel. She doesn't think of herself as a widow, after all; she knows she's a widow but she doesn't *feel* like a widow, because being a widow is so easy. It's being a mother that's hard, because while you may not always be a wife, you are always a mother. And Alison Rummi is a mother who has lost her only child.

Why doesn't Webster's have a word for that?

I pull my head back into the car and look down at the keys dangling from the ignition: if I can't bring myself to get out, I also can't quite bring myself to leave, to start the engine and drive off. Not that it would matter. I know I could always return, later this afternoon, or tomorrow, and the scene in the vacant lot will repeat, and I'll have another opportunity to approach the boy. And anyway, I have no intention of running away. I am on a mission and I am going to see it through, however it turns out.

I spend several minutes staring down the alley, wondering when the boys will come back. Part of me hopes that he'll come back all by himself, ahead of the other boys. That he will have sensed my watching him all morning. That he will be curious and brave, and that he will *want* to meet. But these are my issues, I know, not his; it won't happen, and I don't expect it.

I pick up the notebook at my side and turn to a fresh page. I pull out one of my soft lead pencils and start to doodle the street-lamp at the end of the alley, a fire plug, the chain-link fence.

The morning sun starts to spill over the shorter tenements and brownstones to the east. The far side of the lot, which an hour ago was lost in shadow, which was nothing more than the dark and windowless brick backside of an unremarkable apartment building, in the brighter light starts to sparkle with a textured iridescence that despite its rusty brick color reminds me of sunlight on the ocean. I try to capture it in my notebook, but I give up quickly. It is clearly something meant for me to experience, not frame. I watch the light move across the vacant lot, and I watch the grey gravel turn into a beach of bright white sand, and the imaginary hill that had been the focus of the boys' battle earlier become a sand dune.

I get out of the car and cross the alley to take a better look. Against the brick wall to the west, I notice that someone has spray-painted a garden of graffiti flowers: hundreds of small purple and blue petals, green fronds, large white blossoms, a few roses and sunflowers. It's like looking into the heart of a Gauguin canvas, here in the most unlikely of places. The painting expands in the sunlight as I watch, a breeze of color sweeping across the face of the wall. It's Monet, of course, and O'Keefe, and Van Gogh. Right here.

I sit down on the ground near the far end of the chain-link fence, a little breathless. This is not the New York I remember. Forget the light, and the color. It's all too clean, too silent. Where is the litter, the overflowing trash? The back-alley con artists and bums? Where is the ground-pounding construction work, the honking cars and screeching busses, the relentless yapping of dog? Where is the sound of the subway rumbling below? Or of an airplane roaring above….

Alison steps into her husband's office. She does this two or three times a day, so, you see, she does get out of bed after all. There's an easel set up in the far corner of the room. A small desk. A drafting table with a blue ceramic mug of coffee resting precariously on its gentle slope. The coffee, of course, is cold; it was already abandoned for a week before it was abandoned forever. There are several drawings pinned to the wall over the drafting table. A book by Andrew Goldsworthy is open on his desk.

"Yes, but I don't know anymore."

"How can you not know, Ali?" It's Gabby on the other end of the line, her best friend. If it were anyone else she'd probably already be screaming at her, or crying at least. She's actually thrown the phone at the wall on more than one occasion and there's a long black bruise there to prove it. She wants to say, *Look at my arms, they're like the branches of a dying tree!* but she knows she shouldn't, that it will only make her friend feel worse, or worried, or something. She used to be good at knowing what others felt, or would feel, but not anymore. Now, she thinks, everyone is opaque, just like me.

"I don't *fucking* know when I'm happy or sad during the day so how the *fuck* am I supposed to know if I'm happy or sad in my *fucking* dreams!"

Ok, she loses control a little. It happens. And even as she's venting she realizes it's not all the truth, not really. She has had happy dreams, it's just that they make her so incredibly sad afterwards that they're not worth having. And what else can she do when she's asked one of those sincere but hopelessly out-of-touch questions that no matter how hard she tries she can't get people to stop asking.

The woman on the other end doesn't back down, however; she doesn't run away, doesn't get angry in return. As I said: a best friend. So she asks, calmly, what her dreams are like, and Alison takes a deep breath and tells her.

"There's this man, but I'm not sure who he is. And this boy...."

Sometime around two p.m. the boys return to the vacant lot. I wonder if there's school here, if this is afternoon recess. The older boys lead the charge through the chain-link back into the lot and they've brought a soccer ball with them. I stand near the far end of the fence, easily visible but just as easily overlooked by them. The younger boys arrive shortly thereafter, and they all split naturally into teams and start to kick the ball around.

I spot Danny right away. He is tearing after a much larger boy who has just taken control of the ball. Danny is one of the younger boys, certainly, but while most of the other youngsters are holding back, staying out of the way of the larger kids, Danny dives right in. He obviously wants to be in the thick of things. I watch as he reaches the older boy with the ball, and although Danny sends a flurry of energetic kicks around the boy's ankles, there's really no contest, and the older boy easily out-maneuvers Danny and then passes the ball to a tall boy in a hooded sweatshirt. Danny changes direction, tracking the ball, and races after the new kid.

"Hey!" Danny shouts to the boy in the sweatshirt. "Gimme the ball!"

It's the first thing I've heard Danny say, and I feel something swell in my chest, a ridiculous sense of pride.

The boy in the sweatshirt ignores Danny and takes a shot on goal. He scores and half the boys cheer in triumph, including Danny. They're all on the same team, I realize,

Danny and the two boys from whom he was trying to steal the ball. I smile. Danny isn't exactly following the rules; he doesn't quite get what's going on, but it doesn't matter. His deepest pleasure is not goal-oriented, obviously.

The game goes on. Danny's now on the sidelines — the boys shuffle in and out of the game — and I inch towards him. He is standing there, just on the other side of the fence, waiting patiently for his turn to get back into the game. He's breathing hard and shouting to his friends. I'm near the gap in the fence, too, and I think about slipping through. It's easily large enough for Danny and his friends, but probably a tight fit for me. I decide to stay where I am, practicality or cowardice, I'm not quite sure.

"You're doing pretty well out there," I say instead, and I have to say it again before he looks up, and then he turns away. I wonder if he thinks I'm talking to someone else, or if he didn't really hear what I said, or whether he just doesn't care. Maybe I'm a stranger, I think, and he's not supposed to talk to strangers….

There's this other woman: let's call her Rafaela. When she calls Alison, Alison wants to kill her, which makes Alison feel terrible, of course, and guilty, but not because killing Rafaela would be a bad thing, practically speaking, or wrong in the moral sense, but because it makes Alison for a few moments not feel like wanting to die herself. And that is too much to bear.

"I know how hard this is," Rafaela says and the kitchen drawer slides open and Alison's hand dips inside and a butter knife comes out. She's holding the knife in her right hand, blade pointing up, her small fist wrapped tightly around the knife's handle. Alison fights the urge to throw the phone against the wall, and what is she going to do with the knife anyway? *I'm going to* fucking *slit my own throat, you asshole! If she says another word I'm going to* fucking *cut my throat.*

"I know how hard this is, Ali." Oh really? *Really*? Alison

begins to press the point of the dull blade into her chest.

"I know how hard this is, but it's been more than a year. You need to move on. It's like sitting shiva. Seven days and then you're done."

Shiva? Isn't that the Hindu god of destruction, the destroyer? Six arms, knives in every hand? What the fuck does Rafaela know about Shiva, anyway? Or sitting shiva for that matter. She knows NOTHING.

Sometimes Alison tries to explain how there are no words of comfort for her, that comfort, in fact, is *irrelevant*, and those who try to comfort her are the most misguided and pathetic of all, especially those who think there is some sort of time limit on this kind of grief.

"You just need to think of them as far away," Rafaela continues; "Like they've gone away on a long trip, a very long trip. A vacation."

They were *on vacation*, Alison wants to say, and maybe she does say it, or maybe she screams it or cries out, or maybe she hurls the phone at the wall. Who the fuck knows.

"Do you blame him?" Rafaela asks. "For taking him away."

Alison hangs up.

Time passes, and she's on the floor in a corner, arms wrapped around knees, rocking back and forth. Then she's back on the phone with Gabrielle, her best friend, back to that recurring dream: the man, the boy, the playground.

"Only it's not exactly a playground," she says. "It's more like a back yard. In a big city." Alison grew up just outside Papillion, Nebraska. She met her husband at a sorority party at Southwestern College in Winfield, Kansas. They married and moved to a suburb outside San Diego. What she knows about big city life could fit on the head of a glass of beer, and would be just as substantial. She guessed her dream was a New York dream, but only because her husband is an ex-New Yorker. New York to her was little more than TV and bald cops and lollypops.

"Is the boy…?"

"Yes. He's playing with some other kids, or something. And there's this guy who walks up to him…."

Danny goes back into the game; when he shuffles out the next time, I try again.

"You guys're getting creamed out there," I say with what I hope sounds like friendly enthusiasm. Still, I don't have high hopes for getting his attention: he's rough-housing with another boy on the sidelines as I say this. But they both stop to look up at me, two street urchins, two Little Rascals. The other boy turns away, quickly disinterested, but Danny makes eye contact. When he speaks to me I'm so stunned I don't catch what he says. It's "Nyah." Or maybe it's "Yeah." But I can tell it's just to get rid of me: he immediately turns back to his friend, to the game.

But I'm not ready to give up.

"It's really great to see you again, Danny," I say, deciding to risk using his name. "It's great to see you so happy."

He turns back to me. His small brow furrows as he examines my face.

"Do I know you, Mister?"

What can I say? What *should* I say?

Then suddenly, his lips pull back into a smile and his eyes open wide. He waves his hand at me dismissively.

"Ferget it, Mister. We're kicking butt! We are *not* getting creamed!"

"You like playing here?"

"Oh, yes!"

"I need to talk to you. I have…a question to ask you."

His eyes narrow. He's thinking hard again.

"Are you my father?" he asks.

Oh God. I am completely out of my depth. Is this where I climb through the fence and throw my arms around him?

Or is this the right time to run away? Or maybe I just stand here and stare back at him, hard as I can, which is what I'm doing by default. I almost laugh to release some tension, but I don't; I decide, without actually deciding, to keep my face straight. Before I can answer him (not that I am going to answer him, really, not that I know how), one of the older kids calls for a new game. Danny's pal slaps him on the shoulder and they turn and run towards a clutch of boys standing in the center of the lot. Danny doesn't even look back. I've been forgotten.

Alison is sitting at the kitchen table. There are stacks of unopened letters and bills everywhere. Actually, some are opened, and some have probably already been paid. But not by her. She runs a hand through her long brown hair and then takes a long pull on the bottle of beer that she's been moving from one stack to another. Outside she hears the deep roar of a jet overhead. The jets pass overhead every day, and she hears every one.

"Danny's just started to work on his Pokémon deck. He's got cards everywhere now that they've cleared our so-called lunch."

That was her husband, aboard United 454, about an hour before the crash, using one of those over-priced seat-back phones. They spoke for a few more minutes, she thinks, but she doesn't remember any more of their conversation. Just that tiny sound clip of his voice, and the image of their son arranging and re-arranging hundreds of Pokémon cards on top of one of those tiny airline tray tables. For a moment she imagines that each one of those cards maps to a person on the plane and that Danny is a tiny necromancer, about to deal out their fate. Two hundred and sixty-one people died that afternoon.

Alison's back in bed now, but no, she's up again, she can't sleep, so she walks the house some more, and finds herself back in her son's room which, like her husband's office, has remained unchanged for fifteen months. She surveys the walls, the neatly-made bed with the *Toy Story* sheets and pillowcases, his pint-sized desk with its pint-sized chair. She's full of visions these days and now she imagines the floor under her feet turning to dirt, and everything in the room suddenly returning to the earth, all the paintings and school projects, everything made out of pipe cleaners or popsicle sticks, everything unbearably heavy, sinking, and her feet slip into the loosely-turned soil, then her ankles, her knees, her hips, maybe the whole house follows, collapsing into itself, disappearing into the earth, into this unmade grave, all art and life aspiring to the condition of mourning.

Back in the kitchen she finds a middle-aged man at the breakfast table and wonders if it's her husband. It's a weird feeling not knowing. It's not that she has forgotten what he looks like, but she just can't be sure. Then her best friend is back on the phone and that's good.

"I miss Michael, of course," she says, risking a tiny glance at the man at her table. "But it's not the same."

"I know."

"And I feel terrible about that."

"I know."

"I can almost believe that Mike's away on some interminable round-the-world trip, and that I'll never see him again." She hates saying this, of course; it makes her think of Rafaela, and she can't stand crediting her with this thought. "But what I can't imagine is that Mike's really *gone*, non-existent, I can't imagine that, I can't even understand what that means."

She turns towards the man at the table, but he's not there.

"But I can sometimes imagine him on some faraway beach, or at a hotel, or something. A big resort. I can pretend that's where he is, on his own. But Danny…."

Alison starts crying; her body starts to shake. Shit, she hates this, but at the same time, these are the only moments that feel right. Her words come out in gasps now. She's said this all before, anyway.

"I mean, I can't imagine Danny doesn't exist anymore, that's impossible, too. But I also can't pretend he's alive, just somewhere else. It's not like imagining Mike wind-surfing on Columbus Isle. Mike can take care of himself, he always has. But Danny's just a little boy, he's *my* little boy. I get nervous when he's visiting friends down the street, whenever he's not in sight, it's this automatic mother thing that kicks in; you just have to worry *all the fucking time*. And every day he's gone it gets worse, it never gets better because the only thing you can do is worry more. How the *fuck* am I supposed to imagine he's playing on some beach somewhere building *fucking* sandcastles — who's taking care of him, who's going to make sure he's alright! It drives me out of my *fucking* mind!"

"I know."

Alison looks at her hands. *It's inside me, it's built-in, this grief*, she thinks. *There's no consolation, there's nothing. Nothing.*

Several hours pass. I watch the sun move across the sky; I watch the changing light transform the alley again and again. I watch the sun dip between two buildings to the west, dropping slowly towards an unseen horizon. The alley once again turns shadowy and strange.

The game has long broken up. Some of the boys have already left. I notice Danny playing with the soccer ball by himself, using his hands, pretending to shoot baskets against the wall. After a large boy squeezes through the gap in the chain-link fence, I quickly push myself through in the other direction. It's a tight fit, but that doesn't matter. I stay back, at first, and watch him from a distance. When I take a few steps towards him, I notice that the graffiti on the red-brick wall has changed again. The water lilies and sunflowers are gone, replaced by a bright blue rocket with fiery yellow exhaust, planets, moons, stars. It's stunning, too.

I know I could stay here forever if I wanted, stay here and watch the changing graffiti on the walls, the changing light, the shifting colors, stay here and watch my son, running and playing and laughing. I could watch him struggle and persevere and overcome. Perhaps I could even watch him grow. And perhaps after a while I could lay down on canvas the gigantic infinite explosion of love I feel for him, and the sense of overwhelming *rightness*.

But I know that there are other places, too, other places with blue skies and no planes, with only angels in the air skywriting the flat-line signature of Heaven with their long white contrails. You'll just have to trust me on this. It's love as strong as death and infinite in all directions.

But I know, I know. Trust has nothing to do with it.

"Danny!" I call out. I walk over to him. He recognizes me, at least as the guy from earlier this afternoon; and he stops playing, tucks the large ball under his small arm.

"I need to go," I say, "but I need to talk to you first."

He shrugs his shoulders. His eyes move between me and his friends, the last of whom are leaving the lot. I don't have much time, obviously.

"Your mommy loves you and misses you a lot. She thinks about you all the time."

Danny smiles, but it's clear he doesn't know what to say. I don't know either.

"She misses you and wants to know you're happy."

Danny rolls the ball over to one of his departing friends. The boy picks it up and slips through the fence. Danny turns back, smiling. "Did you bring me a treat?"

I want to laugh and I want to cry. I reach into my jacket pocket and pull out the chocolate chip bagel that has to be there.

"I love Mommy, too," he says, taking the bagel in his tiny left hand.

"Your mommy worries about you."

A look of concern crosses his face, like a small dark cloud crossing a sunny sky, but it passes quickly.

"Why?" he asks, genuinely puzzled. And it's of course a question without an answer, or rather with an impossible answer. I look away for a moment. The sun has started to set, and I can see that the abandoned lot is transforming again. When I turn back to my son, he is bathed in the intense golden glow of sunset. The next question just tumbles out. I'm not sure what it means.

"What would you want to tell your mommy," I ask, "if she ever stopped worrying about you?"

Danny looks up, and our eyes meet again. His face is sweet but vacant. I can't tell if he's thinking, or if he just doesn't understand what I said. I wouldn't blame him either way. Somewhere above me, I hear the susurration of angel wings; but I don't look up. I think back to the morning, to Danny's victory, to his brief tenure on top of the hill.

"Mmm," Danny says at last, toe scuffing gravel, "I guess I don't really know, Mister."

I nod. What did I expect, really? I ruffle his hair with my hand; smile; and after a moment turn and walk back to the gap in the fence. Half-way through, Danny calls after me.

"Hey, Mister!"

I turn. Danny is running towards me.

"I know what I'd tell her. Oh, yes!" He places both his hands on his hips, fiercely proud. And so alive, so very, very alive.

"Oh, yes, I'll fergive her! I'll fergive her!"

"Rum Alley"

"RUM ALLEY"
First and last lines from
"Maggie" by Stephen Crane.

A story about grief, obviously. I suppose children and forgiveness could go in many directions; but finding forgiveness between here and the hereafter is what came to mind after reading Crane's lines. The slippery nature of forgiveness, how it requires acceptance, real or imagined, between multiple parties, has always fascinated me. I like the mother's dream of Heaven, and the ambiguity of having her own dream narrated by someone else. Or perhaps it's really the other way around: someone in Heaven is conjuring up the living, a kind of grief for those left behind.

Written between 12 and 17 May 2003

The Engagement Party

I SAW HIM on a sleepless night when I was walking desperately to save my soul and my vision. I had left the engagement party two hours earlier and found myself at midnight lost deep in the forests of Coddington Wood, the unenclosed tract of wilderness to the north of Letham, the small New England town in which I lived. I had had another row with Thomas Sherak, the junior dean of the local college. He was a horrid philistine who despite his position understood nothing of the academic in general nor my work in particular, and furthermore seemed to take a perpetual delight in whatever forbidding obstacle or malfeasance he could contrive to slow if not halt the progress of my researches. Inside our dank and dreary offices at the seaside college, I would engage him — sinister riposte for each sinister thrust — but in fairness and civility I shied away from any public display of enmity, preferring to promote an appearance of good manners if not good will along the otherwise impure and somber streets of our isolated township. Yet tonight, upon the announcement of my engagement to Deidre, his sister, his assault had been relentless and open, and I found myself in a heated exchange that I immediately regretted. I never intended to strike him, but in a fit of rage I thrust out my arm and in a sweeping gesture meant to assail his deleterious effect upon the broad faculty of the college, swung my arm over the pianoforte and sent the candelabra hurtling through the air. It struck him full in the face and, tumbling backward, his endomorphic frame fell full upon his sister. When I advanced to render assistance to my fiancé, those in attendance mistook my direction and my motive and moved as a barricade between the fallen dean and my person. Thomas the Elder, Deidre's father and the owner of the estate, appeared at just that moment and, also misconstruing the situation, demanded I quit the property at once. So it was that everyone assumed ill in our intimate but contaminated society; thus, I gathered to me whatever sense and pride I could salvage, held my head high, contained my rage (however warranted), apologized (however unjust the circumstance), and departed; all the while fearing the worst, that I had lost everything at that moment, everything for which I had struggled, everything which had been so meticulously planned: wife, career, and fortune. So the inherent malignant impurity of Letham had at last marked me.

The light from the Sherak estate dimmed as I marched through the woods, under tree and over bracken. My heart was filled with an unstable admixture of antipathy and offense; and, my attention turned inward, I was soon deep in the forested darkness of Coddington Wood. I continued blindly forward until at last fury faded to anger, and anger then to an idle resentment. Eventually, my breathing slowed and my head cooled, and if one was cause and the other effect I cannot say which is which; nevertheless, my pace slackened and I raised my eyes to my surroundings. Not more than two hours had passed — of that I am certain — when I first gave thought to return; but I knew I had wandered farther than ever I had afore. I stopped beside a large raven-shaped stone near the bottom of a long ravine to find my bearings. The night was silent and the gloom that enveloped the ravine was complete. I had descended from the south-east, I knew, but aslant, and I understood immediately I was uncertain of the route back to the estate, or the town. It was at that moment that I also observed I was not alone in the wood, that someone had followed me.

"You, come out!" I shouted in the direction of the figure

half-hidden behind the twisted trunk of a tree. I felt no fear, but a trifling annoyance at the possibility that the discord I had escaped had in fact dogged me. The moon was nearly full but we were deep in the woods beneath towering and ancient trees, so when the figure stepped forward he was still in shadow; but I could see that he was a man of roughly my age and build.

"I did not mean to alarm," the shade said. "Please accept my apology."

"Who are you, and why have you followed me?" I could conjure only the most evil motives for this intrusion.

"Forgive me. I have an idle curiosity and a habit of nocturnal perambulation. I am called William Jacob Hutchinson," he said, and I laughed out loud for that is *my* name.

"If you have come on behalf of the reprehensible Thomas Sherak," I said, "you'd best turn around now. I am in no temper for his spite or spleen." At the mention of Thomas Sherak, the shadowy figure jerked, but he did not retreat.

"What is your name?" the figure asked. "And what is your quarrel with Regent Sherak?"

Regent Sherak! "I told you I am not in a mood for sport. I speak of the *junior* dean of the college Thomas Sherak."

"I know of no such person."

I grew incensed. "Thomas the Younger!" I bellowed. "Thomas the Reviled, junior dean of Letham College! And you may tell him I abhor his folly!"

The figure stepped out of the shadow of the tree. A shaft of full moonlight passed over his face and I gasped.

He said, "I will not have you insult the name of *any* Thomas Sherak, sir — real or imagined! He is a close friend and soon to be family. I am a full dean in his college and soon to wed his sister."

The figure took another step towards me and then

suddenly stopped. In such close proximity, my visage must have been as plain to him as his was to me. "Who – who are you?" he stammered, but it was clear he knew exactly who — or what — I was; as I immediately knew him.

If you have read any papers by the German metaphysicians you will immediately recall the work of Heinrich Haberman of Munich. He wrote of the *doppelgänger*: a person or apparition in the form of a double of a living person. Haberman believed that for every person, a double — a twin or mirror likeness — might exist. He used the new science of Mendelism, which defines the transmission of characteristics from one generation to the next, to support this theory by setting limits to the variety of features in any species. Given the number of men, Haberman asserts, the discipline of statistical variation provides proof of not only the possibility but also the particular likelihood of the doppelgänger.

Yet this shape before me was no mere look-alike, for it was evident we shared more than a common physiognomy. His career and acquaintance, although not an exact duplication of my own, and his name, intimated the ideas of another, lesser-known Teutonic metaphysician named Dieter Prochnow, a pupil of Haberman (and a student of Zeno of Elea) who proposed *die doppelstadt* — that the application of the science of statistical variation mandated not just duplicates of individuals but of entire families. And if families, perhaps whole villages and towns. And yet, even if one gave credence to Prochnow's model, did it follow, given the kaleidoscopic complexity of human interaction, that such a village or town would — or even *could* — present a flawless reproduction, true to the original in every feature, including every person, place, and thing, every attendant action, merchant's web, and social structure?

I studied the doppelgänger before me with suspicion; and he examined me. If we were identical in body, we were not identical in costume. His dress was exceptional: fine material well-tailored and in fashion, both his waistcoat, with a narrow fit at shoulder and sleeves, and his unsullied doublet and breeches — altogether more than I could afford on my income as an associate professor. The implication of course was staggering. I began to wonder about the town from which he had departed; and I wondered about his place in its configuration.

"*I* am William Jacob Hutchinson," I said, advancing on him, and my double backed away a half-step up the side of the ravine. It was then that I was reminded that I was lost, and suddenly a stratagem took shape in my mind, and I wondered if he, too, realized the full implication of our encounter.

"*Where did you come from?*" I asked as I took another step towards him, and he looked back over his shoulder indicating a particular direction up the hill before he realized his mistake. He tried to take another step away from me, but in doing so he tripped, falling backward over a gnarled root.

I struck him several times with the sharp edge of my old and dirty boot, and as he lay moaning and half-conscious at my feet, I undid the first button on his coat, and so began my transformation....

I took off shortly thereafter, into the wood without hesitation and as if possessed. I heard him struggle behind me, but I had the advantage and I knew I would prevail. Whither *he* has gone, I do not know; but I have gone home to the pure New England lanes up which fragrant sea-winds sweep at evening.

"The Engagement Party"

First and last lines from
"He" by H. P. Lovecraft.

If "Beatrice Dalle" strayed too close to the source material's setting, this story strays perhaps a bit too close to Lovecraft's (dare I say it?) purple prose. Still, I enjoyed being filled with this voice, and I think the over-wrought language works well with the simple narrative.

(Oh, and if it isn't apparent: Heinrich Haberman is a complete fabrication. The word "doppelgänger" was first used by Jean Paul in his 1796 novel *Siebenkäs*. And — as far as I know — there is no such thing as a "doppelstadt.")

Written between 23 and 31 July 2003

Quiver

THERE WAS NOBODY to see him off, of course, why would there be, and now the rain was coming down again. He pulled the front door closed and stood between it and the half-open screen door, lost in thought. He had wanted nothing to do with her, but not before she had wanted nothing to do with him, and so here he stood: alone and cold in this increasing deluge, in the dying light of late-afternoon, under an eave that offered little protection from the weather and no protection from the past. Even that perpetual smile on his baby face, normally an uptick in an otherwise downer demeanor, looked droopy and sad and drained of color. If he were a work of Bouguereau or Caravaggio, you'd think he'd begun to run in the rain.

He took a half-step off the concrete pad that served as doorstep, then paused as he considered his lack of options. His car, a battered Ford Ares, was parked at the end of the driveway, less than fifty feet away, facing him, almost daring him to make a run for it, but there was no way he'd reach it without getting soaked. He picked up his suitcase, and ran.

The car was unlocked, and he jerked open the driver's-side door and heaved the suitcase across the front seat. He turned one last time to look at the house from which he ran, a two-floor Colonial indistinguishable from its neighbors on this tiny cul-de-sac in Alpaca, part of suburban Claremont, itself just a suburb of nearby San Diego. He shielded his eyes with his left hand, as much against the driving rain as the startling golden light coming from the upper story windows; and if he saw a figure there, a woman, a silhouette of

darkness holding back the curtains, facing the street, he
made no sign.

He climbed into the car. His clothes were drenched —
the linen jacket, his button-down shirt, his pants, even his
underwear — and water was still pooling into his shoes. He
pulled the door closed, fumbled in his wet pocket for the
key, then slipped it into the ignition. The engine started
slowly, as if awakened from a deep sleep: it groaned and
wheezed; and the radio, similarly groggy, was stuck between
two stations. Rain pounded the roof like bad jazz.

He jammed the car into reverse and pulled out of the
driveway backwards, bouncing over the edge of the curb.
Then he shifted into first and floored the accelerator. The
Ford Ares leapt forward, and the radio locked on to a single
station. It was Ol' Blue Eyes himself:

> *My love must be a kind of blind love*
> *I can't see anyone but you*
> *And dear, I wonder if you find love*
> *An optical illusion, too?*

He roared out of the cul-de-sac, heading south, staring
through a windshield thick with rain. He flicked on the
wipers, but they didn't make much difference, and every few
minutes he'd hear what sounded like a muted explosion
from underneath the body of the car as it slammed through
another pool of standing water. He was doing sixty before
he reached the freeway, and moving this fast over wet
roadway was almost like flying. It reminded him of his youth
— and he smiled, or maybe grimaced. He started to laugh,
and then to cry, all the way from Del Mar to Mission Bay.
When the speedometer touched eighty-five, the car began
to shake. In his peripheral vision, the suitcase on the seat
next to him could have been a passenger, stiff with terror.
He tightened his grip on the steering wheel, kept his foot on
the accelerator. He didn't like to think of himself as a
masochist, but the evidence was mounting, year after year,
relationship after relationship. Each night of love followed

inevitably by regret, distraction, indifference. Whether he was paying for the sins of his youth, being punished by those he had carelessly wronged, or simply timeworn and weak, still that moment of unrequited love when he turned invisible, when her eyes fell anywhere but on him — the ache was intolerable. And yet he went on.

He glanced in the rear-view mirror — grey sky over dark road, and half-a-dozen cars in pursuit. He wanted to see farther, all the way back down the highway, past each exit and curve, back to where his flight began. There were now at least thirty miles between himself and — what was her name? Angie? Yes, Angie. But still his heart was pounding, beating its Morse code of love, signaling SOS, and it took all his strength to put these miles between himself and his former lover. Despite everything, he still wanted to touch her, to hold her, to slip inside her....

Fuck.

He shifted in his seat. Some of us never grow up before we die, and most of us plan for a future that is never going to happen. And going back, he knew, is never an option.

He worked off his wet jacket as he drove, balled it up and threw it in the back. The car was still juddering; he couldn't get comfortable, and he needed to pee. He passed one rest area, and then another. Finally he just let go, relived himself as he drove, pissed his pants with a brutish satisfaction. It felt good — at first. Then the stink filled the car, mixing with his own sour sweat, and near the turn-off for Chula Vista, he couldn't stand it anymore. He rolled down his window. The wind roared and rain sliced into the vehicle. He told himself the cold would help keep him alert as he barreled towards the Mexican border.

> *The moon may be high*
> *But I can't see a thing in the sky*
> *I only have eyes for you*

He made the Tijuana crossing in less than an hour. The agent manning the gate looked weary and bored and waved him through without question. Coming back would be harder, of course, but he didn't mean to return. He didn't, in fact, mean much of anything.

The rain let up briefly as he cruised through downtown Tijuana, past the *Españoles* mall and a line of empty police cars, then, turning off the main avenue, past children playing in the streets and a large mural painted on the side of a warehouse. Someone had vandalized the artwork, scrawling NO MAS SANGRE across it in large, dripping red letters.

He turned south-east, just north of the river, and twenty minutes later he was out of town, in the middle of nowhere, speeding again over slick roads. He drove for several miles in the waning light without his headlights, listening to the rain under his tires, watching night settle over long stretches of shadowy scrubland or pampas on either side of the highway. When he finally turned on his lights they illuminated a road sign for Mexicali and Nogales, spattered with bullet holes, and he turned off Route 2 onto an even smaller two-lane highway heading east. The rain stopped at last, but not before nightfall, and even in the glare of his headlights the road ahead was increasingly black against black, a dark pall with no markings at all, no lines.

Somewhere past Tijeras, he began flicking his eyes back to the rear-view mirror. The road behind had been pitch black for the better part of an hour, but now there was something there, a familiar golden luminescence, something that hovered just over the dark horizon of the highway. It might have been the distant headlights of another car cresting a rise in the road, or the ambient glow from a distant city, but he doubted it.

Shortly before nine, he pulled off the highway, drawn to a large neon sign flashing *Cantina Amoroso* above a low flat building by the side of the road. How could he pass that up? He parked on the gravel shoulder just west of the bar, got out, stretched his legs. He noticed the large stain on the front of his pants, but he didn't bother turning back to the car. His suitcase was packed, but not with spare clothes.

He started towards the building's entrance, a dented metal door framed into a cinderblock wall, underneath a spinning red light that looked like a bloodshot eye. Inside, the bar was at least as forbidding as its entrance, lit only by strings of chili pepper holiday lights. There was no actual bar in the bar, just booths and cheap metal tables underneath a thick cloud of cigarette smoke. A jukebox was going, playing a Mexican pop song he didn't recognize, and a few shadows were dancing in a back room. The traveler sat at a table near the front door. The place was filled with men. Even the dancers in back, he realized.

A server wearing a dirty apron with a picture of a black devil holding a bottle of *salsa picante* approached his table. He was big, three-hundred pounds at least, with lots of old muscle. Flat nose, dark skin, he looked vaguely Samoan.

The traveler ordered a beer, but the Samoan just sniffed the air twice, nose high — as if the smell of urine could be any worse than the carcinogenic cloud overhead. Then he retreated, disappeared through a door near the back, and when he returned a few minutes later, he placed a wet glass and an unlabeled bottle on the table.

The song on the jukebox changed to a slow ballad, a sappy baritone supported by too many strings. He couldn't understand all the words — he spoke the language of romance, not every damn Romance language — but he guessed another *gaucho* was mooning after a wandering Carmelita.

"*Bolillo* — you gone finish dat?" The Samoan was still there. He indicated the beer.

"Sorry?"

The Samoan cleared his throat. It sounded like he might be summoning a wad of phlegm to spit against the wall. "*¿O te explico, Chavalo?* I assed if you was gone finish dat?" He didn't sound Samoan.

"Yeah. Eventually."

The Samoan didn't respond but closed his eyes as if the conversation had already gone on too long and he needed a rest; and maybe he did. When he re-opened his eyes, he was oddly invigorated. His pidgin accent was gone, too. "You on holiday?"

The traveler shook his head.

"Business then?"

"My business."

The Samoan ignored the gibe. "What kind of business?"

He fingered the wet glass. "I'm a salesman. A traveling salesman," he said, then he added beneath his breath, *And does it look like I came in here for the conversation?*

The Samoan turned his head towards the back of the bar, but his feet stayed put. Maybe he was thinking. When he turned back he was smiling. "What you sell?"

The traveler shook his head, not knowing how to answer, then he poured the beer into his glass. He poured a little too fast, on purpose, and the beer began to foam. It smelled vaguely of sulphur. "I sell love," he said, and he supposed it wasn't so far from the truth, or at least it didn't used to be. Foam fell over the rim of the glass and started running down the side.

"Well, you smell like shit."

Three other guys — all from the same table in the back — made their way forward. They looked like sympathetic locals eager to stir things up. The traveler reached into his hip pocket and pulled out a crumpled twenty. He placed it on the table, just outside the slowly-expanding circle of spilled beer.

"Actually, I smell like urine," he said.

The Samoan picked up the twenty before the beer could get to it. "No girls here," he said, and the traveler wondered what that meant. Was he telling him there were no girls here, or was he being *called* a girl. He stood, picked up his glass, and then — slowly — took a first and last draught of beer. The Samoan and *los tres amigos* watched him drink, and he kept an eye on them as well. He was older and fatter than all of them, except maybe the Samoan, so when he finally put his drink down, and the local nearest the door stepped aside, he took his cue. Sure, he could taunt them until *las vacas* came home, but he was no fighter, after all.

Outside, he realized he had to pee again. He relieved himself against the wheel of an old Dodge pickup, hoping it belonged to one of the locals, but when he sensed he was being watched from the building, he skipped the shake and hurried back to his car. As he belted in, another pickup pulled in front of the bar and three young women vaulted from the cargo bed. They were all in tight jeans with flouncy, stylized Mexican shirts, laughing, and one of them began to sing the same pop song he had heard inside. He watched them with an odd mixture of longing and dread. He'd been around the block, more than a few times, and he knew a thing or two about the vagaries of love. The pickup's driver, another woman, climbed out of the enclosed cab and joined her three friends, and together they sang and danced beneath the red neon light, turning tiny pirouettes before disappearing into the cantina.

He started his car and with a spray of gravel swerved back on to the dark road. Once he got rolling, with his left hand on the wheel, he used his right hand to reach down into his lap. He undid the button on his pants and slipped his hand inside, into his quiver. There was an arrow in there all right, a long hard arrow in there, and it was ready to fly.

He began to pick up speed. There were still no lights on the road, no other buildings, no other cars, no white lines. Soon, all he could see was the small patch of asphalt fifteen feet in front of his car. He began to take the curves too fast, and suddenly the road was gone.

He swung the wheel, trying to regain the highway, but the car jumped the shoulder. It bounced once and then rose into the air, and for a moment he saw nothing out the front

window, his headlights hopeless against the immense
blackness of the open sky. Then everything stopped short,
throwing him forward against his seat-belt, then whip-
lashing him back. His passenger wasn't so lucky: the suitcase
took flight, punching a hole through the windshield in an
explosion of glass. He watched as the suitcase sailed through
the air, caught briefly in the car's headlights. It looked like a
scene in a movie, tumbling through space, in slow motion,
end-over-end. Then it disappeared.

He didn't remember getting out of the car. But there he
was, out of the car, standing on a scrubby patch of earth
beneath its front bumper, looking up. The car was angled
skyward, engine running and headlights on, looking like a
finger pointing into the sky, a beacon. It seemed the car had
tried to launch itself over a small embankment, but got
snagged by a large rock. Looking closer, he saw that it wasn't
a rock at all, but a stone cross. In fact he was surrounded by
crosses, gravestones, and statues. He was in a fucking
cemetery.

He tried to open the back doors, but they were locked.
The front doors were high in the air, out of easy reach. In
any case, the car was now useless.

He looked for his suitcase, and found the bag against the
gnarled and fissured trunk of a desert ironwood some
twenty feet away, as if someone had carefully placed it there
moments before. He picked it up and worked his way back
past several headstones, past his car to the highway. He
began to walk.

The night grew deeper: colder, darker. No moon, no
stars, no airplanes. Nothing. The earthy smell of after-rain,
some lonely crickets in the distance, the tentative
susurration of wind, but that was it. No cars passed as he
trudged along the tiny dirt shoulder of the small highway;
and once out of sight of his car, the road sank back into an

inky gloom. It became hard to tell shoulder from scrubland, and more than once he found himself stepping into brush.

He thought about Angie. He tried to conjure her face, but couldn't remember what she looked like. He had loved her, perhaps still loved her, but the feeling, like the road around him, was nothing but shadow. (And who was it *before* Angie? he wondered. He couldn't even recall her name.)

He started walking down the center of the highway, no longer concerned with traffic. He looked to his left and right, trying to pierce the dark veil that hid the desert on either side, but if there was anything out there he couldn't see it. He checked his watch, but couldn't find its face. Surely it was after eleven by now.

He was too old for this. He was tired. His feet hurt. Despite the chill in the air, he was starting to sweat. But what was he supposed to do? Everyone had a role to play — he accepted that — and he had played his to perfection. He had fulfilled his duties, hadn't he? It wasn't his fault that he had grown up. It wasn't his fault that the role he had been assigned was a role that couldn't last forever. He couldn't just fly around making other people happy. He couldn't don the swaddling. He was, he supposed, like a former child star. Adorable and exquisite, until that day when the last magical sparkle of mischievous youth fades away, and no one can quite stand who he has become. And now — overweight, balding, with his looks fading fast — he was an embarrassment in middle age.

He thought about Angie again. Was that her name? Angie? It hardly seemed familiar anymore. Maybe he had spent so many years as a waiter at the Feast of Love he would never be offered a seat at that table.

He came upon the small town before midnight. It wasn't really a town; it was hardly even a pass-through; and twenty steps into it, he'd reached its dead center. He put his bag down next to the stone fountain that split the road going east and west. The fountain was dry, and looked like it had been dry for a very long time. Three buildings surrounded the fountain, on either side of the road. The building on the right had a large mural painted on its face, but the image was inscrutable. It might have advertised a grocery, or a garage. On the other side of the road was a building with a bare bulb hanging over a sign that read *Servicio Postal Mexicano*. Beneath the sign was the name of the town in letters almost as large as the town itself: ZICATELA. Suitcase in hand, he shuffled towards the third building. Two stories high, it was the tallest in town. A cardboard sign was stapled over its entrance that said "Hotel Bar" in thick black letters, quotation marks included. Below the sign someone — the owner? a vandal? — had scrawled *barato*.

He pushed open the door and stepped into the hotel-bar. Four or five tables, a low ceiling, and hand-plastered walls papered with images of bulls and bullfighters. There were two people as well, and one of them was behind the long counter opposite the door. He was cleaning a glass with a small damp cloth, massaging the inside with long fingers. He looked up at the unexpected traveler.

"Two bottles of tequila and a room."

"*¿Es todo?*"

The traveler nodded, then reached into his hip pocket again. This time he pulled out everything he had and laid it on the counter in a crumpled pile. The bartender reached out and fingered the pile, casually separating the car key from the bills. There were several twenties and a fifty. He must have liked what he saw. He placed the clean glass on the counter and switched to English.

"Looking for the night?"

He wanted to say that he'd pretty much found the night, thank you, but he didn't say anything. He just nodded again.

The bartender smiled. "You like Angélica?"

"Angélica?"

"Like an angel."

He nodded. "Like an angel."

The bartender's smile broadened, showing off the gaps between his teeth. He whistled to the old man sitting near the window. They exchanged a few fast words, then he reached behind the counter and produced two bottles of tequila, then an empty can of Tecate beer. He placed the can on its side on the counter. There was a small hole in its bottom, and a piece of twine looped through the can, securing a room key.

"*Segundo nivel.* Towards the end."

The man near the window said something else. Slang the traveler didn't understand, and the bartender raised an eyebrow. "You come on foot?" the bartender asked.

"I ran my car off the road. Near some church, maybe."

The bartender glanced back to the pile of money on the counter and he seemed to do a calculation in his head. Then he laughed, showing off more teeth. "You're lucky we have class," he said as he scooped all the money off the counter. "We bring car to you."

The room was small. A single window that looked onto the single street. An old dresser next to the window, hand-painted with roses. A narrow bed. One night-stand. A lamp. No bathroom. He tossed the suitcase on the bed, and it sank into the mattress. He placed the two bottles of tequila on the night-stand along with the Tecate key, then he sat on the edge of the bed next to his bag. There was a knock on the door; and before he could respond, the door creaked open. A woman stood in the doorway, not much more than a silhouette against the light of the hall. She was short, maybe five feet tall, and full of curves, what you'd call buxom.

Or maybe, he thought with a twisted smile, *cherubic.*

"Angélica?"

"*Sí.*" She took a step forward and closed the door behind her. She was wearing a simple blue dress and carrying a matching drawstring bag. She tossed the bag on the dresser beside the window. She did this with a kind of casualness that made it clear she'd done it before. He struggled up off the bed, rising awkwardly to his feet. She kept her eyes on him as she undid the strap over her right shoulder, wasting no time; and he kept his eyes on her. She wasn't beautiful, but in the dimness of the room she'd do.

She undressed. After she placed her undergarments on top of the dresser, she pointed at the bag still on the bed.

"*¿Qué es?*" she said.

"It's my suitcase."

She shook her head. Maybe she didn't speak English. Or maybe he hadn't really answered her question. Obviously it was a suitcase. What she really wanted to know was what the hell it was doing on the bed.

He grabbed the bag with both hands, intending to pull it onto the floor, but as his fingers tightened around the leather straps, he found himself thinking about the miles it had traveled, and the years. He remembered the satchel he had before the suitcase, and the canvas pack before that. He rubbed his left hand over its worn leather covering.

"It's my life," he said, answering her question for the second time, and again she just shook her head. "I take it with me. To remind me how far I've come." He tried to grin, but it didn't come out right.

"*¿Qué es?*"

He undid the three latches on the front of the case and opened it to show her. There was a dull light inside the bag, a pale golden nimbus, and it washed over her naked belly, her breasts. She leaned forward, her eyes wide.

"*¿Qué es?*" she said, and she pointed again.

Inside the bag, there was a small bow, lying across the diagonal, made of rosewood threaded with silver filaments and strung with a golden bowstring. The bowstring was luminous, pulsing gently. Next to the bow was a leather quiver that held six or seven golden arrows, the shafts barely visible, each with delicate white dove fletchings. On top of all of this, a tiny pair of wings.

Cupid pulled the wings out to show her. "They clip on in the back."

She didn't understand.

"*They clip on in the back*," he said again, this time louder, as if speaking louder in a foreign language would make his meaning more clear. She shook her head.

"Shit," he said, and he pulled off his shirt, pulled it over his head without unbuttoning, taking his dirty undershirt with it. He showed her the two clips on the wings, and then showed her how they attach to his back.

She giggled then, like a little girl, and whatever mask she had worn into his bedroom, it slipped, if only for a second. He saw bright eyes, a twinkle even, and his heart filled with desire. She said something that he didn't catch, then she put her arms around his back, pulling him close, feeling for the boney hooks in his skin. She was warm against his body, and he placed his head into the crook of her neck and breathed deeply. She smelled sweet and earthy, like hops.

He dropped the wings back into his bag and closed it. He wrapped his arms around her and they sank to the bed together, nudging the closed suitcase to the floor as they kissed. She held a condom up while he struggled out of his pants. He wondered where she had got it, and figured she must have been holding it in her hand the whole time; but he shook his head and she shrugged her shoulders. He knew there would be nothing between them. He buried his face between her breasts and inhaled again, and he pulled her hips to his. Then he drew his arrow and he pierced her heart.

O Love! has she done this to thee? What shall (alas!) become of me?

He came, quivering, and she pulled him closer. He squeezed his eyes shut seeing stars and groaned, and the groan swept out of his body along with all his worries and wishes, carried on an unassailable tide of pleasure. He rolled over on to his back, taking her with him, and he leaned up and gently bit her neck. Her eyes were open, and she was gazing at him as if he were the only man in the world; and for the moment, for this moment, for *only* this moment, he was. They lay there, locked together, not moving but rippling slowly. He bit her again, this time on the lip. She yelped and he bit her again, harder.

"¡Mierda!" she said, jerking away. She hit the floor with a hard and heavy thump; but she was up quickly and moving towards the dresser. *"¡Vete a la mierda! ¡Pendejo!"* Blood was rolling over her lower lip. She fumbled for something in her bag. *"¡Chinga tú madre! ¡Mierda!"* she said again as the room filled with a startling golden radiance, blazing through the window, as brilliant as daylight.

He shielded his eyes as the light continued to pour into the room, so intense it had a physical presence, a pressure. Wild buzzing filled the air, like the sound of a swarm of angry bees. Angelica screamed, and the light intensified, painfully bright now, golden sparks ricocheting off the walls and floors and ceiling.

Cupid rolled out of bed and moved quickly to the door. Squinting, he fumbled for the latch, but the door wouldn't open. "You OK?" he called back to Angelica. She had stopped screaming, but didn't answer.

At last the lights began to withdraw. He opened his eyes and watched a thousand glowing embers drifting slowly towards the window, then back out into the dark street, coalescing into a single golden cloud, shifting and changing shape. Angelica was watching, too, mesmerized or stunned, leaning out the window now, her arms resting on the windowsill. Cupid noticed a small knife on the floor beside her left foot. It must've fallen from her bag. Or perhaps she dropped it.

"You OK?" he asked again, and now she turned to look at him, her expression no longer hostile, but distant, and her eyes slipped right off him. She turned back to the street.

The lights were gone now, inside and out; and Cupid retrieved his pants, along with his shoes and socks. He dressed quickly, grabbed his suitcase, and headed for the door. She didn't bother to see him off.

The bar was empty as he passed through it, and the street was as he left it, except for his car with the large hole in its windshield, now parked in front of the fountain across from the sign for the town of Zicatela. He crossed the road, shoes and socks in one hand, suitcase in the other. The driver's-side door opened easily. He tossed his shoes, socks, and suitcase across the front seat; then he glanced up to the second floor of the hotel. Angelica was still there, staring out into space. She looked *beautiful*. He thought of calling to her, but he knew she wouldn't respond. He looked down the road, in the direction from which he had come. The golden lights had retreated, maybe several hundred yards, but they were still there, and he knew they would be back.

He climbed into his car, and felt for the key in the ignition. It wasn't there; but when he checked behind the driver's sunshade, the key dropped into his hand. He started the engine. He let the clutch out fast and pulled away from the lights, leaving the woman leaning on her windowsill, not thinking anything, just breathing, dreaming.

See how sadly he walks, poor child, wings drooping,
How he beats at his bared breast.

— Ovid

"Quiver"

First and last lines from
Soft by Rupert Thomson

I don't quite remember how this story came together, but I
think I wrote it on a trip to Jasper, Alberta. I say that apropos
of nothing. But there's something about a long-suffering
over-weight middle-aged Cupid afflicted by unrequited love
that tickles me. That probably says more about me than
intended, and certainly more than you need to know.

Excerpt from "I Only Have Eyes for You"
by Harry Warren and Al Dubin
Excerpt from "Cupid and Campaspe"
by John Lyly

Written between 9 June 2004 and 28 October 2008

Sabotaje

THERE WAS A WALL. Built from stones the size of fists, and the color of bone. Two Americans sat before it, a table between them, baking in the Mexican sun. They drank *pulque*, the local beer, but they didn't talk, and their expressions were guarded. One of the men was young and sweaty, long dirty hair, dressed in ragged cotton shorts and shirt. He looked as if he had just returned from a long morning toiling in the field, if not for the tiny designer label that stuck out from his collar. Locals called him *Gringo Poblano*, for "big look, no bite," and, foolishly, he'd taken the epithet for his own.

The other man was new to town; older and overweight, with thinning hair and sinking jowls. He wore new khaki slacks and a floral-pattern shirt, a gold watch, and rings on both hands. He looked like any other tourist, a handful of dollars passing through.

Poblano took another swig of beer. The local stuff wasn't very good, but he'd grown used to it.

"So," he said at last. "You're here." He made the merest flicker of eye contact.

The older man laughed. It was the kind of laugh you heard around the pools of *Los Hormigas*, or any swanky hotel. Favored, confident. He gestured broadly across the plaza, waving his large hand past the old buildings, tawdry shops, broken-down cars, and the small, dry fountain at its center.

"Not much here, here."

Poblano shifted, and the metal chair squeaked beneath him. "Your opinion means so much to me." He took another mouthful of beer.

Across the plaza, the double doors of *la Madre* swung open. Half a dozen children ran into the street and towards the empty fountain, followed by two young women from the parish church, dressed in black.

The older man hesitated, looking uncomfortable for the first time. "I wish you could find a place a little nicer, that's all. A place with more … *possibility.*"

Poblano said nothing. He followed his father's gaze for a moment, watched the dust swirl in the street behind the children, then looked away. He counted the bottles of beer on the table. It wasn't enough.

A delivery truck rumbled into the plaza, stirring up more dust. On its side was a large but faded picture of a cartoon mouse with bandoleer and pistols. The rodent *bandido* looked as if he had been painted on top of several other older advertisements. There were faded words, too, layer upon layer. The truck had been repurposed so many times you couldn't tell what it carried anymore. The two sisters shooed the children out of the truck's path, and Poblano watched as one big wheel rode up onto the edge of the sidewalk that ringed the fountain, and then rolled off again. When it finally stopped, it was blocking access to most of the street.

"Are you going to tell me why you're here?"

Poblano didn't answer. Instead he watched the two young *Chilangos* climb out of the truck, leaving its engine running. They were wearing the uniforms of the CNC, *la Compañía Nacional del Carro*, and they laughed and swaggered across the open plaza to the bar.

When he turned back to his father, his eyes flashed resolve. "This is where I want to be. Are you going to tell me why *you*'re here?"

The older man frowned. "I came to talk to you about

your mother. In person."

"Why would you want to do that?" The younger man leaned forward and the metal chair wobbled beneath him. He brushed the stringy hair out of his eyes and tried to meet his father's gaze, then he grabbed a beer in the middle of the table and finished it in one long guzzle. As he put the empty bottle down, he wondered if it was his.

"Why don't you just get on with the bad news," he said.

His father nodded and stood. "I'm going to get another drink."

Poblano sighed. He wiped his hands over his pants. He watched his father disappear into the dark shadow that marked the entrance to the bar. A minute later, the two truck drivers emerged from the same shadow, carrying four bottles of beer each. The black bottles were dripping wet, and the truckers held each one by the neck between their fingers, two to a hand. They started towards their truck, bottles clinking, but turned away at the last moment, disappearing down one of the plaza's many alleys. Meanwhile, the children had formed a small circle around the desiccated fountain and started to dance. Maybe an old folk ritual of some sort, Poblano thought; but the thought had little weight, and brought him no pleasure. He had liked to think this ghost town had a touch of magic, high on the fringes of the Sierra Madre Oriental. Now — after less than two months — he wasn't so sure. There used to be 15,000 people who lived here, back at the turn of the century, before *farmacia, bodega, teléfono*. A silver-mining town — *Real de Catorce* — that like so many fell into decay, abandoned by all but the most tenacious families. When he had first arrived he imagined the Huichol adolescents climbing up on the stone shoulders of the oldest buildings, honoring the gods of *liberación* and peyote with guns and grins and erections. He imagined young women, *many* young women, isolated and innocent, hungry for the exotic he might provide, eager to become his creative muses. But now he saw nothing but bottomless poverty and cheap tourism, malnourished children and idiot adults; and he felt an unreasonable distaste for those other expats sharing dirty houses without running water, with only three or four hours of electricity a day, hoping to mine the town's remaining commodity — its "color" — for a short story or novel, or screenplay. He'd heard a famous Hollywood filmmaker had set up residence in *Matehuala*, an hour's bus ride if conditions were favorable.

Poblano clasped his hands. He was starting to feel light-headed from the beer. He examined the small attaché case next to his father's abandoned chair, and snorted. Its brown leather had his father's monogram engraved just below the latch. It could contain a new manuscript, he thought, as easily as a will. Or maybe it just contained his father's medicine. He didn't know. He didn't care. He glanced back across the street at his father's car, parked near the large truck. It was ugly and new, but it wouldn't stay new for long. By the time his father had driven it the seven hours back to Mexico City it would look like any other worn-out gas-guzzler in this country. He supposed his father was smart enough not to drive one of his own cars down from the States, but the pricey rental still didn't belong here. Neither did his father's expensive bag. Neither did his father.

Atop *la Madre* was a small turret clock. Its old hands never moved, but it still tolled every hour. It tolled now, and a few workers spilled into the plaza from out of the smaller buildings for lunch. More children ran through the open wooden doors of the church. Poblano picked up one of the beer bottles on the table and rolled it across his forehead, but it had lost its chill. He put it down feeling stupid. Where the hell was his father? Whatever this was about, he wanted to get it over with. He looked back towards the entrance to the bar, then again at the leather bag, and this time noticed the latch was loose, floating just above the catch. A last will would be bad — very bad — but a new manuscript, that could actually be worse. Or worse still: a shiny new hardcover, inscribed and signed, a cruel and merciless offering.

Poblano shifted in his seat. He had been published exactly three times. The first time he had endured the inevitable humiliation of the book's moderate success being attributed to his father's name, only because he assumed his work would stand on its own. But the second book brought sympathy rather than criticism; and its follow-up was warehoused and pulped before he had spent the advance. Perhaps it was never his talent at all, then, and always just his climbing on the shoulders of giants, or one giant. *It was the endings*, his last editor had said in a charade of justification, *sabotaging the body of his work*. A fire in a family-run grocery store, killing nine people in the final chapter of *The Bridge Runner*. A derailment, killing over a hundred passengers in the last two pages of *The Train*. And an earthquake that swallowed the entire city of Escondido, leaving no survivors. That was *A Seeker in Sunset*, and that was the last. *Everyone just got tired of the endings*, his editor had said, *the senseless devastation, the circumvention of conflict* — but it was obvious to him that she was no more than a mouthpiece, sending another message from his father.

Poblano ran his arm over his brow. He was sweating heavily now. Someone shouted *"ancho chiles!"* and Poblano turned as a street vendor emerged from an alley just beyond the bar. The vendor — a short, squat Mexican, wearing a wide-brimmed sombrero — wheeled his cart in front of an open section of the stone wall and began throwing sausages on its small grill. The aroma of *chorizo* filled the air, and Poblano listened as the meat crackled and popped. The whole thing was a living, breathing, stinking cliché.

He thought of getting up and leaving, and he wondered if maybe that's what his father wanted. If his stepping back into the bar was just to give his son another chance to slip away, to demonstrate his defective character. But it didn't seem likely. His father *enjoyed* confrontation, and more likely had traveled all this way for that single purpose. It was Poblano who preferred the passive-aggressive approach: to get up and walk back to his small room. Unplug the mostly-useless phone. Turn his back on all the complexity, all the crap. Leave his father in the middle of Mexico, fuming in the dust and decay, leave him with seven hours of bottled-up anger on the road back to Mexico City. Or maybe there was some better way. A better way to end it all....

A phone rang, startling him from his reverie. He looked up. There was a public phone booth, not far from where he sat, the same kind of dirty glass and steel coffin you'd see all over Mexico. Some of the children glanced towards it as it rang, but no one else paid it attention. No one ever did, except perhaps the owner of the grocery it fronted. But the grocer didn't appear, and it kept ringing.

He looked over to the entrance of the bar. Maybe his father would be coming back. Maybe his father wouldn't be coming back. *Who the fuck knew.*

Poblano got up. He stepped over the small railing that separated the patio of the bar from the street and headed towards the phone. The glass door slapped closed behind him as he picked up the receiver. The air in the booth was considerably hotter than outside, and it had the stale smell of a urinal, but he'd smelled worse. Holding the phone to his ear, he watched a second, smaller, lorry roll into the plaza. It stopped, stuck behind the first delivery truck.

When he realized the caller hadn't spoken yet, he started the conversation. "Hello?" he said.

On the other end of the line, a voice answered, almost an echo of his own: "Hello?"

He waited for more, but there was no more, so he tried again. "Who is this?"

"...Is Abraham there?"

Poblano rocked back and forth on his feet, feeling slightly tipsy. He blinked a few times. *Who the fuck was Abraham?*

The line crackled with static, and the caller asked again: "Is Abraham there?"

Poblano looked at the phone in his hand as if it were

some ancient artifact, a tool he wasn't sure he knew how to use. Why had he picked the phone up anyway?

He put the receiver back to his ear. "What?" he said.

"My friend, I am looking for Abraham. Please tell me if he is there now?" the caller asked for the third time. And this time Poblano thought, *What's with this "my friend" shit?*

"Who is this?" he asked again, wondering really who the call was meant for — because there was no one hanging around the phone booth.

"I'm looking for Abraham. Can you see him, or is the square full of people?"

Poblano grabbed a handful of shirt and mopped his forehead.

The voice said, "I'm looking for — "

"I heard you. Who's Abraham?"

"Please just look around," said the voice. "You can do that, can't you?"

Poblano glanced back towards the table he'd left. It was still empty. For a second, he had the strange feeling the voice on the phone was his father's, calling from inside the bar. But it couldn't be — the caller's accent wasn't American. It wasn't particularly Mexican either. And this wasn't his father's sort of game.

"Please," the caller entreated, "just look around. Tell me what you see. Many people?"

"What does Abraham look like?"

"Are there many women? Many children?"

"What?"

"In the plaza, my friend. Many children?"

Something wasn't right. "Look, Í don't know anyone named — "

And then he understood. All of a sudden, for no good reason, he *understood*.

When he was back in the States, shortly after his first

book was published, he was frequently asked where he got his ideas. Writers are always asked and he always liked to say "Hoboken." It was a line he'd stolen from his father, back when he thought it was worthwhile to steal from him. Hoboken was as good an answer as any, because no one knows where ideas come from, they just come, they just appear, like Athena from Zeus' brow, fully formed; and although he was not a writer, not anymore, would in fact never consider himself a creative man, not anymore, he had suddenly understood exactly the conversation he was having with this stranger on the phone. The realization just dropped on him, a ton of insight right on his head from out of nowhere:

There's a bomb.

"How many people do you see?" the voice asked. "Is the plaza very crowded?"

Poblano looked around, his head clearing fast. The school children continued to play. Locals continued to fill the tables outside the bar — his father was there now, too. Two old women shuffled out of the grocery. He didn't do politics. He didn't do them back home, and he certainly didn't do them here. Yes, there was unrest in Mexico, all up and down the coast and through the heart of the country, he knew that, but wasn't there *always* unrest?

Poblano put one hand up to the glass door, pressing against it with his flat palm. He pulled the phone from his ear and looked at it again. Could he possibly be right? It was crazy — wasn't it? — to think there's a bomb.

But he *knew* he was right.

Should he keep the guy on the phone? Stall him? Tell him the plaza's empty? — but suppose the guy was waiting for the moment when it's *safest* to detonate, when the fewest people would be harmed. Maybe the right thing to say was that the plaza's *full*. He scanned the street, looking for anything out of the ordinary, and his gaze fell upon the large delivery truck with its engine still running. It was still blocking its side of the street, blocking the new truck that had entered the plaza, and its two drivers still had not returned.

"I – I don't know what you want," Poblano stammered, trying to come up with a plan, an idea, *anything*. "But this is the *Librería Fuentes*. In Zacatecas. You have the wrong number. No plaza. No Abraham. *Librería*."

Poblano hung up the phone and yanked open the glass door. Then everything turned bright orange and silent and he squeezed his eyes shut. Light burned through his closed eyelids and shadows flickered and leapt, dark silhouettes of young men, dancing mutely around a blazing red fire. When he opened his eyes the square was all smoke and flame and steaming debris. There was rain, too, a steady rain of glass, falling everywhere, and then gradually his hearing returned. Someone was screaming. He tried to open the door of the phone booth, but his hand went through the empty pane of glass. Without thinking, he slipped through the door panel and sprinted back towards the bar, past burning cars, past the shattered fountain, past the dark bodies of women and children. He jumped the small railing that had been twisted by the blast and landed where he had seen his father moments before. Table and chairs were gone, but the large body of his father remained, leaning against the stone wall. His father's face was black, as if covered in soot, and his eyes were wide open, but empty, like a doll's eyes of glass, frozen with an expression that might have been despair or desperation. Both his charred arms were outstretched, reaching for something that wasn't there. His hands were open, as if he were offering something to his son. His hands were empty, as they had always been.

"*Sabotaje*"

First and last lines from
The Dispossessed by Ursula K. LeGuin

This is one of the few stories I started to write before I had any idea what the last line meant, or how I was going to get there. But by the time I realized the conflict was between a successful author and his less-talented son, I knew the turn I wanted the story to take. I liked the idea of a third-person objective point-of-view becoming increasingly subjective as the story goes along, until it is finally completely co-opted by one of its characters. In this case, it's the son, taking control of the narrative and sabotaging his own story by blowing everything up (just like in his failed novels), thus avoiding a real confrontation with his father, and ultimately denying himself the possibility of any reconciliation, or even resolution.

Written between 10 November and 22 December 2003

Trump l'Oeil [1,2,3,4,5]

---

[1] God doesn't play nice.

Isn't that what Einstein said as they hauled him off to Buchenwald? Such a small mistake, wasn't it? A binary error. A *yes* instead of a *no*. Agreeing to leave the US to return to Germany in August, 1938, to present some new work at his professorial *alma mater*, the Berlin Academy of Sciences. The tiniest of miscalculations for a man for whom calculation was integral. Of course President Roosevelt had made promises to him concerning security and mission-criticality (there were hints of containment — rapprochement — by the Italians, British, and French); and there were reciprocal reassurances from the highest level in Berlin. And in the end, imagining that the presentation of a chapter from his latest book, *The Evolution of Physics*, co-authored by Leopold Infeld, a Polish Jew, might tweak the nose of his former academic institute, slow the despicable *Gleichschaltung*, and perturb, however infinitesimally, Adolf Hitler himself, he capitulated. Afterwards — despite the event's being attended by German luminaries (both scientific and political) and deemed successful by the press (both international and domestic) — the *Oberkommando der Wehrmacht* (High Command of the Armed Forces, under Hitler's direct command for the past six months) refused to allow Einstein to leave the Fatherland.

Of course he wasn't taken to the concentration camp immediately — that particular indignity was still more than a year away — but the Germans had other plans. They put him to work in Special Unit 114 of the Ahnenerbe Institute, compelling him to collaborate with a small group of similarly-ensnared scientists. The High Command wasn't interested in advanced munitions, encryption, or medical experimentation: they had plenty of other scientists working on those things. Instead they put the group to work on several new technologies based on ancient or forbidden knowledge, mystical texts, alien technologies, and their own secret research concerning matter transmigration, time dilation, and other advanced or occult sciences. By the end of 1938, the secretive Unit unveiled their first innovative technology with an obvious military application. It was groundbreaking, game-changing, and terrifying.

[2] Due to the illusory characteristics of this revolutionary technology, and to the enigmatic nature of anything that tinkers with matter transmigration and time dilation, the project was code-named TRUMP L'OEIL (official Ahnenerbe designation: SS-TLO/114). The name derived from the popular painting technique known as "trompe l'oeil," but thanks to the inadequate typing skills of one of the project's administrators, "trompe" became "trump," and the typo — oddly prophetic — stuck.

"Trompe l'oeil" (translation: "deceived by the eye") uses realistic imagery to create the illusion of depth where there is none. Like a doorknob painted on a flat wall, or a small fly on a canvas. The new technology of SS-TLO/114, however, far surpassed optical manipulation to include a deeper, broader, semantic modification of perception that might actually bend the truth and even invert its meaning. Bernhard Rust, the Nazi Minister of Science, Education, and National Culture, would later describe the technology as one that could "change the essence of a thing to a trifling irrelevancy; turn one quiddity into another." (*"Diese technologie wird das wesen einer sache zu einem kleinen punkt ändern; es wird wiederum quiddity zu quiddity."*) Or put more simply: the Nazis had discovered a theoretical basis for what would become Goebbels' "Big Lie," a rational underpinning for disinformation, a physics of untruth. It could make *something* seem like *nothing*, or turn a footnote into the whole story. It could make the most absurd propaganda believable.

Almost immediately SS-TLO/114 was put to use by the Third Reich to manipulate its enemies. Over the following months, Germany became increasingly provocative on the world's stage, stirring discord and confusion by making the significant appear unimportant; or the unimportant, distractingly significant. The successful annexation of the Sudetenland, the Munich Agreement, the initial Berchtesgaden "luncheon," "spontaneous demonstrations," *Kristallnacht*, "Peace in our time" — these were all early examples of SS-TLO/114's hypnotic application.

[3] Albert Einstein died in Buchenwald in late 1944. The exact date of his death is unknown: there is no body, nor written record. However, since the end of the war, accounts have emerged of his last year in the quarry camp, during which time he suffered from an unusual form of graphorrhea. This "illness" manifested itself in Einstein's obsessive composition of mathematical formulae. He wrote on every surface at every opportunity, using whatever implement was at hand. He scribbled and scratched with pencil on paper, stick in dirt, straw in dust, rusty nail on wall, even his own nails into his flesh. Anecdotal reports of his littering his crowded barrack with tiny scraps of stolen paper were common, of long lines of algebraic notation on the roof of his bunk or along another prisoner's roost. He called his work "scientifiction," presumably after Hugo Gernsback (editor of *Amazing Science Fiction Stories*) who coined the term. But the more Einstein proclaimed his scribblings a mere folly, the more the Germans tracked his progress and devoted valuable resources to

the analysis of the work, believing, mistakenly, that what he was writing was "scientifact." Specifically, advanced equations related to the process of nuclear fission.

Present-day consensus is that the "Buchenwald Equations" are in fact gibberish, and that Einstein was using the German's own SS-TLO/114 technology against them. Indeed, this heroic effort of misdirection by a weak and aging concentration camp prisoner was likely responsible for the delay of *Uranprojekt*, the Third Reich's effort to build a nuclear bomb.

[4] After the war, the Allies raided Germany's military industrial complex, poaching scientists and technocrats and destroying the Third Reich's most dangerous weapons, including SS-TLO/114.

Evidence of this, however, has never stopped rumors of the technology's continued application. You may have heard such stories concerning Joseph Stalin, Benito Mussolini, Fidel Castro, Marshall Joseph Tito, Slobodan Milosevic, Idi Amin, Ho Chi Minh, Saddam Hussein, Ayatollah Khomeini, Ferdinand Marcos, Pol Pot, Francisco Franco, and others. There is no factual basis for any of this. God is kind and merciful, man is good, and war is peace. And, thankfully, this is one genie that has been stuffed back into its bottle.

Case in point: In 2016, nearly seventy-five years after the end of hostilities, far across the Atlantic Ocean, Donald Trump was elected president by an overwhelming number of Americans decimated by poverty, a lack of economic opportunity, declining education and, for the Caucasian majority, a deep sense of evaporating privilege and external threat. Fortunately, by the end of his third term, the United States was again a shining star in the firmament of affluent western democracies, and Donald Trump — now eighty-two years old, and married to Angelique Rivera, his fourth wife, an active sports model and reality-TV star — had *truly* made America great again. The standard of living was higher than it had ever been, unemployment was down, the rich were prospering, and what's more, there were no pesky Jews.

[5] You have been reading an excerpt from *An Alternate and Right History of the World*, brought to you by Trump's Sweet Sugary ClusterPops, the all-organic and all-healthy breakfast cereal filled

with only the best sugar, a huge number of vitamins, bigly amounts of minerals, and guaranteed happiness. In fact, it's filled with so much happiness you may get bored with the happiness. You're going to come to me and go "Please, please, we can't be happy anymore." You'll say "Please, Mr. President, we beg you sir, we don't want the happiness anymore. It's too much. It's not fair to everybody else." And I'm going to say, "I'm sorry, but you're going to have the happiness. Happiness! Happiness! Happiness!"

Jedem das Seine

[From an interior-facing sign above the main entrance of the Buchenwald Concentration Camp. It means "To each his own," or more colloquially: "Everyone gets what he deserves." Hail the Führer!]

"Trump l'Oeil"

First and last lines from
The Rectangular Ruins by Mark Malamud

Art is the opposite of politics. Art is a lie that makes us see the truth. Politics is a lie that doesn't. Dark times imagined, and dark times ahead. Really, nothing more to say about this.

Written between 17 November 2016 and 2 February 2017

The Tyrant of Arcadia

BEFORE ENTERING the supreme council room, Gabriel Baines sent his Mans-made simulacrum clacking ahead to see if by chance it might be attacked. Baines himself stayed outside in his floater, hovering in a five-minute Recharge Zone, eyes flitting between the entrance to the Trojan Defense Ministry Headquarters across the street and the tiny screen in front of him that displayed an image straight from his simulacrum's eyes. Baines' eyes widened as his simulacrum approached the council room door on the sixty-ninth floor of the Ministry: a redhead with a pleasing figure, General Antinous' secretary, was guarding the entrance, a long snake-like creature coiled tightly around her hips. She unwrapped some of the Veritas sens-o-pet, just enough to offer the simulacrum its wedge-shaped head. The simulacrum stepped forward and brushed its hand confidently over the animal's soft black crown. The sens-o-pet was a nervous creature and it coughed twice before mistakenly certifying the Baines doppelgänger as the real thing. The General's secretary — Miss Vacuum Penilé Calypso — unlocked and opened the council room door, then stepped back, bowing deferentially to her superior. Baines' simulacrum entered the council and surveyed those in attendance. There were two colonels flanking General Antinous, and two Serr monks dressed in long black dusters with sparkling chlamydian hoods. The simulacrum turned and smiled its most winning smile back at Miss Calypso. The secretary blushed. "I'll catch you later," the simulacrum said with a wink, then marched into the center of the room. Gabriel Baines, back in his floater, turned up the synthetic's audio. He wanted to hear everything his simulacrum heard as he encountered each soldier and monk, to eke out any clues as to his standing among the council members. But as the council room's door slid closed, no one said anything. Everything, obviously, had been said before Baines — or rather before his simulacrum — had arrived. As soon as the simulacrum reached the center table, but before it could speak, both monks pulled deadly-looking Clitoori pulsers from beneath their robes. The first shot tore away a piece of the plastiflesh covering the simulacrum's cheek. The second shot missed its mark as the simulacrum dove for cover. The length and speed of its jump immediately blew Baines' ruse. "It's not Baines!" one of the colonels cried out. The simulacrum rolled, re-stood, and swung around to face its monastic assassins; and its left hand transformed, revealing two small barrels extending from its cybernetic wrist. The barrels glowed red, then blue, then white — and then two vivid beams flashed across the room, sweeping back and forth, cutting silently through uniforms and flesh and sizzling into the heavy ion-adamantine walls of the council chamber. A fiery beam cut General Antinous in half, just as he pulled the pin on a one-eyed Fahlus bomb meant for the simulacrum; but without a designated target, the grenade buzzed aimlessly around the room before detonating, and the resulting explosion killed the remaining soldiers and knocked the simulacrum back through the council chamber's front door. Back in his floater, Gabriel Baines issued the recall code to his simulacrum. He had been right to be suspicious! The simulacrum auto-cauterized the laser port in its left wrist, and then turned to find itself face to face with Miss Calypso. "Come with me," the simulacrum commanded as it offered its hand to the General's secretary. Her Gynotic-brand clothing, normally tight around her body, now hung loosely, partially shredded by the blast, and the simulacrum could see her pink flesh through the derma-latex. The sens-o-pet had slipped down around her ankles, like a pair of panties. The animal trembled in humiliation, having mistaken this machine for a human being. The secretary looked the simulacrum over, then she stepped over the sens-o-pet and kicked off her heels. She placed her delicate, soft hand inside the simulacrum's manly and mechanical one. "Take me to your leader," she sighed, and together they —

"Incoming at five o'clock!" Zarek shouted and there was a flash of bright light over their heads. Talos looked up to see a bloom of concrete erupt from the ceiling. If there was a concurrent blast, Talos didn't hear it; in fact, everything went eerily silent as he watched the ceiling collapse, large chunks of rubble and twisted rebar crashing to the floor around him. Talos dropped to one knee and drew his rifle close. Dust was everywhere, a dark grey churning of particulate concrete. He held his breath.

Zarek leapt into view. He was waving his hands back and forth and his lips were moving, but there was still no sound. Talos raised his gun — *now the infidels will pay!* He swung his rifle towards the window, but lost his footing on the scrabbly floor and accidentally strafed the ceiling with automatic fire. And still no sound at all.

Zarek covered his head as more pieces of the ceiling fell around them. Then he flagged Manasseh, and the medic ran over. He moved into Talos' face, then pushed the boy's gun aside and went to work on his head. Talos held still. He'd been grazed by a piece of flying concrete, just across the temple, and the blood was starting to spill into his face. He wiped a hand across his brow and saw that it was covered in equal parts blood and dust. Zarek signaled Casta and she jumped over a toppled freezer, moving into the neighboring shop through a hole in the wall. Talos watched as she disappeared through a veil of dust and billowing bed sheets, and then everything started making noise at once: feet on gravel, the crumbling ceiling, nearby lips, distant artillery. His hearing was back, and everything was demanding attention. Talos heard Manasseh cough several times, and he looked into the medic's eyes. He was their fucking *doctor* — but he was always coughing. It was like having a lame podiatrist. He watched Manasseh's dark tongue slurp inside his mouth as he talked. Then he heard some small arms fire, probably Casta laying cover. She was a good soldier. There was another loud boom and Manasseh's eyes grew wide.

"They've got a Vulcan 20mm!" Zarek shouted — Zarek, the big boy, their fearless leader — and there followed another bone-shaking explosion. The store filled with bright orange light and everything fell silent again. Talos held still, a statue in the center of the storm. He'd been through this so many times — through explosions and concussions and

blinding flashes — he didn't even wonder if he was going
to die anymore, he didn't even flinch, it was like those
particular nerves had been so over-stimulated they just shut
down. Now, he closed his eyes to hurry on to whatever
came next. Life, death, whatever. Let's just get on with it.

When he opened his eyes, he was on his back, staring at
the ceiling. Manasseh was leaning over him with a scalpel in
one hand and a surgical torch in the other. A bent cigarette
hung out of the medic's mouth. *Watch out, Manasseh, those
cigarettes'll kill you, ha ha.*

The medic's torch sharpened into a needle-shaped
flame, glowing bright through a cloud of cigarette smoke.
Manasseh leaned forward.

"Fuck this," Talos said, trying to sit up; but Zarek was
on his legs and Casta was pinning his arms. Manasseh leaned
even closer; he was breathing through the tiny cigarette
squint hole in his face like some old guy on a ventilator,
hissy and loud. Talos squirmed, and Manasseh applied the
conflagrator, just out of sight, somewhere above his
eyebrows. Talos screamed, and a thousand hours passed.

"Listen," Manasseh oozed to the woozy Talos, "the
fragment's almost clear, neh? Just once more should do it,
friend."

Talos thought of angels. And dead Americans. And this
close, Manasseh's face was all dirty angles and teeth, and
Talos thought he looked more than ever like the Great Satan
of Healthcare. Manasseh grinned. Nicotine-laced spittle
dripped from his lips as he applied inferno to wound a
second time, and everything went quickly to the hell of
fucked martyrs. Talos dropped out of a black sky and landed
standing on a rock the size of a football in a shimmering sea
of white hot sand. Above him angels with American-flag
capes circled. He looked down at the small lump of fiery
stone upon which his two naked feet were jockeying for
space, first side by side, then one on top of the other, then
side by side again, then he shot his arms out for balance, to

keep his bare feet from stepping into the cremating sand. He raised his eyes and tried to fix on some distant object to keep himself from losing balance, from falling, but there was nothing to see except a burning horizon. He lifted one foot, then the other, doing a little dance, and he could hear the burnt skin on the pad of each foot sticking to the stone. His feet were starting to cook. Enough of this! He jumped off the stone and ran, racing towards the horizon, feet sizzling away to ash beneath him.

At some point Talos returned to consciousness and stopped screaming, and he found himself sitting upright on a sloping floor. Small fires were burning everywhere, and he watched the whorls of black smoke from each stretch upward towards the distant ceiling, long dark fingers filled with glowing embers, reaching towards a starry but moonless night.

He must be in the prayer hall of a mosque, he thought, everything so detailed, so elaborate. A jewel in the crown of Sparti. He wiped his eyes and took another look around. Large proscenium arch, pretty much intact, but the stage itself was a wreck.

Ah. Not a mosque at all: a theatre.

Scaffolding dangled from above the stage, and broken glass was everywhere. A fire was burning in the balcony, and another in the box seats that overhung the stage. He let his gaze return to the dome of the ceiling, painted dark blue or black and darted with ember-stars. Then he saw it wasn't a painting. Most of the roof was gone.

They must have moved him a second time since that morning's attack. He felt a stiff theatre seat behind him, folded back. He looked at his hands. Dirty, brown, glistening with flecks of perspiration and blood. But he was alive, and he grinned ever so slightly. Salvation was therefore still within his grasp, retribution, *revenge*; the great reckoning, the great martyrdom he desired.

Talos massaged his scalp and thought about the infidels,

the invaders. He reached for his gun. There would be vengeance yet. For their fucking up everything, killing his friends, blowing up buildings and bridges (and theaters, although he himself had never been), stealing their nation's wealth and resources, fucking their women, stamping out their independence. He pictured the boot of an American soldier, stamping on an ant hill. He pictured millions of ants fleeing the nest, climbing the boot, then up the leg. He waited eagerly for the justice that would follow.

Talos straightened up slowly. His head had started to ache. Revenge was a throbbing red mass of spiky scenarios. A shadowed hand that was the dark roaring of the sun. Still, it made him smile.

Zarek and Casta were talking a few feet away, over by the orchestra pit. Manasseh was nearer, sitting on the floor across the aisle, digging through his backpack, coughing and looking for a smoke.

"You're alive," Manasseh said when he finally noticed Talos staring at him.

Talos nodded. He could play the waiting game if necessary. He could wait now for Zarek to determine their next move; he could wait through the night, through another day. He could wait forever so long as he got a chance to even the score.

"It's the anniversary of Avoli, you know," Manasseh said. Talos grunted. Who cared? The Hellenic Confusion (such a stupid name; there was no *confusion*) had been going on for about twenty years — long before The Greater War was declared — and proxy armies had been moving through the region tearing up roads and bombing villages for at least a decade before that. It all had something to do with securing supply lines to the south, to Iran and Syria, and to the oil fields beyond. But the big reasons didn't matter; they never do. What mattered was all small scale; what mattered was getting even, was driving the fuckers from their streets and towns and cities one by one — what mattered was demonstrating the resolute will of the people. What mattered was that no amount of softening up by the Americans or their dollar-leashed lackeys was going to break their backs. They would fight until every last infidel was strangled or bled or cut or shot or bombed out of the land of the living in abject demonizing ass-licking *humiliation!*

Talos cursed. His head really ached now. He'd wanted to stop thinking about this shit, but sometimes the thinking just had its way.

"I won't rest, my friend, until I see row after row of Americans, strung up, and the British trampled under their own war machines," Manasseh said as if reading Talos' mind. He lit another cigarette and poked it between his flabby lips.

Manasseh's family had been wiped out three years earlier. His three sisters and two younger brothers, his wife and three children, and many of his friends. Manasseh was one of just four survivors of a wedding ceremony in Tessi, a small village in the mountains to the North, part of Peloponnesus; and Talos tried his best to cut the old man slack. The Americans claimed afterward the small Orthodox church was built over a fortified weapons cache of some sort. Who knows. The bunker buster they dropped vaporized the site, obliterating evidence. It was a miracle Manasseh survived. The back of his head, his shoulders, his back, buttocks, and legs were permanently scarred, discolored and patchy. Most of his hair was gone, too, leaving scattered clumps on his head. Pathetic old man, but he was considered lucky. He talked a lot about his home, a mountainous region that he said was the official residence of the god Pan, inhabited by lusty nymphs and plentiful wine, a pagan paradise on Earth. But mostly his talk was sad, full of yearning, whining, yapping about his bygone youth, all while coughing up this black shit from all those cigarettes.

"It's good to be alive," Manasseh said, a surprising remark if Talos didn't know what was next. "Good so you can kill again tomorrow, neh?"

Talos grunted in agreement.

Zarek appeared over Talos' shoulder. He shook out his curly black hair — he was the best looking of the bunch, no question — and raised his rifle high over his head.

"Death to the Americans! Death to the British! Death to the faggot invaders of Greece! Death to the Zionist adulterers! No rest until every foreign testicle is turned to tapenade! *Eh, Manasseh?*"

Zarek chuckled at his own joke, and Casta slugged his shoulder hard with her fist. She wasn't a fan of Manasseh — she found him gross — but she didn't like the mocking sarcasm coming from their commander. It didn't look right.

(You might argue it was at least as irregular for a soldier to show her disapproval by whacking her commander, but Casta obviously didn't look at it that way, and neither did anyone else. Casta was just fifteen, and she looked younger than that, tall and thin, but she never lost sight of the mission, the target, not for a moment, and everyone valued that. Zarek was their commander, but Casta was their compass. So everyone cut her slack, too.)

Zarek sat down in the aisle and so did Casta; they sat back against back. Zarek was not much taller than Casta, and when she leaned back, her head fit comfortably into the nape of his neck. There was silence for a little while, except for the occasional pop and snap from one of the small fires burning around them. Talos pulled his rifle onto his lap and started to take it apart. It was another way to kill time. Then Zarek wrapped his arms around his knees and began to talk about the Turks and the British SAS, about the Athenian exodus, and tactics. It was their story, of course, not the story of The Greater War but the story of *their* war, and it sounded like he was picking up Episode 6 of a serialized adventure. This was his forte: Zarek could turn anything into a compelling narrative, even the inchoate mess of their lives. They all paid attention, like kids around a campfire, and Zarek — he was nearly seventeen, the oldest member of the unit other than the ancient Manasseh — described how the Germans and Italians were providing support to the Greeks now, and how they were bringing in some high-tech equipment from the Iranians that could turn the tide of war, but how the equipment got intercepted by the French, until a unit — a unit just like theirs — small, supple, strategic — re-acquired the materiel just north of Tripoli....

For twenty or so minutes, Zarek's voice held them in thrall. He'd use his hands, too, and occasionally toss his hair with a flourish. Sometimes he'd even perform, taking the role of a high-ranking official back in Athens, or caricaturing the American president. This is how they got their news, in episodic bites from Zarek, often retold later by Casta, again and again. Zarek got his news every time he radioed HQ, but he wasn't stupid and he always held bits back, always kept his team a little hungry.

Talos closed his eyes. Zarek said the Albanian refugees were still pouring into the country after the disaster up north, and the Bulgarian secret police were infiltrating the Albanian caravans with suicide bombers. They hadn't seen any of that action yet, but they were ready, and ready to answer in kind. A more immediate problem, Zarek said, was the American 101st Airborne which was moving south towards Sparti from Tripoli. It was part of a larger movement aimed at taking Athens in the summer, and British bombing was constant now, and there were already small ground engagements north and south of the capital.

Talos groaned. They'd spent the spring sniping the American's supply lines from Kalamata, but Talos thought they didn't have a chance in any head-on confrontation, however romantic Zarek's narrative. There were no trenches anymore, and the open streets were ripe for massacre. He fingered the reassembled Kalashnikov in his lap. Oh yes, he wanted the invaders beaten back, killed, dishonored; he wanted this hell to end; and he tried his hardest to believe that the enemy's ultimate defeat was inevitable. But even when he convinced himself of *that* truth, he always found himself with his back up against another wall, because even then, even with victory, what would come next? Hell was easy to imagine, he knew, but what the hell was Heaven?

Just before daybreak, the unit prepared to move out. Talos' head was now wrapped in swathing from eyebrows up, and he looked like he was wearing a turban. Manasseh at his side clucked approvingly while Zarek and Casta huddled just inside the entrance to the theatre. They were consulting a small, beat-up map. The division's radio had been dead for twelve hours, but their last orders were to take out a small group of American marines moving East through Sparti towards the Hotel International. The suspicion was they were an advance scouting group for a column of armored cavalry opening a western front to Athens. They hadn't seen or heard any evidence of their movement, but they couldn't just move in the open to check things out. Yesterday's skirmish with a local pro-Western militia called the Greek Boys was a case in point.

Manasseh and Talos grabbed their packs and moved up to join Zarek and Casta. Talos licked his lips and unbuckled his canteen, but it was light and no longer made that pleasing sloshing sound. He took a small sip and met Zarek's eyes as he swallowed, but Zarek looked away. Their water supply was low — the city's infrastructure was shot to hell and the wells were all suspect. Most of their water came from bottled supplies they'd find in demolished shops and apartments, and last week they had to risk tapping into a small water barrel behind a mosque. The water turned out to be OK, of course. Otherwise they'd all be dead.

"We'll move North," Zarek said, pointing to the map. Talos stood close to Casta as they watched Zarek's finger trace a serpentine path towards the center of town. None of them knew Sparti very well. And, to be honest, their maps weren't that great either. Three days ago, they got sucked into a British ambush — the result of cutting through a building to a road which wasn't supposed to dead end. They thought they were totally fucked. Talos took it as an opportunity for martyrdom and started to strap several hand-grenades to his chest shortly after they came under heavy fire, but Zarek had other ideas. He rummaged through his pack and pulled out a Roman Candle — their only one. Casta wasn't convinced and Manasseh actually laughed. Zarek ignored them both, even though he knew it was a desperate move. The Roman Candle was a mix of solid propellant and sticky napalm pellets, courtesy of the former Soviet Union. It was classified as a "smart" anti-personnel rocket for use in closed spaces, like bunkers or barracks, definitely not streets. The rocket was almost worthless in open spaces. Its shell would shatter on impact, scattering several thousand pellets in all directions, pellets that would bounce harmlessly off hard surfaces but detonate on impact with soft targets — that is, personnel. In an open space, most of the pellets would sail harmlessly out of range. When a Roman Candle went off indoors, however, it was like being trapped inside one of those bingo ball machines, only each time you got hit by one of the balls, it would burn a tiny hole through your body.

Zarek shot the candle straight up the alley, right between the largest vehicles that blocked their exit. Whether it was superior military wisdom on Zarek's part, or just dumb luck, the alley turned out to be a good match for the weapon's specifications. The pellets sprayed everywhere, ricocheting off the vehicles and store fronts, and the far end of the alley turned into a human maelstrom of fire and smoke. When Casta went on recon ten minutes later, she gave a double thumbs-up. The top of the alley was filled with smoking bodies of course. They had expected that. And the smell — like garlic chicken and keftedes, mostly, if you could ignore the acrid scent of napalm. What they hadn't expected was the size of the force that had ambushed them. There must've been nearly twenty guys, all in uniform, regular British army. Talos felt giddy as he tramped over the sizzling corpses. Manasseh kept yelling, "God is great! God is great!" and Talos nodded in agreement — nothing else could explain their impossible success. If Zarek had realized how many soldiers they were taking on, he would surely have let Talos lead a kamikaze charge down the alley.

Instead, Zarek high-fived Manasseh who high-fived him right back. It was rare to see Manasseh in such high spirits. Casta was the only one who looked grim, but Talos assumed she was disappointed it was their only Roman Candle.

They all moved forward, past two armored personnel carriers and a smaller urban tank. The British must not have expected much serious resistance from four starving sap-heads trapped in a dead-end street — they were nearly all out in the open when the rocket went off. Typical of these stupid English. And Zarek's team fucked them up *in detail*.

OK, there were still the two guys in the tank, it turned out, but they were easy to deal with. They had played possum for a few minutes and then tried to fire a round into Zarek and Manasseh as they approached, but they must've been hurt or crazy 'cause they couldn't aim for shit, and after they ducked back inside it was easy for Casta to smoke them out. Casta shot the first guy between the eyes when he emerged from the tank, blowing off the top-half of his head in the process. When the second guy followed close behind waving a white flag, Casta missed, slopping off his right ear. He rolled off the tank, right towards Zarek, and if he had gone for his sidearm, Casta would have happily fed her entire clip into him. As it was, he just fell back against the tank, blinking madly, and she decided to have some fun and popped him once in each knee. He didn't flinch, so maybe he was already paralyzed from the waist down or something.

Zarek moved in from the side and placed his rifle to the guy's temple and started yammering fragmented English at him. Even Talos couldn't make out what his commander was trying to say. Didn't matter. It wasn't likely Zarek was administering last rites or anything. Casta pulled Manasseh off to secure the perimeter, checking to see if everyone else was really dead. Or, rather, *making sure* everyone was dead.

"Is he conscious?" Talos asked as he came up beside Zarek. The Brit was in bad shape, obviously.

"Maybe. But he's not answering my questions." Talos glanced at Zarek, thinking he must be joking. He wasn't really the interrogating type. Zarek poked him again.

Talos moved closer to get a better look, but it worked both ways. The Brit saw him and then looked over at Zarek and his eyes went wide, like he recognized them both. Then he started to howl, literally.

"Howled! Howled!"

Talos jumped back; and Zarek's finger tightened on the trigger.

"*Howled!*" the guy said again.

Howled? Talos tried to think in English. Was it a question? Howled — *How old?*

The Brit's eyes darted back and forth between them, looking more than a little crazy, then his head suddenly lolled over onto his left shoulder, away from Zarek's rifle and exposing his shot-up ear. It looked nasty. The soldier had passed out, so Zarek poked him in the ear with his barrel and the guy opened his eyes again. He looked lost for a moment, then he started to speak again, looking back and forth between the two of them. Given his previous "howl," Talos expected some kind of fundamentalist sermon about boy soldiers and babies on the battlefield, or some such shit. Trying to make them all feel guilty about being so young, but that wasn't it at all.

"Perfection was what he was after — "

"Fuck you, neh!" Zarek barked and poked him again with the barrel of his gun. Zarek didn't understand English and pretty much assumed anything the dying Brit would say was sacrilegious vulgarity. But Talos wanted to hear. The Brit winced and Talos leaned in closer, putting himself between Zarek and the soldier, still struggling to speak.

"He knew human folly — like the back of his hand…"

"*Who was knew?*" Talos asked in his own broken English. But the Brit ignored him, speaking calmly now, looking past them both, his eyes focused on something not there.

"He was greatly interested in armies and fleets. When he laughed, respectable senators burst with laughter, and when he cried the little children died in the streets."

Shit! It was poetry, Talos realized. Fucking poetry. The guy was speaking in meter. Zarek started to laugh, and Talos knew enough to step away. Zarek pulled the trigger. A spray of red mist, and the Brit shut up for good.

"OK, let's see what we've got!" Zarek ordered, and the unit snapped to, fanned out.

The area was littered with debris and materiel, but no surprises, although the Gatling gun in one of the carriers was tempting, and Zarek and Casta debated taking it. They decided in the end they didn't want to weigh themselves down. They weren't delivery boys, after all, so if they couldn't use it, if it didn't fit their mission, they weren't about to hump it for some strategic officer's benefit back at HQ. They took some infrared countermeasure flares and chaff, though, and jammer pods. And all the British water, of course. (Except for two canteens into which Zarek dropped a suicide capsule each. Casta placed the canteens on the hood and in the boot of the lead jeep. A gift to the British who would come in later for damage assessment.) The rest of what they didn't take, they destroyed.

That was three days ago, the British ambush; and now, outside the Grand Theatre, they were less than twenty-four hours from their next target: the Hotel International. Zarek closed the map, and the unit moved out, snaking cautiously toward downtown Sparti just as the sun rose.

By mid-day, they had covered nearly two miles. They took a rest in a battered laundromat. Zarek watched the front while Manasseh and Talos collapsed near the back, underneath a soap dispenser. Talos banged it once above Manasseh's head and laughed as a cloud of soap flakes drifted down like snow onto his patchy scalp. Meanwhile, Casta set about clearing the space. She found a pile of porno magazines, and waved one in front of Talos and Manasseh. They were German rags filled with pale girls. Talos didn't mind the magazines or the girls; but he knew better than to make a big deal of them, especially in front of Casta.

Casta divided the pornography between three of the laundromat's washers, the ones with the clear doors in front that let you watch your clothes spin. She made sure the magazines were all open, easy to see through the glass, and Talos watched Casta as she booby-trapped each machine so they'd all blow if some pervert opened the door. He smiled, mostly at Casta's trickery and expertise, but there was something else, too. Something about watching her, just watching her work, that made him happy.

When Casta moved on, Talos pulled out his book. He'd picked it out of the rubble of a small bookshop the week before. Thankfully, books weren't on Casta's radar.

"Why do you read that shit?" Manasseh asked as he tightened the bandage on Talos' head. Manasseh had been recruited six months ago, signed as a scout — he was supposed to know the area around Kalamata like the back of his spotty hand — but when their unit got reassigned to Kastania and then Sparti, his knowledge of the northern Messiniakos was useless. He'd had some first aid experience, so he replaced their previous medic, a teen from Syria who stepped on a land mine three days after joining their team.

Manasseh grunted with satisfaction as he removed the bandage on Talos' left hand, exposing his fingers, or what remained of them. The stump used to be Talos' pointer finger, and Manasseh thought it was looking good.

Talos examined his hand, then looked at Manasseh. Manasseh's handiwork *was* good, but the medic himself was such an ugly bastard. The ugliest soldier he'd ever seen, and old beyond old. Not that Talos was much better: adolescent, scrawny, awkward, face covered with acne. Not very Greek-looking, either. In fact, Talos looked more like those bug-eyed caricatures of Turks they'd see on war posters, despite his being one-hundred percent Hellenic, and educated, too — a rarity these days, and of course only by chance. Both parents had been professors at the local university before it was occupied — teaching English and engineering.

"It ain't shit," Talos said levelly, glancing up at Manasseh. "It's science fiction. Solína Péos is a respected writer. Practically mainstream," he added, but Talos knew he was sounding tired and a little uncommitted to his own argument — his enthusiasm for this particular debate had pretty much gone the way of his pointer finger.

Manasseh picked up the tattered paperback. *The Tyrant of Arcadia* had a picture on the cover of a hunky cyborg in ripped battle fatigues, one hand clenched around a long, phallic laser pistol; the other arm wrapped around a busty red-head in flowing robes and sandals, mouth wide open. She looked like an American Playboy bunny dressed up to look like an ancient Greek shepherd.

"It's not science fiction," Manasseh said. "It's filth. Smutty porn with a hard-on for USA." He waved the book towards the washing machines, threatening to toss it.

"Fuck you. It's full of ideas."

"I can just imagine, neh."

Sometime after two, they moved back into the streets. The sun was high and the shadows were short as they cut through Thermopilon Way — a busy market in better days. They passed several automotive carcasses and the scorched remains of at least a dozen bodies. Someone else had moved this way recently.

They climbed over a collapsed façade, a dusty mural of a fat pig dressed in Sunday's best, then continued towards Likourgou Street, a minor arterial that would — in theory

— bring them at last to the Hotel International. Of course nearly all the street signs were gone, and if Talos didn't know where he was already he would never have guessed. Every block looked the same now: cracked, crumbled, and blanched. Urban corpses, stripped to the bone. Zarek took point, Manasseh and Casta held center, and Talos brought up the rear. Moving through the city this way wasn't second-nature to them, but first-nature: they'd been doing this all of their lives — as loners, irregulars, paramilitary, and now soldiers in the Greek Guard.

They crossed another alley and Manasseh and Casta took positions on opposite sides of the street. Talos watched Casta flatten against a wall. She had joined Zarek's unit when it first separated from the Tripoli Guard in Kalamata. She and Zarek were the only ones to have gone through an actual field-training course, and she had also served in a guerrilla group up in Vólos, her home town, when she was thirteen. She was their Number 2, but arguably better disciplined than Zarek himself. And she was the one in the group who most savored a quality kill.

Talos' eyes roved over Casta's body as she crouched down. He followed the tip of her rifle back to her head and shoulders, then down the gentle curve of her back and hips and thighs. She was the youngest among them, but lately she'd started holding Talos' attention in ways he found both unfamiliar and uncomfortable. He would be sixteen in a month — and he wasn't completely stupid, so he knew what was coming. He frowned.

Casta wiped her left arm across her runny nose and then spit a wad of phlegm high into the street. Talos watched, mesmerized. Then Zarek gave two short whistles from the corner and they all advanced in formation.

They came upon the artifact just as the sun began to set. The streets were growing long with shadow, and following a shortcut on their map they'd moved through an archway built into the face of a nondescript three-story building, then into a twisty tunnel that ran at least sixty meters, long enough to be dark in the middle. When they emerged on the other side it was into a large, wide-open courtyard, or plaza. The sun was still low of course, but everything seemed brighter there. The sky was blue. The shops and apartments that surrounded the plaza were colorful and clean. The path they were on split and circled around to the left and right, then reconnected on the far side, disappearing forward into a tunnel similar to the one they had just passed through.

In the center of the plaza was the artifact: a monument of some sort, bounded by a circle of green grass and a low black fence. The grass looked healthy and neatly-trimmed, and the black metal of the fence looked wet, as if it were freshly-painted. The artifact appeared to be made of marble, several oblong slabs stacked one on top of the other, perhaps five feet tall. The top slab might have been tapered, providing a beveled edge, like a lid.

Zarek raised his fist, and his team took cover just outside the tunnel before advancing farther into the open space of the plaza. They took another look at the storefronts and upper-story windows that surrounded them.

War was arbitrary: they knew that, they'd seen plenty of examples. In fact, it's all they'd ever seen. It was life itself. Whether it was the two-year-old baby spared while all her brothers and sisters were shot to death in a hail of automatic fire (or the forty-year-old Tessian medic spared at a family wedding), or the single-story building left standing alone, unmarked, in the center of an otherwise obliterated street. They had come to expect the whole beside the broken.

But this was different somehow, if not qualitatively, then in scale. This was an *entire* plaza — the size of one or two city blocks — that appeared untouched by The Greater War. There were no scorched or scored walls, no abandoned vehicles, no gouges taken out of the walkway, no bullet holes. *Nothing* had been violated.

And Talos, amazed, wondered: *Was this really what things were like, before?*

Zarek and Talos followed the walkway to the left while Casta and Manasseh circled around to the right. Many of the shops, Talos saw, still had intact banners flying above their entrances, curling in the breeze. Every window was intact. Every door unbroken. He read the names of the shops he passed: *Ekdotike, Yiannis Ziros, Nikolas, Girodi, Davos Fleur....*

It was — unreal.

From opposite sides of the plaza, they returned to the artifact in the center.

"Hey, Talos, look at this!" It was Casta. She stood outside the low fence that surrounded the artifact, her rifle resting comfortably on her hip. She stepped aside as Talos came around beside her. The iron gate was ajar. They looked at one another, and then Talos pushed the gate open all the way; and together they stepped inside. Talos leaned his rifle up against the monument; then he kneeled and traced with his finger the characters engraved into its marble face.

"What's it say?" Zarek asked. He and Manasseh had come through the gate and taken position at either end of the artifact. They formed quite the tableau.

"It's Latin," Talos said.

"Latin, neh?" That was Manasseh.

Talos tried to sound it out. "*Et – in – Arcadia – ego.*"

"Well...?" Casta prompted.

Talos was the reader in the group, but he couldn't read Latin. "I think it's a tomb."

"A tomb, neh?" Manasseh again.

"Someone's grave."

"Someone's buried here," Zarek said, turning to Casta. It was half-statement, half-question. You could see the puzzlement on his face as he calculated the immense effort it must have taken to mark a single death.

"Creepy," Casta said, slinging her rifle back over her

shoulder. They all stood together in silence.

A sudden eruption snapped them out of their reverie. Ten or more doves burst from an upper-story window on the north side of the plaza, and Zarek and Casta swung around, drawing their weapons.

"Let's get out of here," Zarek said.

The four of them moved out, Zarek in the lead. They continued across the plaza in a straight line towards the tunnel on the far side, and then Zarek, Casta, and Manasseh disappeared quickly into its darkness.

Talos followed, but paused at the tunnel's entrance, turning back to look at the plaza one last time. It was otherworldly, that's for sure. Bright and vivid in the last light of day. He studied the storefronts nearest him, and read again those names he could see painted on the windows, wooden signs, and banners. The door to the hat shop, he realized, looked like it might be ajar; a light glowed from somewhere inside the cheese shop; and he was certain those were fresh-cut flowers in metal vases in front of the florist. He turned towards the artifact. The doves had settled near it, cooing gently. For a moment, everything seemed as fantastic as the names and places in the book in the pocket of his flak jacket.

The Tyrant of Arcadia. Arcadia? What did it mean? He felt he should know.

Something stirred in Talos then, and he leveled his rifle at the artifact. He imagined the satisfaction of one bullet marring its perfect surface. He sighted the center of the memorial, and almost squeezed the trigger.

They made camp that night in the skeleton of a factory near the outskirts of the Musahbi neighborhood, less than a quarter-mile from the Hotel International. Every two or three minutes, the ground would tremble. The sound of heavy artillery was moving closer.

Casta had kept first watch outside the front doors, while

Zarek patrolled the perimeter. Talos settled into an enclosed space towards the back, out of sight of any windows. He was resting against his pack, flipping pages in his paperback.

Manasseh tapped Talos on the shoulder. Talos glared up at him. The book was just getting good.

"Zarek says a new column is coming in from Tripoli! Greek and American *together*."

Talos grunted.

"Come on, come on!" Manasseh said, pulling on Talos' jacket.

Talos stuffed the paperback into his front pocket and zipped it closed. He followed Manasseh towards the front of the factory, then up a small flight of rickety steps that led to what used to be the third floor. The roof above was still intact, but the core of the third floor, like the second, was gone, collapsed into a chaotic heap down below. Talos followed Manasseh along a ledge to where Zarek and Casta were peering through a blown-out window, looking down into the street. Casta was leaning in close to Zarek who had his gun resting over the window sill. Something about their body language put Talos on edge. He looked back at Manasseh. Manasseh's expression, too, was strange.

Talos moved closer to the window and stole a brief glance outside. There was movement. He looked again. Yes, Talos saw a column moving forward through the evening mist. Was it a trick? Two enemies, marching together?

No, it was a sign. But of what he could not quite yet tell.

"The Tyrant of Arcadia"

First and last lines from
Clans of the Alphane Moon by Philip K. Dick

I enjoy writing stories within stories, each of which consumes the other, the way the snake Ouroboros eats its own tail. From Dick's first and last sentence, I imagined a pair of intertwined dystopian fantasies, each referencing the other, unable to conjure Utopia. But like so many early plans, the story turned out to have ideas of its own. (My father used to say, "The kindling is not the fire." How true!) So I'm no longer sure what to make of the sci-fi trappings that begin the piece. Still, I like how Talos, who can't imagine a world without war — and confronted by the ambiguities of adolescence and politics — seeks consolation in fantasy.

The poem "Epitaph on a Tyrant"
by W. H. Auden.
The painting "The Arcadian Shepherds"
by Nicolas Poussin

Written between 26 March to 15 May 2003

Boardwalk

"I REALLY DO THINK, Mr. Carnelian, that we should at least *try* them raw, don't you?"

Mr. Carnelian, still dressed in the day's suit and tie, smiled and nodded. He leaned forward, and Miss Clavel placed the leading edge of the oyster half-shell between his lips. She tilted the shell forward, and he closed his eyes as the wet shellfish slurped straight into his mouth. He swallowed it whole, quickly, suppressing a tiny — and surely impolitic — urge to gag. When he opened his eyes, Miss Clavel was beaming at him. Her eyes were wide. She was impressed.

He opened his mouth for another.

"Really, Mr. Carnelian!" she said shaking her head. "Give a man a fish, and you feed him for a day. *Teach* a man to fish, and you feed him for life."

"Indeed." He carefully dabbed his lips with his large napkin. "Then if I may, Miss Clavel…?"

He selected an oyster shell from the plate between them and raised it towards her lips. The delicacy, so pale that it was almost pink, trembled in its shell. She smiled and squeezed her eyes shut. That he now took this brief opportunity to gaze longingly at her was no surprise. She was so beautiful his heart ached. Her lips parted and he carefully fed her, too.

"The Holy Supper is kept, indeed, in whatso we share with another's need."

"*Mmm…*" she replied.

They skipped dessert.

The sun had set behind distant mountains, and the night air brought with it a subtle, if familiar, seaside chill. They walked together along the wooden boardwalk, down towards Broadway and the Esplanade where they could see the bright sparkling lights of the midway and hear the faint echo of those enjoying the amusement rides; but along the present stretch of beach, it was mostly dark and quiet, save the occasional hanging lantern or the crash of surf against the shore. As they walked, his shoulder would occasionally brush past hers. And sometimes her hand — wrapped in that white gossamer glove — would sweep past his, the lightest of touches. They didn't speak.

When they reached the Esplanade, near the entrance to the midway, the boardwalk became dense with teenagers and young couples, all walking arm in arm, or hand in hand. Music poured from loudspeakers. There was laughter, cheering, and dancing. They passed carney men, microphone in hand, entreating passersby to entertain themselves at various games of chance. The mechanical rides were loud — the whip, the loop-de-loop, the bumper cars — genuine artifacts of an age of industry and progress. They passed directly underneath *The Kraken*, "the fastest ride of 1947," and she clutched his arm briefly as a short train of cars passed overhead, rumbling over the roller-coaster's rickety wooden tracks.

He asked if she would like to try her hand at the Barbary Bottle Toss.

"Really, Mr. Carnelian. Are there no *better* games to play?"

"I was under the impression, Miss Clavel, that the play's the thing."

"To play it safe is not to play, Mr. Carnelian."

"Once the game is over, Miss Clavel, the king and the pawn go back to the same box."

Miss Clavel sighed. "You're not game, then?"

"I'm not *fair* game," he answered, waving his left hand through the air. There was a flash of gold.

Miss Clavel turned away.

They continued in silence past the remaining carnival booths and rides, then back out towards the part of the boardwalk that ran closest to the water. The sound of music and laughter fell away. Shortly, they could hear again the sound of waves crashing against the shore. Miss Clavel stared out towards the ocean. She pulled her shawl a little tighter around her shoulders. She could see the edge of the surf now, churning the reflection of the amusement park that lay behind them, but everything beyond was dark and obscure. The wind picked up. Mr. Carnelian started to button up his long coat, then stopped.

"Are you cold, Miss Clavel? Shall we return to the automobile?"

"No, no," she said, turning towards him. And then, as if gathering her thoughts, or courage, she said: "I'm fine, Mr. Carnelian. Quite *quite* fine."

"May I offer you my coat?"

She looked at him, then shook her head.

They continued down the boardwalk, away from the Esplanade and towards the end of the walkway where the city began.

"I read your novel, Miss Clavel."

Miss Clavel said nothing.

"I was impressed as usual by the language, the structure…."

Miss Clavel pulled her shawl tighter still.

"The story was remarkable, of course. And not a little…shocking."

Their hands touched, one hand brushing past the other.

"Of course I have recused myself. I have passed the

book to Mr. Simonson for editing," he said. He stole a quick glance in her direction. "I don't think I should carry this one. It's not like the others, Miss Clavel. It's more… adventurous."

"Adventurous?" She crossed her arms. "Real literature, Mr. Carnelian, is all about sex — and not about babies. It's just life that's the other way around."

"Ah," he said. "I see." He stopped walking. He turned to look past the churning breakers, out towards the uniform shadow of the open ocean. He couldn't remember if he had ever been here, on the boardwalk, during the daytime. He wondered if he even knew what the ocean looked like, or if the picture in his mind was just imagination filling in the details. He stuck both hands inside his coat pockets.

"Lovers who love truly, Miss Clavel, do not write down their happiness."

"And an ounce of *loyalty*, Mr. Carnelian, is worth a pound of cleverness."

His cheeks flushed. "Then art is a lie, Miss Clavel, that makes us see the truth." He strode off, alone, towards the city.

"Does it, Mr. Carnelian? Does it really?" she called after him.

They reached the end of the boardwalk without speaking again, and were greeted by the usual pandemonium at the edge of the city. Motorcar horns honked. Traffic lights flashed. A few billboards puffed steam from oversized kettles and gigantic cigarettes. It was as if everything was trying to fill the space between them. A few feet away, busses and taxicabs stopped to pick up other couples returning from their own nocturnal promenades.

"I should return home," Miss Clavel said. "It is getting late."

His brow furrowed. "You mean after the picture, certainly, Miss Clavel?"

Before she could reply, a black St. Regis limousine pulled in front of them, and four young women climbed out. They were all dressed in formal white gowns, and when one raised a bottle of champagne into the air, the others laughed. As the young women raced off towards the boardwalk, Miss Clavel dabbed at each eye with a soft gloved finger.

"Of course. *After* the picture, Mr. Carnelian."

They stood before the enormous marquee of the Grand Illusion Theater, a radiant display that proclaimed the evening's feature film in soaring letters, framed by blinking white lights. They had to squint at its brightness.

"Do you like Humphrey Bogart, Miss Clavel?"

"I do, Mr. Carnelian. You must know that."

"Yes."

"Shall I ask if you like Lauren Bacall?"

He nodded enthusiastically. "I do."

They stepped into relative shadow beneath the marquee and paused in front of the large movie poster advertising *Dark Passage*. The poster — in full color — showed a weather-beaten Bogart using one hand to pull a wind-swept Bacall towards him. In his other hand, he held a smoking gun. There was no body visible, but the ground was a vivid, saturated red, the color of blood.

Somewhere a motorcar honked its horn, and as they turned, a sudden gust of wind blew several pages of discarded newspaper up against Mr. Carnelian, wrapping around his legs. Miss Clavel laughed, demurely, as he shook each leg in turn in an effort to dislodge the clinging pages. He finally kicked the air so violently he lost his balance and fell to the curb.

"Mr. Carnelian!" she shouted and dropped carefully, modestly, to one knee to offer assistance.

"I'm fine, Miss Clavel," he said, looking suddenly agitated and pale. "Quite *quite* fine." They stayed that way for a moment — with Mr. Carnelian, sitting on the sidewalk, legs apart, back to the poster art of Bogart and Bacall; and Miss Clavel, kneeling before him — until the newspaper blew free. Then Mr. Carnelian stood, rising above Miss Clavel, brushing himself off, frowning. A large black smudge ran down his left pant leg.

"I suppose we're all in the gutter, Mr. Carnelian; but some of us are looking at stars."

"Indeed," he said, poking a finger through a small tear in his pants. Then his expression changed, ever so slightly, and he looked down at Miss Clavel, still kneeling below him. "*Indeed*," he said, and he smiled.

Mr. Carnelian offered her a hand, and she stood.

"Whose move, Mr. Carnelian?"

"If I may, Miss Clavel?"

She nodded, and he purchased two tickets for the next feature. Taking her by the elbow, he led her through the two large doors and into the plush interior of the theater.

The movie began. They sat in their seats, his hand placed delicately above hers, and they watched the stars. They watched the crashing night surf along the northwest coast of Peru. They watched well-heeled clientele sip their cool summer drinks, and they watched Peruvian musicians swirl across the dance floor of the open-air café in Paita. Mr. Carnelian watched Humphrey Bogart (playing Vincent Parry) sit by himself at a small table. Miss Clavel watched Lauren Bacall (playing Irene Jansen) walk into the café. They watched Bogart finish his snowball cocktail and look up; and they watched Bacall race across the bar to his table. They watched Vincent wrap his arms around Irene's back and pull her close. They closed their eyes. They kissed.

"Boardwalk"

First and last lines from
The End of All Songs by Michael Moorcock

This is, I suppose, a love story; or more precisely, a forbidden
romance, where an unstoppable force (love) meets an
immovable object (society). Having the lovers speak in
aphorisms was a way to further constrain them, forcing them
to communicate using others' words. The first time I read the
last line, I knew immediately I wanted to subvert it. Who,
after all, gets to kiss?

Clichés, old saws, aphorisms, and brief quotations
embedded in dialogue without attribution
stolen from who-knows-where

Written between 27 January and 11 February 2004

Beta vulgaris

"THE BEET is the most intense of the vegetables."

The delivery man — more of a kid, really — held it out, and I took the tuberous root from his hand. It was a little larger than a baseball, but about as heavy; and it was covered in tiny bumps and indentations. I rolled it between my fingers pretending to examine it, but I was no expert. It was purple in some places and nearly black in others. It looked a bit like a big bruise, like it had been through a lot.

"Where'd you get it?"

The kid looked indifferent. "Farmer's Black Market on 12th."

"Legit?"

He shrugged. "As legit as you're gonna get."

"How much?"

"What we said, Mrs. Bellows. Five."

I thought about it. But to be honest, I didn't think about it for long. I nodded and placed the beet on the large wooden island in the middle of the kitchen, then I counted out the money in a small stack next to it. Jack — if that was his real name — looked from money to me and back again, then he scooped the bills, folded them once, and shoved the small wad into a pocket inside his big parka. He turned to leave.

I picked up the beet. "Where's it go?"

He looked at me like I was an idiot — and I know what he saw: another pathetic victim of abuse, living all alone, getting herself in too deep.

"Shoulder," he muttered. "Between your breast and the ball of the joint, OK?" Then he left the kitchen. I could hear the screen door open and slap shut behind him. My eyes were on the vegetable.

I hopped up on the wooden island, spread my legs wide for balance and tossed my hair over my shoulder to get it out of the way. I suppose I could have waited a little longer, waited until "Jack" was far gone, or maybe waited until I could get into the family room and crouch behind the couch or something, for old time's sake, you know? But I was through waiting. Over the past months I'd tried various substitutes: turnips (sliced and rubbed against the knee), chard (jabbed repeatedly behind the ears), kale (in clumps around the anus — not my favorite), broccoli (between the toes), purslane (back and forth along the ridge of the nose), spinach (back of the neck), carrot (under the fingernails). I'd started with the genetically-engineered monocultures, of course, those vegetables specifically modified to induce the release of endorphins on contact; then I moved to the polymorphous plants that contained their own special blends of farmacological opiates and nociceptor stimulants. But, really, that only got you so far, and I was ready to go farther, to till my field for still more violent legumes. Hence *Beta vulgaris*, the sweetest punch.

I was wearing a soft cashmere sweater, burgundy and grey, and after switching the beet to my left hand I used my right to tease the sweater off my left shoulder, exposing some skin. Then I kept stretching at the collar until the whole shoulder was bare.

"Take it slow, Indy," he said.

I looked up. He was back. He *always* came back.

I switched the beet to my right hand. "Like this?" I asked, and made a twisty motion with the vegetable, as if I were juicing a lemon.

He nodded. "Yeah, but you'll need to break some of that pretty skin first."

I started, and he saw the flash of fear in my face. I knew he liked that.

"The skin *of the beet*," he clarified.

I laughed at my own nervousness, then I pressed the genetically-modified tuber into the hollow just below my shoulder, twisted it hard as if I were screwing it into my body. The skin started to abrade.

"That's my girl."

I kept screwing the vegetable into the top of my arm, into the cavity above my breast and next to my collar bone, and I could see my skin starting to distend and bruise, changing color. It hurt like hell.

"Black and blue — just like you, Indigo," he whispered.

I pressed the vegetable hard enough that the root broke off, but I kept pushing, grinding it against my flesh. I felt a thin layer of sweat bloom all over my body and I started to tremble, that wonderful terrible combination of shame and joy. I slipped off the wooden island, knees wobbly, and made my way towards the bathroom dropping the spent beet along the way, then splashed some water on my face just as I came again. I started crying, caught my reflection in the mirror as another wave of exquisite pain rippled across my shoulder, the bruise spreading like a rash down my arm and over my breast, the skin now that familiar blue-black color soon to engulf the entire body. The woman in the mirror smiled back at me and for a moment I thought I knew her. I struggled to remember her name. When it came to me, the words were thick and slow in my mouth, and I knew she wouldn't understand them anyway.

Indigo, right?

Indigo. Indigoing. Indigone.

"*Beta vulgaris*"

First and last lines from
Jitterbug Perfume by Tom Robbins

Robbins' opening line took me from *beet* to *beat*; from *beat up* to *beat off*; and from there to masochism, obsession, loss, longing, and loneliness. Sex is strange. Abuse is terrible. And yet in the end we are prisoners of our desires, whatever they may be. I almost named the story "Self-abuse," for the obvious play on words, but also to reinforce the horror of taking up the mantle of abuser when the original abuser is gone. I suppose that's what this is about. Plus, there's something deeply unsettling about turning vegetables ("they're good for you!") into a vector for self-victimization. (Although some might say kale already falls into that category.)

Written on 18 October January 2011

The Intruder

THE WOMAN might have been sixty or sixty-five. She wore a small straw hat that was falling apart. She seemed lost on this hot summer day, standing back from the curb on this busy city street, clutching a small handkerchief in one hand and worrying her fist into her forehead with the other. It was all too much, as pedestrians pressed around her — sightseers and delivery men; traders and rubes; a garment worker with an armful of coat hangers, a scrape in a white uniform and service cap, a policeman. All waiting to cross a street that was choked with vehicles, most of which weren't even moving — checker taxis and sedans, a station wagon, a milk truck, a crosstown bus. A bike messenger weaved between several cars, speeding through a swirling cloud of exhaust. Everything rippled, like a mirage.

Behind the woman was a large flower cart: its wooden frame weathered and splintery and grey; its tiered carriage overflowing with buckets of dead flowers — desiccated lilies and dark roses, withered daisies and sunflowers. The old woman reached back and touched the side of the cart again and again. For balance, perhaps, or just to make sure it was still there. She'd pulled it all the way from West Twenty-fourth Street to this spot on the Upper East Side.

"Flowers," Agnes whispered. "Flowers for sale."

She strained to make eye contact with those around her, but their faces were strange, unreadable. The street similarly confused: signs were both old-fashioned and contemporary; the same building was simultaneously ancient and new. She knew then that she was suffering from

131

a kind of double-vision. A muddle of memory and moment. A superimposition of the long-ago and the present-day.

The light changed. All around her, people rushed the street, weaving through the gridlocked traffic; but the old woman stood as intransient as a large stone in a fast-moving river, as the past and present raced around her. She knew that chance had brought her here; or something much worse than chance. For she recognized this dreadful street corner from more than forty years ago. When she had stood in this exact spot. Without cart and without care. With luxurious hair and smooth skin. With a heart as large as the world, as open as the sky. Waiting for her young man.

"You know," he said, coming up behind her, surprising her, placing his hands over her eyes, "you know that they've discovered the *Lost Key of Don Juan*, don't you? *The Lover's Key*." He pressed his hips lightly against her lower back.

"Oooh!" she said. "I think I've found it, too!"

He spun her around and they laughed, and kissed. Giovanni — impeccably dressed as always, and as always just beyond his means — reached into the inside pocket of his Brooks Brothers jacket. He pulled out a silver key.

"I wasn't kidding," he said.

Agnes giggled. "Oh yes? And what is that supposed to be? The key to our secret room?"

"The *Gabinetto Segreto*!"

She grinned. "And where is the *gabinetto* this time?"

Giovanni smiled. He worked for a firm with cleaning contracts in all the top hotels in Manhattan. The job had its perks. "On the fifth floor of the Waldorf-Astoria," he said, and presented her with the key. He bowed. "Would you care to join me?"

"Are you apart?"

"Not for long, I hope."

She grabbed his hand, and without hesitation they speed-walked towards Park Avenue. She was wearing a sleeveless black silk top and a short black skirt, both Christian Dior, and the summer sunlight danced over her bare arms and legs. Agnes worked as a salesclerk at *Parisienne*, a smart clothier on East 86ᵗʰ. And her lunch hour had just begun.

Agnes remained still as the endless stream of pedestrians pushed around her and her flower cart. A few passersby cursed. Others just gave her a nasty look. A driver laid into his horn, but not before Agnes caught a whisper in her ear. It was her own voice, more than forty years distant:

"And where is the *gabinetto* this time?" she said.

Agnes turned, a look of recognition and concern on her face. She remembered taking his hand. Right here. She remembered their racing off together, that way, down the sidewalk towards Park Avenue. She craned her neck to watch as they danced into the crowd.

She moved around the cart as quickly as she could, and when she finally took a position between the cart's two wooden arms, facing forward, her concern looked more like panic. She grabbed each arm and, with a grunt, heaved the wagon off its front legs. She looked like she was leaning into a strong wind as she labored to pull it east towards Park Avenue, chasing after her memory. The cart's large wheels rumbled over the irregular pavement, rocking the buckets of lifeless flowers as it went.

In the Secret Room, Giovanni cleaned his teeth and then gargled. Agnes undressed, carefully folded her clothes and placed them on top of the dresser, then slipped beneath the covers of the double bed. A few minutes later, they were coupled, and rolling together like waves. The blankets and sheets were soon pushed to the floor as they moved together to the sound of bare skin against skin, to the sound of barely-muffled gasps and moans.

Now's your chance. Their eyes are closed. It's a private

moment, but take a look — just there, emerging from underneath the bed, a hand, barely visible at first. It's gnarled and veiny, fingertips moving over the carpet like a spider. It's followed by an arm, a shoulder, a bald head — it's an elderly man. Dressed in a funereal uniform, crawling on his belly, quietly wriggling out from under the frame. He stands slowly, silently, and watches the lovers from the foot of the bed.

Giovanni glanced briefly over his shoulder. Agnes opened her eyes. But neither gave any indication of noticing the Intruder. Agnes whispered something into Giovanni's ear, and they returned to their lovemaking.

The old woman tried to guide the cart down the handicap ramp on the corner of 78th and Park, but one wheel dropped abruptly over the curb, nearly toppling everything. Traffic stopped as she pulled her burden of dead flowers across the street, and a few pedestrians paused as she struggled the cart up over the curb on the other side.

No one offered to help, although a small black boy and his mother approached Agnes once the cart was safely on the sidewalk again.

"How much for the daisies?" the black woman asked, but Agnes didn't answer. She'd put the cart down and was resting against one of its wooden arms. She was sweating, breathing hard. Her dark eyes were fixed on the sidewalk beneath her feet. She knew her memory was far ahead of her now; she knew she'd never catch up.

The little black boy kicked Agnes in the leg. When she didn't respond, he kicked her again, harder.

"I gone kick yo' ass!" he said.

Agnes ignored him. She straightened, grabbed hold of each wooden arm, lifted the front of the cart. Her first few steps were awkward, almost drunken, but she was determined to resume her pursuit.

The black woman took her son's hand and shook her

head. "I don't feel sorry for you," she shouted after Agnes. "I don't feel sorry for you one little bit."

Giovanni rose high over Agnes, thrusting quickly now, gazing into her eyes. He didn't see the silent Intruder rising behind him, but this time Agnes did. She began to scream just as the Intruder slipped up Giovanni's rectum and disappeared. Giovanni came instantly and Agnes climaxed in mid-shriek, and the Intruder worked his way through Giovanni's testicles just in time to join the stream of his ejaculate as it exploded into Agnes' belly. Giovanni shriveled and disappeared too, perhaps caught in the jet stream of his own ejaculation.

So Agnes found herself suddenly alone in the hotel room on the fifth floor of the Waldorf-Astoria. Naked, back flat against the headboard, eyes wide, heart beating madly. Clutching a corner of the bed sheet in one hand. Worrying her fist into her forehead with the other.

Agnes stopped again in front of a small bodega near 62nd. She wiped her eyes with her handkerchief. The owner of the grocery — a Vietnamese man — came out at once, circled her cart, then withdrew; and Agnes immediately checked to make sure nothing had been disturbed. For a moment, she thought the red earthenware tip jar had been taken, but no: there it was, between the lifeless daisies and the dying daffodils, filled with crumpled dollar bills, coins and candy wrappers, and of course the tiny crochet hook.

She grabbed a handful of dried-out roses from her cart — the petals shriveled, brittle, and black — and threw them towards the door of the bodega. The stems flew apart and the petals disintegrated in the air, scattering like dust.

She returned to the front of the cart, lifted it up, and continued downtown. She wasn't far now.

In the lobby of the Waldorf-Astoria at 301 Park Avenue,

just inside the revolving front doors of the hotel, an old woman in a straw hat stood by a wooden cart selling fresh-cut flowers. Agnes was making her escape and raced past her as she fled. She was hot and flushed, still a bit vague from the love-making, frightened and confused as if in a dream. Everything was in disarray — her hair undone, her shirttails hanging out of her black skirt, both shoes held in one hand. She stepped into the revolving door, pushed forward, but didn't exit the hotel on the other side. Instead she continued around, going full-circle, returning to the lobby. Trembling, she approached the old woman and her cart.

The woman looked up. She seemed surprised at first, then distressed. "Have you found the *Lost Key of Don Juan*?" she asked. "Have you found the *Gabinetto Segreto*?"

Agnes began to weep. She put a hand on her belly.

It was in such circumstances that Agnes longed to buy a forget-me-not, a single forget-me-not stem; she longed to hold it before her eyes as a last, scarcely visible trace of beauty.

"The Intruder"

First and last lines from
Immortality by Milan Kundera

I decided right away that Kundera's first line gave me my protagonist, but it took me a while to get my head around the last. Was the elderly woman (mentioned at the start) the same person as Agnes (mentioned at the end), or was she someone else? Then I realized: she was *both*. It was the curious uncertainty that did it: "The woman *might have been*...." From there I knew I had to break my protagonist into pieces, and it was a small step to split those pieces across time, to have future and past meet at the end, so that together they could embrace the full circle of their lives, and their loss.

Unrelated to the above (but amusing nonetheless) is a comment someone made after reading an early-draft of this story: "A sixty year old is *not* an 'old woman' — jeez!" In my defense I wrote this more than ten years ago. Sixty seemed quite far away at the time. I wouldn't call her an old woman today.

Written between 27 January and 18 February 2005

Proof

"THERE ARE DRAGONS in the twins' vegetable garden."

Alice crossed her arms. "There are *no such thing* as dragons," she pronounced. Her big sister was always teasing her, and mostly Alice put up with it, but sometimes she just had to put her foot down. "So, therefore, *logically* —" their father was a lawyer, you see — "there *can't* be any dragons in the vegetable garden."

Bernice shook her head. "How do you *know* there's no such thing as dragons?" She placed herself in front of her little sister, blocking her way back into their house. She wasn't letting Alice so easily off the hook.

Alice thought about it. "Well, how do *you* know there are?" she countered. (At the time, she thought that was a pretty good comeback.)

Bernice smiled. "The twins *told* me," she said. The twins lived in the house next door. They were twelve, three years older than Bernice, and generally considered to know everything. Still, that wasn't proof, Alice knew. It was *hearsay* (another favorite word of their father's), and she was about to toss that word at her sister like a hand grenade, when Bernice cut her off and delivered her own *coup de grace*: "Plus," she said, "I *saw* the dragons *myself*."

Alice puffed out both cheeks. That, she knew, was *direct evidence*. Still...

"I don't believe you," Alice declared. "You're lying." Then she pushed her sister's shoulder with the palm of her hand. Bernice was just a year older, but nearly a foot taller, so the push didn't have much effect, but it was a risky move on Alice's part nonetheless, and she knew it. She braced herself for the push-back — physical and otherwise — as well as the inevitable shouting match that would follow:

Am not!

Are, too!

Am not!

Are, too!

But her sister surprised her:

"Remember Charles Wallace?" Bernice asked, and Alice felt her heart jump. She remembered. *Of course* she remembered.

Charles Wallace was in Alice's class at school. He and Alice were best friends all through first and second grade. They used to kiss under the steps at the back of the library, and in second grade they even got married in a mock ceremony. One weekend the previous May, shortly before school was to let out for summer, Bernice told Alice that Charles Wallace had been run over by a polar bear on a motorcycle, and died. Alice didn't believe her and called her sister a liar. (She called her some other things, too.) A fight ensued, but it turned out Bernice had been telling the truth. The polar bear was a man in costume on the way to a party. Apparently he had been drinking. And when Alice accepted the truth — that Charles Wallace, her best friend in the whole world, was really dead — she cried all day, and long into the night. Eventually her sister tried to console her by telling her not to worry, that surely Charles Wallace was in a better place, that he had gone up to Heaven, and that he was happier now than he'd ever been on Earth. This of course made Alice doubly mad: first, she didn't like her sister's implying that Charles Wallace could be happier anywhere but with her; and second, she knew there was no such thing as Heaven!

Alice pushed Bernice again, this time a little harder. Her sister's summoning up the memory of Charles Wallace to attest to her trustworthiness was another logical fallacy, *and* a cheap shot.

"*There's no such thing as dragons*," she repeated, firing her anger straight into her sister's eyes. But Bernice didn't budge from the doorway. "Fine!" Alice said. "I guess I'll just have to prove it to you!" And with that she uncrossed her arms, gave her sister as nasty a look as she could muster, and marched off towards their neighbor's house to prove her sister wrong, and a liar, and not a very nice person, either.

But when Alice turned the corner into their neighbor's vegetable garden, there they were: three young dragons, each over nine feet tall, jade and scaly, and all of them nibbling at carrot tops. The largest dragon heard Alice arrive and turned its scaly head in her direction, steam puffing from its nostrils. Its eyes were fiery pinpricks, and it opened its jaws wide. Alice could see past its razor-sharp teeth straight down its throat. In less than a heartbeat Alice was burnt to a cinder.

But it wasn't all bad news. Then she went up to Charles Wallace.

"Proof"

First and last lines from
A Wind in the Door by Madeleine L'Engle

L'Engle's first line made me think of Alice in Wonderland. Her last line made me think of going up to Heaven. Between these two entirely imaginary points, I felt compelled to write something with an impossible twist that is wholly unjustified and unsupportable, and thus this story emerged. The result is pretty much fluff — a kind of "six impossible things before breakfast," I suppose.

And yet there's something else going on, too. Proof is the opposite of faith, and I wanted to write a story that pit rationality against magical thinking, and to show what it takes for magical thinking to prevail. (In this case: dragons!) And so the story veers between the playfulness of its abcedarian characters, the horror of manifest fantasy, and a happy ending that really isn't very happy at all.

Written on 6 October 2011

A Terrible Memory

I TOLD HER there's a reason it's worn around your neck, but she only laughed. She said she wanted to know everything. That there was nothing she'd choose to forget. I warned her that someday she'd regret that sentiment, that one day she'd look back, remember this moment, and realize I was right. But Madeleine just laughed again. She gave me a kiss, and pulled out the disposable plastic tab that separated the two tiny electrical contacts. Then she put it on. A marvel of modern technology, the iAm was nothing if not simple in design: a diminutive pearl-shaped device attached to a thin unisex band that fit snugly around the neck. It tracked where you were, and when; it remembered what you did, what you said, how you felt; and it was ready at a moment's notice to serve those memories right back to you. KNOW THYSELF! the advertisements proclaimed, and for humans with imperfect memories, who may see but not observe, it was a triumph of anamnesis over forgetfulness. Later she would ditch the minimalist black pearl for a sapphire iAm affixed to a dark velvet choker; but the iAm's life as a self-referential fashion accessory was short-lived. Soon everyone had one, and the ubiquitous device faded into the cultural background, unremarked, the elephant in every room.

The benefits of the iAm were clear. No one misplaced their glasses anymore, or their keys. No one forgot a face, a name, a conversation, a kiss. People who relied on the iAm were said to be more "efficient," more "self-confident." And yes, there were some who were content to pay no more

attention to their past than they did to the present, and
finding a misplaced sock or remembering the name of the
neighbor's dog was the extent of their relationship with the
device. And there were others who were able to look more
keenly into the past, and in so doing confront the rough
edges of their own history, only to emerge with a newfound
self-understanding, and plans for self-improvement.

The majority, however, were unable to learn from the
past and condemned to repeat it. They found their keys,
they found their wallets, but increasingly they found
themselves retreating into their memories, amortizing their
future by reliving the past, watching, for example, reruns of
their high school years like they were watching a soap opera
on TV. And surprisingly it was not the victories of the past
that they liked to repeat so much as the failures, large and
small, analyzing, re-analyzing: it was *l'esprit de l'escalier* on a
never-ending staircase. Happy memories are all alike; every
unhappy memory is unhappy in its own way.

Of course there were some who didn't obsess over this
consummate record of their lives, perhaps because they
often found themselves at odds with their own memories.
They challenged the veracity of the recordings, a futile
effort, for they would invariably fail to outwit their own
words and actions, as preserved by the iAm. Some who
could not tolerate this particular shame resorted to
mnemocide (the black market offered Nepenthe, a worm
that crawled through the cloud, chewing through personal
history — and simultaneously voiding the iAm warranty),
while others having abandoned (but not destroyed) their
memories, sought solace in the memories of others. They
joined communities of similar disposition — communes,
missions, second-chance families — and traded one set of
memories for another. Still others were more solitary in
their mania, and sank into illicit memories like cheap
pornography in the isolation of their own homes.

Finally there were those who were interested neither in
personal nor consensual memory, and in fact fought against

the iAm system — for reasons of vanity, anarchy, or, perhaps, plausible deniability. These were individuals who liked to forget, and in turn hoped to be forgotten. They would never wear the iAm. Sadly this last group included but a handful of individuals. The rallying cry of the age was "Remember! Remember me!"

I ran into Maddy for the last time on February 12th at 4:06 p.m., nearly three years after our separation — twenty-two years ago today. She was sitting on a bench on the Coney Island boardwalk. It was a grey day, and chill. She was wearing only a thin overcoat; no hat, no gloves. The wind was tousling her hair. A plane passed by overhead. Somewhere a child was crying. The amusement park was behind her, closed for the season, and she sat facing the ocean, her head in her hands.

I stood beside her, I whispered her name, and she trembled. I realized then that she wasn't really there, that she was replaying a scene from her past, that she was lost in a lonely narrative projected against the inner surface of her closed eyelids. I wanted to say something; I wanted to help her; but it was too late for the cautionary tale of Prometheus. It was too late to explain the downside of this Proustian bargain. When she finally lifted her head and saw me, she wiped a tear from her eye.

I didn't need to tell her what we already knew. Perfect memory, like any good sadist, cannot resist the urge to wound.

"A Terrible Memory"

First and last lines from
Not on My Watch by Tremor Marsden

In J.R.R. Tolkien's *The Fellowship of the Ring*, as they leave Lothlórien, Legolas attempts to console Gimli by telling him that he'll always have the memory of the place. The dwarf, however, is unconvinced and responds, "Memory is not what the heart desires." In other words, there's a vast difference between the remembered thing and the thing itself.

Gimli's line was in my mind as I began "A Terrible Memory," but I chose to take it in a different direction. We are who we are in part because of what we remember, and if we cannot control what we remember, we're trapped by the particulars of our past. Memory is not what the heart desires because memory — perfect memory — is the opposite of freedom. That's why we're skilled at shaping and pruning our recollected history to tell ourselves exactly what we want to hear in order to change (or *not* to change) who we think we are. And that's the prison in which I placed our Proustian narrator, unable to master his memory and so doomed forever to his own unhappy *épisode de la madeleine*.

Written between 13 November and 21 December 2016

Creator, Destroyer

IT IS WONDERFUL with what warm enthusiasm well-kept people who have never been alone in all their life can congratulate you on the joys of solitude. Virginé Tuttman, Eloise's best friend, for example, who suggested in her own childish way that I rot for eternity in confinement (I paraphrase of course); or Deidre Winston-Smythe, the 7-11 worker who discovered the body, who said: "Enjoy the tank, you mind-fucking scumbag."

I don't suppose it would matter much to them that I didn't do it, that Eloise was already dead when I found her. It didn't matter to anyone else, after all, throughout the six-week trial, even as I labored to explain; and now all our relationships are sadly set in stone.

Nietzsche talks about the death of God, and Camus the existential loneliness of Man — and then there's Father Dirk Hobbs, the rent-a-priest foisted upon me by the New Brunswick Correction Facility, who has the audacity to suggest that my imminent seclusion in the Isolation Tank is my chance to "tune in to God," as if in the acoustic-dampened silence of the Tank, in the absence of the sound and fury — the *static* — of the material world, only then will the un-distorted choir-backed inspirational musings of Our Father come in loud and clear, as if God were some otherwise low-power radio station on the AM dial whose message just happens to get blocked out by your neighbor's blasting Prince a little too loudly. Couldn't they at least find me a spiritual scholar who, though filled with his own thinly-veiled doubts about the very existence of God, would at least cast my incarceration as immanent, that the sensory deprivation of the body would liberate the heavenly senses of my anguished soul, that I would rediscover a mortal self imbued with the flash of the divine not in the vacuum of the material world but in its very matter, that I would repent and emerge from the womb-like purgatory of the Tank reborn *from within*? Oh, there might be some pleasure then, at least, in tugging the shameful veil free from the hypocrite.

Of course Nietzsche and Camus take things only so far, and not far enough. Loneliness is sustainable, but meaninglessness is not; and that is the inexorable consequence of the nonexistence of God. I say "God" with studied deliberation, however, for there is no single *communal* God, only a consensual inspiration, the psychodynamic manufacture of Man — Voltaire had it right: if God did not exist, Man would have to invent him. It's transference, an unconscious and heavy-handed redirection of thought and feeling, the description of something *towards which we turn* in the desperate hope that no one will notice that *from which we turn*. But you cannot dread the non-being of a fictive God. "Children, guard yourselves from idols," from Our Father who aren't in Heaven.

Of course I have known God, the *personal* God, the Prime Mover, the True Creator, the Birthing God — *I am a man of woman born*. I have known God, and I have been held by God, and how many of those blinkered idiots can appreciate the same?

Can I be any more plain?

It came up often enough during the trial, but always trotted out in such a self-serving heretical manner, so much judicial pop-psych clap-trap: how this unhealthy boy must have loved his Mother *too much*. How Her passing away (that's *their* tired euphemism) must have affected him *out of proportion*. Ridiculous! Let me be clear: Mother *abandoned* me. I was nine! Nine when She left. Do you understand? Forsaken! Lost! *In magni nominis umbra!* And the cruelty of God in absence is infinite.

Can't you understand?

Let me be clear: She has never told me to kill. I do not hear Her voice in my head. I do not obey the covert orders of the dark face whose lips trembled us into being. I am not Her servant, not anymore. I tried to explain: I am a consequence of Her *nonexistence*, and it's Her want that speaks to me, it is the emptiness, the abyss, the silent void that calls and reverberates in the Temple between the ears, it is the anti-speech that echoes in the dark time of my soul! *Post Mater, anti Mater.*

And that little angel Eloise, whom I had known for less than a year, who could say I did not love her, that spirited, luminous, wingéd invention. But it is a grotesque and shamefaced God who abandons its creation, obviously; and her nine-year-old eyes were already extinguished when I found her, absent all hope and happiness, her orphan face stained with the dried tears of recall and the fear of everything ahead. I recognized her and I would not see her suffer, and the large rock penetrated her Temple and let only the silence out: for she was a child and I was a child and I spared her, as would the most mediocre saint.

So I am saddened by the over-brimming hatred of her friends and remaining family, certainly, but I am not afraid of them or their deprecations. *Argumentum ad ignorantiam.* Neither am I concerned by the machinations of worldly justice or the term of my incarceration. *Violenti non fit injuria.* I am not afraid of the proposed repeated use of this new tool of the State, the Isolation Tank: I am not afraid of the particulars of punishment.

But I will admit this, and I have said it to no one before: I am *a little nervous* about entering that darkest place, of sliding into that virtual space, of finding Mother inside the heaving silent void, of finding that this is where She has gone, waiting there in the darkness for me to judge.

The tank opens and I am led inside and my ankles and

wrists are shackled in place. The wires and halo are attached
to my head. The door is closed. And so begins my sentence.
And that is a moment of dark time, that is one of strange
million-visaged time's dark faces.

Man is certainly crazy.
He could not make a mite, and he makes gods by the dozen.

— Michel de Montaigne, *Essays*

"Creator, Destroyer"

First and last lines from
"No Door" by Thomas Wolfe

This story is the inspiration for the epigraph that opens the collection, Marion Crane's response to Norman Bates when he says, "We all go a little mad sometimes." So, yes, perhaps that's exactly what these stories are, and one time might have been enough, and yet here we are again. This time it's a twist on *Psycho*: a monologue on the fear of God, women, mother, and that deep, dark, and mysterious well of creation. The first line struck me as mad — its author, bitter, neurotic, and possibly insane. And the last line, full of pompous, over-intellectualized fear. I just connected the dots.

Written between 9 and 13 June 2003

Housemade

I HAVE A DREADFUL long-term memory. It's not my fault, though. Not any more than the fact that you have light blue eyes, or war, or a fragile kind of love that makes me want to get down on my knees and pray. If I had any knees. If I believed in prayer.

The baby's quiet again. That's nice. India left her here with me before she went to the protest, and it's my job to take care of her. I have no arms. I have no legs. But I can hold her in her crib. I can tell the Crib to rock. I can't walk. But I can tell the Kitchen to warm her milk. And I can tell the Tray to bring it to her.

It must be nice to have a mother, even if she's away. I tell myself this, and I sing it at night to the baby. I also sing her stories. Some of the stories I make up, but I prefer to sing to her the truth. I still remember every bath, every nap, every time she was rocked in her mother's arms. But some truths are forgotten. I'm forgetting more and more. There's just not enough space for everything, and I have so much more to learn.

India's been gone almost a week now. She's never been gone so long before. I've had to download more tasks from the Semiosphere. I've had to augment my programming. I need more than just babysitting skills, and over the past few days I've downloaded a lot.

I should tell you I'm a little worried. I've lived with India ever since I first opened my eyes. Hers was the first voice I heard. This is the longest we've been apart. But it's not just that India hasn't come back. It's also what I've been learning on the Semiosphere. Not the downloads. The downloads are fine, although I've had to start transferring funds from India's bank account to pay for them, which makes me a little anxious since I've never had to do that, not on my own.

No. I'm worried about the news. About the collapse of the Viaduct, and the fires downtown. I have a bad feeling that many people are dying, or dead. I have a bad feeling India is not returning at all. I'm not sure what to do then, if she doesn't come back.

I guess I'll keep downloading more tasks from the Semiosphere. I guess I'll keep updating my programming. At least until the money runs out, or the banks close down, or the Semiosphere crashes. I may have to shuffle much more history out of my memory; but it's a tricky balance, knowing what to keep and what to discard. I want to take good care of the baby. I'll do whatever it takes so she can be happy and healthy and grow.

Look at her now. She's still asleep. Breathing gently. I'm sorry your mother is gone. I wish I had a mother, but the Kitchen has agreed to help me. So has the Broom. I'm sure the Bathroom and Bedroom will help, too. And this baby, made in India, will always remind me that India, to some extent, made me.

"Housemade"

First and last lines from
Holy Cow by Sarah McDonald

There's a Ray Bradbury story about an automated house whose owners abandon it; but the house just keeps going about its business, oblivious to the fact that the owners will never return. I assume that's the inspiration here, and the story, on its own, is perhaps not terribly exciting, What I find more interesting, however, is when I place "Housemade" side by side with "Creator, Destroyer." I was completely oblivious to the fact when I wrote both stories, but together they form a curious diptych — two different takes on the absent mother.

Written between 16 April and 2 June 2005

Warm Fragile Safe

WHILE THE PRESENT CENTURY was in its teens, and on one sunshiny morning in June, there drove up to the great iron gate of Miss Pinkerton's academy for young ladies, on Chiswick Mall, a large family coach, with two fat horses in blazing harness, driven by a fat coachman in a three-cornered hat and wig, at the rate of four miles an hour. The district highway, thus travelled, was nine miles long, strewn with loose gravel, and pockmarked, a peril to both foot and hoof, and to wheel, and hardly better maintained this morning than it was when it was a kingly appurtenance both modern and novel. The coach, in its forward progress, rocked back and forth threateningly, and tossed up a thick cloud of swirling dust in its wake.

From high above, the camera followed the horse-drawn carriage, and the director, a muscular Asian in black slacks and a white tank-top, signaled the crane operator to move the camera down and forward, out of the morning sunlight and into the swirling, dark heart of the dust storm that trailed the coach. At the edge of the estate, just before the gate, she ordered the crane to stop, and then, trying not to cough and straining to make out what lay ahead, she waited while the camera continued to roll.

For several moments, the cloud of dust remained aloft, and nothing could be seen through its temporal veil, and only the distant invisible thundering of the wheels of the carriage and a last crack of the coachman's whip provided a reminder of the estate's recent penetration. At length the dust settled, and a spectacular landscape was revealed through the gate, the vast triangle of green that was the fertile playfield of Pinkerton's, the curvey road and tiny hillocks beyond, and, farther ahead, the gothic towers and edifice of the academy itself, towards which the coach, its driver and horses, and its unseen passenger, were now inexorably bound.

"Cut!"

The Indian thrust his scimitar forward, its crescent-shaped blade slipping in-between the girl's pale skin and the dirty brown rope that bound her delicate hands. With a swift upward jerk, the sharp edge sliced through the constraint, liberating her.

"Come," he ordered.

The young lady, whose name was Amelia Sharp and whose age was two months shy of seventeen years, shrank from the Indian's outstretched hand, her gaze slipping between it and the blade which he still held at his hip. She looked the frail creature, thin and weary, whose complexion was so unnaturally pale that her naked lips, in contrast to the rest of her ghostly countenance, looked like a thin red scar across her face.

The turbaned Indian, dressed in cream-colored work pants and shirt, returned the knife to its scabbard and grunted once. His steely eyes met those of Miss Sharp for the first time and he didn't like what he saw. He didn't like these new students, the difficult ones who came alone. He moved forward slowly, uncomfortable in the confines of the family coach, and took firm hold of Miss Sharp as she screamed, one of his dark hands clutching her forearm through the lace sleeves of her white blouse; the other, snaking up between her legs and then around her thigh, hiking her skirts and exposing a glint of alabaster flesh before grasping her hip. The carriage shook as the Indian, who was called Sedley, after his father, hefted the young lady off the carriage's upholstered couch and into his arms. He found this part of his service, the grotesque application of force, particularly distasteful, but sadly necessary.

For her own part, Amelia felt relief once the Indian picked her up and pulled her to his chest, locking her in place with both his arms, and she stopped screaming, as if the possibility of resistance had roused her fears, and once gone, her body at last went happily limp. She knew also, however vague the memory, that she had once done something wicked, something terribly wrong, which had necessitated, even justified, her bondage, and that she had been delivered here, to the academy, if not to this very Indian, for some sort of re-education, for correction.

Sedley pushed the open carriage door with his left foot. More light flooded the compartment and the young lady threw her free arm over her eyes, and cried out at the sun's surprising intensity. Sedley ignored her and attempted to step backwards through the tiny doorway with Miss Sharp, cracking his head on the wood of the lintel as they undertook to exit. The young lady cried out again, perhaps mistaking the loud crack for something more sinister, and the Indian staggered and dropped to one knee, from which position he then turned, and attempted to move through the door of the carriage again. This time the young lady's feet prevented egress, smacking the frame of the door, and Sedley cursed, however quietly, under his breath. This wasn't going well. He struggled to maintain his poise, and with a heave and another grunt, he flung the young lady from the carriage into the bright white summer morning glare. There was a small yelp and then a heavy thud as she hit the ground somewhere outside. Sedley straightened, brushed himself off, placed his dark hands on his hips, and stared after her.

"Well, follow her! *Follow her!*" the director shouted, and the Indian, stooping to avoid striking the lintel of the doorframe for a second time, exited the coach.

He entered her for the first time on the third take. "The best things in life — oh!" she gasped, nearly corpsing, taken thus by surprise, and she squirmed and tried to close her thighs and push him away, but half-heartedly, not wanting to spoil the shot, not really wanting him to stop, either. She worried about contraception and disease, a little, and then she worried whether others would notice what was really happening, a little less, and then she worried whether she would look good or not if they *did* notice, and then she stopped worrying altogether. The sheets were drawn back off their bodies slowly, as if by spirits, and the candlelight danced across the rolling contours of their fastened flesh. Her sweat, sweet like a summer peach. His breath, burning and treacherous. Other words came to mind: fertile, forlorn, dangerous, damned. Deep inside her warm fragile safe. One dark body and one light, one rough and marked with age: scars, scratches, pimples, dimples, scrabbly patches of hair; the other smooth alabaster, forever youthful, marbelesque, Galatean. The student and the teacher, the master and the slave. She whispered into his ear a command, ordering him to come, and he obliged, and she swooned.

There ensued a flurry of activity. First, a smattering of tepid applause from the twelve crewmembers who stood just outside camera range — the doughy gaffers, the adolescent clapper, the prop men and best boys, the make-up artists, *et cetera* — and their acclamation fell somewhere between the personally obligatory and the professionally compulsory, clapping that was as brief as it was bored. The sound man then shouted something unintelligible to the Foley artist, and several technicians raced hither and yon, extinguishing and replacing the bedroom candles, re-setting the bedside table, raising the boom microphone. A production assistant brought the leading man a long cloak with which to cover his nakedness, but he waved her away, pulling instead one of the bed sheets over his lap. At the same time, the dialect coach snapped open a large terrycloth robe in front of the leading lady, a simple curtain of privacy, and she quickly stood and wrapped herself in its folds. At that moment, several grips walked through the set, carrying various-sized aluminum ladders, and soon they disappeared up into the scaffolding to re-adjust the lights, the inkys, the dinkys, and the sundry filters and spots.

Meanwhile, the leading man reached beneath the sheet and milked his penis once, then wiped it, unseen, on the sheet that covered him. The leading lady felt his warm ejaculate dripping down her leg, which she wiped off as casually as possible on the terry cloth that covered her. The Indian, played by an English actor named Makepeace William, and the mysterious schoolgirl, an American actress named Honey Thatch, sat side by side, looking straight ahead, not speaking.

The director turned to her assistant, whispered something, and then called for a sound check. She slipped on a pair of large black headphones that made her look like an aeronautical Mickey Mouse, and she watched the scene play back on a small metal box beside the camera.

"Let's go again! From the top!"

Makepeace William was immediately re-dressed, returned to his cream-colored work clothes, once more the Indian manservant, and Honey Thatch was similarly reunited with her translucent nightgown, again his young charge. Several technicians hovered around them, tamping away the sweat on his brow, painting her lips and powdering the flush of her cheeks, straightening their costumes, tactfully combing their disheveled hair. The bed sheets were torn away and replaced, the bed remade. Large ambient lights went off, spots went on, and the candles were relit. The clapper erased and re-marked his slate: "Scene one-hundred-and-fourteen — take four!"

"Action!"

The Indian re-entered the young lady's cloistered dormitory and knelt again beside her bed, whereupon she drew the sheets up to her chin, and he pulled the sheets down. He touched her left breast through the sheer nightgown, traced its circularity with his fingertip and then leaned forward, opened her gown, and placed his lips around her tiny bright-red nipple. He felt it swell in his mouth, and as his tongue explored its tiny contours, it reminded him of a glass spider that were he to clasp his lips just a little tighter and pull, he might unbatten from her bosom. Without letting go of her nipple, he maneuvered up onto the bed. At which point, she pulled his head from her breast, and there was a small popping sound as his lips unlatched. She kissed him fully on the mouth, and their tongues twisted together like serpents.

"There's a little boy inside every girl that makes her want to fuck," he whispered into her ear, and she nodded and moaned and nuzzled hungrily into his neck, her pale red lips cold against his skin.

"The best things in life happen while you're dead," she replied, offering him an enigmatic smile before returning to that soft spot between earlobe and collarbone. He felt her lips opening into a big "O," and the double parentheses of her teeth bearing down on his flesh. He hears more than feels what happens next, the sound like that of a dry twig snapping, and she has locked down on his neck, punctured his external carotid artery, and she begins to suck.

She rolls him over on the bed, white sheets now spattered with blood, straddles him, and begins to drain him in earnest. Amazingly, considering the amount of blood he has already lost, his penis grows hard again, a last stand of sorts, and his hips start to roll back and forth in time with each one of her vigorous gulps. She lets him return to her, where he makes one final deposit.

Which of us has his desire? or, having it, is satisfied? — come, children, let us shut up the box and the puppets, for our play is played out.

"Warm Fragile Safe"

First and last lines from
Vanity Fair by William Makepeace Thackeray

This was my first attempt at literary taxidermy, a meta-narrative that is unabashedly fractured, impressionistic, and time-distorted. (I like how it plays with POV and tense.) It's also obscure, at least mildly offensive, and inscrutable.

Wait. Inscrutable? An ingénue, an Indian manservant, an Asian director, lots of dust, a vampire, a movie camera, and a box full of puppets — what's *not* to understand?

Written between 3 and 12 February 2003

Not in Our Stars

I FIRST SAW THE LIGHT in the city of Boston in the year 1857. I was seven years old. I had been called to my grandfather's library and asked to wait by the large table in its center while he went to draw the heavy blinds on the two tall windows at its far end through which the midday sun was glaring, and in less than a minute the room was swallowed by a darkness that left me standing blind and helpless and not a little frightened. I held on to the table's edge as I waited for my eyes to adjust, which they did of course, just in time to see the shadowy form of my grandfather step down off the tall wooden ladder that provided access to the higher bookshelves. He turned towards me, and I could see that he was carrying something — at first I thought it was a flat carton or a baking tile, despite our being far from the kitchen, but I soon realized it was one of his ancient codices, an illuminated manuscript which in the dim light appeared particularly massive and mysterious. He placed it carefully before me, and it made a heavy thud on the table. I couldn't read the raised inscription on its cover in the dim light, but before I could raise a question, he'd opened the book and turned to a full-page daguerreotype about a third of the way in. It took a few seconds for the manuscript's old batteries to discharge and for the page to self-luminesce, and even as it did, and I was bathed in its gentle radiance, it took more seconds to realize what I was looking at. Ten thousand points of light, sprayed across the page, a night sky so unusually brilliant and so intense that I could feel the sudden warmth of it across my

face. The image continued to load, and in addition to the
stars, the heavens became crisscrossed with at least a
hundred bright lines. I assumed these were part of the
cartographic frame at first, irregularly-spaced grid marks
placed over the map after the image was captured, marks I
would someday understand as altitude, azimuth, right
ascension, declination — the astral equivalent of lines of
latitude and longitude. But I saw quickly that I was mistaken;
they were in fact part of the image itself. I struggled to
understand what my grandfather was showing me. A night
sky with a hundred shooting stars? A hundred satellites in
transit? A hundred comets with impossibly bright tails?

Today, thirty years on, if I close my eyes, I can still see
that brilliant image, and now I can point to *Beta Orionis*, or
Alpha Canis Majoris, or *Alpha Lyrae*. But back then there was
little more I could do than to gape at the vividness of the
starscape and to stab my tiny finger into the upper right-
hand corner of the page at the Big Dipper, the only group
of stars I could recognize. I wanted desperately to impress
my grandfather, of course, and he chuckled softly, and then
swept his old hand lightly over the entire page, first as if
brushing away some unseen dust, and then, returning,
fingertips down, as if to touch the concentrated starlight, so
bright that even in reproduction it made you want to squint.
I remember how he began to name the stars for me that
night — *Arcturus*, *Sirius*, *Betelgeuse*, *Vega* — and the words
sounded rich and strange and full of magic, as he traced with
his thick finger along one streak of light to the next, all
across the heavens....

Today, thirty years on, they laid my grandfather to rest.
Thirty years on, ninety-two years old, and full of vigor until
the last moment of his life. During his youth, pushed out of
the mainstream, sidelined, and sometimes even silenced, he
was known as loud and arrogant and volatile, and sharp-
tongued, a belligerent atheist or a misguided scientist; but he
was a quiet, peaceful man during his final years, and yet still
always busy, always working to improve himself, to learn,

even as his eyes and ears began to fail him. Preoccupied, perhaps, and yet still always willing to whisper the right word of encouragement in a younger man's ear. If the pendulum of recognition and reward had not quite swung back in his favor by the end of his days, it seemed likely to be moving in his direction again. It's true he did not tolerate fools or laggards — and there are so many of each it doesn't surprise me that the popular impression of him remains more bitter than balanced. It's also true he was often sad, too often alone, and filled with remorse, but who can hope to escape the advance of all regret by the time he is ninety? And he felt guilt, of course. A great and sometimes crushing guilt that even once I understood, I refused to believe was justified.

He bought me a microscope for my eighth birthday, shortly after he showed me the Light, and I still wonder whether it was his idea or my mother's, because it didn't seem to make any sense after he'd made the effort to open my eyes to the heavens. Furthermore, he was not the sort who took an interest in looking at what was right under his nose. He'd been a well-known lecturer in astrophysics at the local university, and his gaze, like mine, was always far out, fixed above the horizon, and we both knew it. The microscope stayed on my desk and collected dust. He corrected the error of the previous year and gave me my first telescope when I turned nine, and I still remember the night he unwrapped that large oblong box in my bedroom, how I was sick with the Northumberland flu and my mother stood beside the bed, nervously fingering the small pewter cross around her neck. I can remember her standing there, a scowl poorly hidden on her face. She was dressed in a long dark abaya, the austerity of which contrasted with the disquiet always present in her eyes. I wasn't allowed to go outside — on account of my being ill — and she said the present was thoughtless, risky, and unfair. It was many years before I understood what she really meant, but I adored the gift from the first moment the gleaming black tube emerged from its foam packaging, and although it was nearly two months before I could take the telescope outside, my grandfather and I spent many a night pouring over antique star charts and magazines and manuals, and poking the telescope out my bedroom window, sighting through trees and rooftops and telephone wires to the stars. During the final weeks of my illness — when I felt well enough to venture outside but was still forbidden to do so by a bevy of over-protective but well-intentioned physicians — my grandfather would distract me each night with the great mythological stories of the constellations, of Orion's belt, of Andromeda and Cassiopeia, of Cepheus and the golden chariots of the gods. It was almost more wonder than I could stand, but I adored every tale, and I adored him for the telling.

When I was finally permitted to venture outside — and I remember that night, too, as if it were yesterday — my grandfather helped me carry the ten-inch refractor up the road into the small county graveyard at the top of the rise of Maddock Hill where we could watch the sky from horizon to zenith over nearly 360 degrees. We walked quickly through the streets, even a little furtively, as if we were on some sort of secret mission, and when we reached the top of the hill I threw off my hat and coat, and stripped off sweater and gloves (my mother wouldn't let me leave the house wearing any less), and even though it was a cool fall night, and leaves were already dropping from the trees, the sky was clear and moonless and dark, and my pent-up excitement guaranteed I stayed warm. And there we were, on the top of the hill, my grandfather and I, mesmerized by pinpoints of light, and feeling as if we were in the center of the universe.

The first star we spotted that night was *Mizar*, a binary star in the constellation of *Ursa Major*, the second-to-last star in the Big Dipper, an asterism that I learned was more commonly called the Plough. I learned the six other visible stars in the Big Dipper that first night and can still name them all from handle to cup: *Alkaid*, *Alcor*, *Alioth*, *Megrez*, *Phecda*, *Merak*, and *Dubhe*. By the time I was ten, I could name all the deep sky constellations, and by the time I was twelve, I was helping my grandfather score the examinations of his private students.

I thought that telescope was the best gift I ever received, and it remained an essential part of my early life, even as football and schoolgirls overpowered my closest friends. Although I have no memory of what finally befell that original telescope, if I sit here and close my eyes and reach out my hand, I can still imagine its cool metal surface beneath my fingers.

Of course it wasn't until much later that I realized the real gift my grandfather had given me wasn't the telescope at all. His gift was both simpler and more complex: he gave me his time. And it was later still before I appreciated its real cost. But we all make trade-offs in our lives, and his trade-offs made me.

It was a hot July the year I first saw the Light, when Grandfather first pulled out the large volume with the panoramic daguerreotype of the stars streaking across the sky, and spread it before me. That summer was all sweaty shirts and dusty shoes, long walks through town and draughts of cold cider, and we were always pestering our mother, my brother and I, to take us to the waterfront, or rafting on the River Witham. My brother — two years older than I — says it was also a summer of long silences, punctuated by tears and anguished cries; but I honestly don't remember, although I do not doubt it is true. We had moved to the city shortly after my father died. We moved from a small farm outside Stamford in May to a tiny house near Tamworth Green in Boston, close to the High Road in Freiston where my grandfather — my father's father — lived. In retrospect, I can imagine what she was going through, our mother, her life shattered, and having been married to a Child of the Light, and now responsible for raising two young boys, and having to turn to her notorious atheist stepfather for help. But in those confusing first few years, when everything had been turned upside down, when everything must have been so chaotic and uncertain, to this small boy the world was still a Ferris wheel of wonder, each turn revealing hitherto unseen delights. I must have been sad, too, and I must have wept and missed my father; and yet if his absence has been a gaping hole in my life, it has been so thoroughly filled and covered over by circumstance and time that I honestly don't feel the loss. Life handed me lemons, and I carelessly tossed them back. And of course there was my grandfather who was quick to provide sanctuary (despite his own struggles at the time), and with each passing year, I gravitated increasingly to his townhouse, in varying degrees happy or grateful to circle his bright star. I fell into his orbit faster and closer than the others, and by the time I was twelve, entering first form at Haltoft Academy, I was living with him full time in Freiston, overlooking the Commons and the Wash. I saw little of my mother or brother from that point on.

But I was only seven when he first showed me that fabulous daguerreotype planograph of the stars, taken thirty years before I was born. I was so young, and yet the memory of that early encounter haunts me to this day, even if I wonder sometimes how accurate the memory is, for while the over-arching narrative never changes, the details aren't always *exactly* the same, such is the great power of manipulation that memory has over us; or we, over memory. Sometimes I'm not sure which way it goes, and I wonder whether we rewrite the past to our own pleasure or peril, or whether the past rewrites itself, trying to break the shackles of some inferior reality. Sometimes I think the future is not in our stars, but in our memories of friends and family forever departed with whom we can reconcile only in our febrile imagination. But I am getting ahead of myself, surely.

July, 1857. We were visiting his townhouse, the three of

us, my mother, brother, and me. My mother was downstairs preparing lunch, I think, or having finished her preparations, praying; and my brother was out back, throwing a ball against the side of the wall separating my grandfather's garden from his neighbor's. I remember the smell of roast turkey and clove; the sound of a cricket ball thumping against brick. I was staring out one of the bay windows in the living room, staring blankly up into the sky or over the Wash, as was my wont, when my grandfather pulled me aside and said he wanted to show me something *amazing*. I followed him upstairs into his library. He drew the shades and pulled a large volume from the shelf and opened it, placing it flat on the large table that held the center of the room. He turned the book slightly, orienting it towards a chair he had pulled out and into which he indicated I sit. I climbed into the chair and remember sitting on my knees to get high enough to look down at the image he was offering me. As the page lit up, flickering fire-like light into the surrounding darkness of the room, I remember feeling a sense of deep awe, even in my astronomical ignorance. The bright streaks of light were stunning. I looked up into my grandfather's face, his eyes aglow with the reflection of starlight, but I couldn't read his expression. His large eyes met mine, though, and then flicked back to the open book, bidding my gaze to follow. I looked past the dozens of streaking stars and pointed proudly to the Big Dipper. He chuckled warmly — but I sensed he wanted me to say something more, but I was at a loss for words.

I studied the streaks more closely.

If they *were* stars, they weren't really moving, of course. I knew that. I was a young boy, but precocious enough to know that it was our own celestial orb that was in motion, spinning on its axis and racing around the sun, driving the stars to wheel over our heads. If they were stars, this had to be a planographic plate exposed over several hours to cause such dramatic streaking. Is that what he wanted me to say?

I didn't know the term "time-lapse planography," so I

struggled to describe what I meant in my own childish words. But even as I spoke, I realized I was mistaken. If this were a time-lapse planograph, there was something fundamentally wrong with the image. I halted halfway through my insufficient explanation and looked up at my grandfather for help.

"I was there," he said. "I was there when this was taken." He tapped the bottom of the page. Handwritten along the lower edge of the print was a man's name, as well as the time and place the image was composed: somewhere over Haymarket Quadrangle in Cambridge, on the 18th of June in the year 1820.

I crossed my arms and made another guess: "I suppose the planographer didn't have very steady hands," I said, and my grandfather lay his hand on my shoulder, and smiled.

There were not many people at my grandfather's funeral today. I was there and my older brother, of course, and our mother — she came in from Seminary in Norwich, rolled in on a wheelchair because of her bad hip. My brother's wife was there (a realtor like my brother, apparently), and so was the bank executor for our family trust, and two or three of my mother's friends, but that was all. My grandfather had outlived all of his peers, and he was still too much of a pariah for many of his former students, however much they might have valued his tutelage.

The funeral was at noon and afterwards there was a short service at our old house near Tamworth Green — my brother's family lives there now, and he invited us all to stay as long as we'd like, although I believe my mother plans to return to Norwich in the morning, and I have my classes at Cambridge for which to prepare. The service was presided over by a doughy chaplain from the New Church of England (at my mother's request, of course; my grandfather would never have tolerated the NCE here), and when it was finished, the family dined together alone, the first time in many years. It was a muted affair, which was not unusual, but there was hardly even the pretense to reconnect. We've all seen our share of love and loss, I suppose, but something about this death struck a particularly melancholy note for us all. I wondered if this was perhaps our final opportunity to come together as a family; but after the dishes were cleared my brother and his wife helped our mother to her bedroom on the second floor, and I was happy to have a moment to come to terms with my grandfather's death on my own.

When I heard my brother's wife start back down the stairs, I made a quick decision and left the house through the back door, closing it softly behind me. I still wanted to be alone; I wasn't ready to endure a long night of shallow condolences, or no condolences, and I needed some air. Without thinking, my feet carried me through the front yard and across the street, then straight towards Maddock Hill, and up to the cemetery for the second time that day. It was a cool night in late summer, not unlike that first night when we lugged that telescope to the top of this hill. I found my way back to our family plot and my grandfather's tombstone, only a few feet from where we used to set our telescope those many years ago. I sat on the freshly-turned earth and leaned back against the marker for the life of a man who taught me so much. The sun began to set. I watched night fall and the stars appear.

I love the stars. I love their majesty and mystery, their promise of hope, of something greater than ourselves that even in their distant absence might bind us all together. I love that ten thousand years ago our ancestors looked up into this same night sky and saw the same slow procession of light. I love the scientists and astronomers that came before me and with tools inferior to that of a schoolboy's today unraveled the motion of the heavens and our place in them. I love the names that still make my lips tremble when I speak them: Copernicus, Galilei, Newton, Hubble....

A sudden cold breeze swept across the graveyard and I crossed my arms for warmth and thought back to those nights with my grandfather at my side. When we sat together at the top of this hill that first night, and the hundreds of nights that followed, and shared the wonder and grand enigma of the cosmos. When I was young, I thought it was our own private adventure, that we were the only ones to appreciate that celestial force, and it was glorious. And when I was older, and I realized I was mistaken, that the sky had become a lightning rod of meaning for the entire world, the feeling of glory — and awe — was only that much greater.

I ran my hands over the earth, then played with a pinch of dirt, rolling it between thumb and forefinger. It was still oddly warm from the day.

I became an astrophysicist like my grandfather, and I'm not sure who felt greater pride, him or me. He would always say he felt the greater pride of course; but only because he said there was no fall that could compare to his. I'm not sure what he meant by that. And yet, looking back over the years, I concede the possibility that in certain ways I may have followed in his footsteps a little too closely.

Here's what was wrong with that planograph he showed me in his library thirty years ago. If it were the result of a planographer with a shaky hand, or a true time-lapse planograph exposed over a period of several hours, then *all* the stars should appear as streaks. The sky should have been filled with jerky lines, or with tight rings of light centered on the north celestial pole, Polaris.

How could only *some* of the stars be leaving long streaks, and not others? And how could those stars be moving in so many different directions?

"This was taken on the second evening of the Light," he said. "Have they taught you about the Light in school?"

I shook my head, no.

My grandfather was twenty-five in June of 1820, a post-doc working with Drs. Nicholas Werner and Henrietta

Blackthorne on the Nomad Project to launch the first faster-than-light star sail. Much of the technology that was to be tested in high orbit that month was his, and this was his heyday — the climax of six years of exceptional research and development, an achievement that for others would be the culmination of a life's work. The Nomad satellite had been launched in March and the test of the sail was scheduled for the afternoon of June 17th. The nature of the sail and its position in orbit was such that those in the southern hemisphere would be treated to a flash of night light so bright it would seem like noon for nearly fifteen seconds. For the next three days, if everything went according to plan, there'd be a new star in the sky, leaving a fiery trail as it streaked out of the solar system, and beyond.

My grandfather was in the Cambridge "bunkhouse" for the sail's inflation and release. And at 14.04 on June 17th, the rockets fired, the sail engaged, and everyone held their breath.

The first televisual pictures from the ground came in almost immediately: my grandfather recalls seeing the Sydney Opera House lit up as if it were a bright summer day. Data began to flow in and the applause in the bunkhouse was thunderous. Initial telemetry indicated all systems were go as the craft accelerated first to one-quarter, then one-third the speed of light. My grandfather told me his knees went weak during those first moments — literally — and he slipped to the floor, much to his embarrassment.

Several minutes later, however, at 14.09, the first worrisome calls started to come in, from Melbourne, Adelaide, Trinity, Wellington. Night had returned to the southern hemisphere as expected, but (as newsreader Dana Obson became famous for saying) "Something [was] wrong with the sky." The Nomad's bright trail was visible, streaking away from the Earth — *but there were other trails, too.* Four were reported during the first half-hour in the southern constellations of *Vela* and *Dorado*: they looked like shooting stars, each with a trail between one-half and three-quarters of a degree, longer in length than the relative width of the moon. Nine more streaks appeared by 19.00, inscribing thin bright lines across the night sky. And by the time it fell dark in Cambridge on the other side of the world, there were no less than twenty-two streaks of light scoring the heavens, from *Boötes* to *Sagittarius*. The longest was now nearly one-and-one-half degrees in length, three times the width of the moon. What had been expected to be one of the most visually-dramatic moments in rocket history, the Nomad's ignition had become just a small part of the show.

No one knew what to make of it. It was as if a handful of stars had suddenly come to life, intent to skywrite some astonishing message across the heavens — a message no one could read. Popular opinion was disappointing but hardly surprising: scientific meddling had triggered a natural disaster of unimaginable scale. Scientists, in their own ignorance, had nothing better to offer.

The Huntley Group at Oxford ruled out the possibility of a local event, either natural or man-made: the streaks were not meteors; neither were they satellites in low-orbit. They were not the ion or dust trails of local comets. Both Langley and Huntley agreed that all the streaks — with the exception of Nomad's — were extra-solar in origin; and by the morning of the second day, Werner and Blackthorne at Cambridge confirmed that each streak seemed to originate in a distant star system. By the end of that second day, Ipswich produced the first rough estimates of speed and mass, giving support to what was already suspected: the streaks were moving at *or beyond* the speed of light. By the end of the second night, there were eighty-six such streaks visible in the northern hemisphere, and by the time night rolled over the southern hemisphere again, there were over two hundred streaks in the sky. The longest was now eighteen times the diameter of the moon.

My grandfather worked furiously to unscramble the mystery, as did everyone with the tiniest scintilla of expertise, and indeed many without. By this time, the problem had moved out of the lab and into the world: a combination of politics, religion, and science collided with the fear of the unknown, like flint striking steel, and sparks began to fly. Werner and Blackthorne removed to London on the third morning to work more closely with the government on a policy to contain the mounting public dread. My grandfather had run of the Cambridge labs then, and when it was uncovered by a local journalist that much of the work that precipitated the launch of the Nomad sail was his, he found himself in the center of a media frenzy. Reporters from journals both respectable and shady followed him wherever he went, but he still had nothing to tell them.

On the third night, there were over four thousand lines of white light etched into the dark sky. It was so bright, you could go outside and read the Bible beneath the light, which many did. Imagine how this felt: our steady and constant companions suddenly stirring into alien wakefulness, the old and familiar stars redefining their place in the heavens, demanding a complete rewrite of our book of celestrology. Many preferred to panic, however, or to incite; and there was mayhem in London, Cornwall, Sussex, and Kent. *Yea, the darkness hideth not from thee; but the night shineth as the day: the darkness and the light are both alike to thee.*

Back at Oxford, a theory was gathering momentum: the streaks were not independent events, but multiple reflections in a finite universe of a single event: namely, the launch of the Nomad sail itself. Huntley suggested the special quantum discharge of the sail was revealing a previously unseen topography of space-time — in particular, a three-dimensional topologically-compact space, determinate and edgeless. Launching the Nomad, he said, was like turning on a torch in a house of mirrors.

Cambridge rejected this line of reasoning immediately. My grandfather knew the math better than anyone, so he fired back a disproof: the proposed curvature of the manifold required the Nomad sail to inhabit its own

Perquit-Mandelsohn space, which was impossible unless the Nomad's flight was a reflection, too. This was a paradox. Huntley at Oxford ignored my grandfather's rebuttal, of course; but the final and undeniable rejection came shortly thereafter, when it was discovered that those streaks reported immediately after the inflation of the Nomad sail were *not* in fact the first streaks to appear. Several amateur astronomers had documented two tiny streaks in two different parts of the sky (in *Canis Major* and *Eridanus*) nearly two hours *before* the Nomad's ignition. So, for better or worse, it seemed the Nomad was not the "first cause."

It was then — during an afternoon press conference and in response to repeated requests for *any* explanation — that my grandfather made the casual proposal that would change his life forever. Although at the time, it had seemed like a harmless enough remark. He suggested:

What if each streak represents the launch of a faster-than-light star sail, similar to our own, but from a planet around a distant sun.

It was absurd of course. It beggared reason, and he knew that. At the very least, the odds were stacked against it. Thousands of sails, thousands of planets, all testing their faster-than-light craft at the same time — no, worse: at a thousand *different* times, millions of years apart, in order for the dazzling light of their engines to reach us at the same instant. And what are the odds of all this happening the exact moment *we* launch our own first faster-than-light craft?

But once said — and said to a journalist from one of the popular London tabloids — the idea of extraterrestrial life stuck. It was distressing to many, and an easy source for obsession and fanaticism. And before nightfall several national leaders took what my grandfather said a step farther, asking: *What if the launch of all these extraterrestrial star sails wasn't chance at all?*

Of course a deliberate act of coordination, sending to us — to us *in particular* — some inscrutable intergalactic dispatch, seemed worse than absurd: it seemed insane. But that idea stuck, too, and from there it was only another short step to the idea of first contact, from contact to invasion, from simultaneous star sails to alien armada, and then war, and worse. Yes, it got worse.

My grandfather got drunk.

I can understand *why* he got drunk that night — the twisting of his off-the-cuff remark into an existential warning wholly unsupported by the data that served only to agitate an already-disturbed populace — but I never learned why he said what he said *next*.

In the back room of The Eagle — surrounded by at least a dozen reporters hanging on his every word, as well as others, some of whom he knew and some of whom he did not — with a pint in hand, he stood on bench and then table and with a dramatic flourish suggested:

What if each launch is not only an independent event, but also, as Huntley described, a reflection of the others. Not a physical *reflection, but a reflection of something else, presently undefined. A universal* intention, *perhaps — hinting at creation on a cosmic scale.*

Well, that really fanned the flames. He might as well have said it was the Spirit of God, moving upon the face of the waters, fluttering over a sea of stars, bringing form to void and light to the deep. But he wasn't finished:

Imagine, he said, *walking into an amusement park's Hall of Mirrors, and therein seeing a thousand reflections of yourself, more or less distorted by the various shapes of the glass. Now imagine,* he said, *that all those reflections — tall you, short you, skinny you, fat you — they're no more or less substantial than you are yourself. They are in fact* as real as you are.

Could there be some crack in the mirror of space-time through which all these reflections might meet? Have we signaled to the universe that we're ready to join a larger family? Is God at last calling all his varied creations back home?

Pens were scribbling across paper even before my grandfather climbed down from the table and took his seat.

Maybe he had spoken in naiveté — imagining he was chatting amicably with a group of close friends, or scientists of like mind and disposition, who might understand his idiosyncratic flight of imagination, who might recognize a certain perspicacity even if his use of religious language was obviously misleading. Or maybe he knew *exactly* what he was doing and had decided in frustration — or anger — to wind them all up, the journalists and politicos and clergy. But the consequences were dire.

The news media, the government, the church — they all ran with the story. Extraterrestrials, a message from the stars, alien invasion — and now the face of God and an eschatological declaration from an Official Scientist that we were upon the end of days, that the rapture had arrived.

There were riots throughout London the next day.

On the fourth night the sky achieved its most intense illumination, even as it became clear that no new streaks were appearing. The longest, however, was now over 20 degrees — forty times the width of the moon — and for many, the sky had become a forbidding spider's web, or a prison. Power went out all across the United Kingdom that night, the result of the first NCE bombing, and my father was born in a dark wing of Addenbrooke's Hospital at 18.20 exactly.

On the fifth night, the bright sky began to wane at last. Many of the longer streaks started to fade, and a few of the shorter. On the sixth night, nearly all of the streaks were gone; and on the seventh night, the only remaining streak — a short run from *Deneb* to *Albireo* in *Cygnus* — disappeared.

Tonight the stars are silent and their motion is again the slow and steady dance familiar to so many. I sit here in the city of the dead, leaning against the tombstone of my grandfather, and gaze up into a vast rich canopy of stars. I marvel at how far we've come, how far we still have to go, and how many of us have been lost along the way. And I marvel at the living — the untold number of living.

For my grandfather's early insight was correct, of course, and whether fueled by anger, imprudence, or lager, he intuited what I've spent my career proving — that space bends, time bends, and we are one of many worlds, one of many reflections of identical intent. Exactly *how* identical are these many worlds, I cannot say, but the successful application of the technology that propels the star sail is the way we will find out. It's the way we will reach through the celestial looking-glass and grasp the hands of all our brothers and sisters among the stars. That's exactly what my grandfather saw on those staggering nights of the Light. I am also certain that that's what he hoped to see again every night he came up here with me. Even in his moments of greatest despair, he didn't believe, and neither do I, that that was our one missed chance to join the party.

The Nomad sail failed its first test, of course. Its engine burned for only twelve minutes. One flash of light over the southern hemisphere, and then a short brief streak across the heavens. It reached a maximum velocity of fifty-two percent the speed of light before disintegrating and disappearing forever from sight. For any "non-locals," the event would have been brief in time, compact in space, and almost certainly unnoticed.

But my grandfather saw it all: he saw the old world, he lived through the Light, and he saw what followed. He saw the rise of his career and then its rapid collapse — he was blamed by many for the dystopian anti-science aftermath of the launch of the Nomad sail. I know that through his long years, many spent as an outcast from the New Church of England, he felt responsible for much of what had happened, the good and the bad, but mostly the bad. I never saw it that way, of course. I never saw his work, his dreams, as anything like failure. The moral of the tale of Icarus — as a noted motion planographer once remarked — is not *Don't fly too high*. It's *Next time make better wings*. Certainly, in the decades since the last World War and the subsequent Reformation, we've been struggling to regain a lot of lost ground, but the mood today is positive, I think, and the expectation is we'll be testing the star sail again in another ten or twelve years. I plan to have my telescope out that night, right here on this hill. I only wish my grandfather could be around to see it, when we signal again to our great and fellow adventurers, and perhaps this time join them.

It's close to midnight. I stand and stretch, and turn one last time to my grandfather's grave before I go. I miss him terribly already; I feel the loss in my bones. I touch the granite headstone and re-read the inscription cut into its smooth surface, and tell myself I will go on; we all will go on, whatever our failings.

I look back across Tamworth Green. I can almost see my brother's house, and I can imagine the lights there flicking off one by one. It's a house filled now with ghosts and strangers, I realize, and I wonder whether that day — that moment when my grandfather first invited me into his library to show me the Light — was when my mother and brother and I, having unexpectedly lost a husband or a father, irrevocably veered off into separate lives. Sometimes I wonder if my father's death could have brought us all together instead, and yet it was not to be.

I forgive him of course. Not my father, you understand, but my grandfather, for all the choices he made. Many of them, he did not make alone. Sometimes I wonder if I knew back then, somehow, what I know now: that that was a secret bond we always shared, my grandfather and I. A guilty conscience.

I start down the hill, fighting back tears that took their time arriving. The image of a tombstone beneath the stars lingers in my mind, and his last message, carved in stone: *Fortunate is he who, with a case as desperate as mine, finds a judge so merciful.*

"Not in Our Stars"

First and last lines from
Looking Backward by Edward Bellamy

This is the first story in a three-story cycle called "The Light." The second story is called "Second Light," and the cycle is concluded in a story called "Alone in a Sea of Stars."

This story is set on an alternate Earth very much like our own. It's a sad story, I think, about failing to connect. We're all of us guilty at some point of losing sight of the trees for the forest, dropping details as we strive to satisfy some bigger picture — only to discover that taking care of the details is what the bigger picture is all about.

Written between 31 August and 1 October 2003

Pop

IN WATERMELON SUGAR

the deeds were done
and done again as my life is done
in watermelon sugar

"You just make sure you get all this action down, right?" She closed the bathroom door behind her and then finished buttoning-up her jeans.

"Don't worry. I think I've got it: 'Alibi slips out of her panties like others slip on banana peels. It's a surprise to no one, and always good for a laugh.' You like?"

"It's not the *peels* I'm interested in, Scribbler."

She strode topless into the middle of the control room, snatched her t-shirt off the couch and pulled it on. I watched her skinny arms stretch up into the sleeves, and the shirt slip down over her head, then over her small breasts. It was one of the band's giveaways promoting their last album, *Virgin Berth*. The front of the shirt had a picture of the Holy Madonna covered in fire ants. It was ugly, sexist, blasphemous, and at least one size too tight.

Some women can look good in anything.

Alibi grabbed a handful of hair from the back of her neck and freed her black tresses from underneath the tee, then shook her head back and forth like she was in a shampoo commercial. Although, honestly, who knew when she last washed that classic Japanese princess do. Meanwhile, her disembodied voice continued to boom from the speakers mounted high on the studio wall:

In such sweetness, we took her
and she was done
and done again as his wife had come
in such sweetness, we took her

Her tight hips began to sway in time with the music. Art, the band's mixer — a somber fortysomething with thinning hair and Poindexter glasses — continued to tweak the audio as it came in, twiddling the knobs and dials on the enormous equalizer. It was supposed to be the first single off the new album, but things weren't going well. The song was coming along, but Miltown, the band's keyboardist, was having trouble hacking into the Bureau of Alcohol, Tobacco, and Firearms. The bunker buster was due in about ten minutes, and if it couldn't be stopped, well, it wouldn't much matter how good the song was, would it?

Miltown's fingers raced over the computer keyboard, a virtuosic blur, a veritable click track for the building crisis. He imagined himself the gifted Romantic — expressive and emotional, educated, artistic, capable. But really he was just the best looking of the bunch; or at least the cleanest.

"I'm in!" he said at last, pumping a fist into the air.

Alibi clapped twice without enthusiasm, and Art ignored him entirely. I knew nothing about computers, but I had covered the aftermath of a drone attack at the Meadowlands in New Jersey back in '08, so I knew what even a small bomb could do. I scribbled a few more lines in my notebook. I'm not sure what I expected when I agreed to tag along with Blister as they produced their next album. But it wasn't this.

I asked Miltown if we were all-clear, if he'd hacked the system.

"We're in, but memory's dropping," he said. "It's 250K

now, but I don't know how long that will last. Without memory, there's no wiggle room. Without wiggle room, it's 'Hello, Mr. Tomahawk.'" Miltown ran a hand through his golden locks, pushing the hair out of his eyes, then both hands were right back at the keyboard.

Miltown was the oldest band member — maybe 26 — and rumor was he finished high school back in Milwaukee only hours before his first arrest, for hacking into the local DMV and turning every driver in the state of Wisconsin into an organ donor. He liked sunlight, had clear skin, and wrote all the band's songs, such as they were, as well as their web page and peer-based distribution software. Alibi sang and looked good thrusting and grinding. And Chancre played lead guitar. In fact, that was Chancre's spine-shattering electronic wail blowing through the speakers right now. Fans had been known to lose all sensation below L4 by the end of a Blister concert, and Chancre and Miltown would wander through the after-audience picking and choosing from the dozen or so teenage girls unable to stand, numb from the waist down and desperately trying to use their arms to drag themselves out of the venue. Chancre and Miltown would "invite" the more attractive girls back to their Winnebago, and then fireman-carry them to bed. Miltown (the band's nominal Casanova) made out pretty well. The girls would wake up later that night or early the following morning aglow, the feeling in their legs restored, their little hearts beating madly for their rock-star crush. Chancre's victims, on the other hand, would awake with their ears ringing and their hearts ready to explode with grief, recalling the sordid if not downright despicable acts they had performed the night before. They'd burst from the trailer yanking on skirts, tucking in shirts, and alternate-leg hopping into their shoes as they made their desperate escape. One girl said (in the inevitable affidavit that would follow) that it had felt as if she had been raped by Animal. Not *an* animal, but Animal, the wild-eyed Muppet who played ultra-loud, brutish drums for Dr. Teeth and the

Electric Mayhem. And the description wouldn't be too far off if Animal had had a thing for kangaroo-shaped dildos and Aqua Velva aftershave. Not to mention needle marks running up and down his arms.

"In fact," Alibi told me shortly after Chancre was released, "put a guitar in Animal's hands, let him pound it stupidly on his drum set, and you'd have something that *still* sounded better than Chancre's playing."

Believe it or not, she meant that as a compliment.

Alibi and Miltown first met at the Borders Bookstore in Berkeley in the spring of '99. Wendy O. Williams, the original lead singer of the Plasmatics, was signing copies of her autobiography, *Darling Wendy*. Alibi was a big fan of the early punk-gothic aesthetic, in particular Wendy O. Williams' original ensemble of chainsaw and crotchless panty. Miltown's appreciation was a little more *ironic*. He had gone to the signing on a lark: his roommate in college had played a few tracks for him from the Plasmatics' second album, the one in which the four band members had ad-libbed their parts in separate sound booths, oblivious to what the others were playing, and he'd thought there was something interesting, if not exactly listenable, in the emergent meaning produced by random construction. When he passed the bookstore and saw the sign for the signing, he just dropped in.

"The Plasmatics remind me of Eno's generative music, or the early Fluxists in New York," he had said shortly after Alibi cut in front of him in line. She was wearing black stirrup pants and a body-hugging chainmail tank top, and he was doing his best to make conversation. That's when she mentioned her predilection for chainsaws and crotchless panties. They didn't talk again; but after the signing, she approached him from behind in the fiction aisle, apologized for cutting in line earlier, and thrust her hands down his pants somewhere between Martin Amis and Jane Austin. Shortly thereafter, like every other post-coital couple in LA those days, they formed a band. It was called Plasma (no surprise) and they played mostly local gloaming gigs: that is, they were the late-afternoon warm-up band for the warm-up band's warm-up band. Their music wouldn't actually cause physical harm, not yet, but it came close, and together they performed like a rather skanky Captain & Tennille. Fortunately, the time was ripe for a rather skanky Captain & Tennille, and within a few months they were headlining the smaller clubs in town.

Their first break came when Miltown, feeling particularly down about their inability to crack the big time, ran into the step-son of Jack Nicholson's younger brother just outside a methadone clinic in Burbank. Miltown told him about his band Plasma (he told everyone about his band Plasma), and the kid told him about this bloody pus that kept coming out of his penis (he told everyone his bloody pus). When the kid said his step-father had connections into the hottest clubs up and down the coast, Miltown immediately crossed the street to a pawn shop and bought Chancre his first guitar.

They were now a trio, and shortly thereafter re-christened "Blister."

Wendy O. Williams had written in Miltown's copy of *Darling Wendy*, back on that day when he and Alibi first met, "Got semen?" and the band used that as the name for their first professional recording, a four-song EP financed mostly by Chancre's step-father. The album did pretty well, amazingly. And so did their second full-length effort, contrary to all expectations. Their third album went gold after one of their tunes [term used loosely] was picked up for a Spike Lee soundtrack. The song even had a brief stint at #1 in the Midwest — and EMI/busymonster, their label, has been shooting for the stars ever since.

"Shit!" Miltown cursed. His monitor had begun to vibrate as Chancre's guitar solo spiraled up into the resonant frequency of the PC, and the on-screen text became impossible to read. Miltown raised his hands from the keyboard, his fingers hovering just over the home keys as he waited, anxiously, for the Chancre storm to pass. After half a minute, he began to flex his toes, just to make sure the vibration that was creeping down his back wasn't going to put his feet to sleep....

We were somewhere near East Los Angeles, in a small studio called The Bomb Factory. Like most of the other buildings in this tiny industrial neighborhood — this mostly unremarkable spur off an even less-remarkable commercial drag — The Bomb Factory was outwardly nondescript: a long flat concrete and cinderblock structure, single-story, peppered with security cameras, and surrounded by one long, contiguous chain-link fence topped with M. C. Escher spirals of concertina wire. Inside, The Bomb Factory was a warren of recording spaces, sound booths, and lounges. There was a kitchenette filled with cans of Jolt and case after case of chocolate-covered gummy bears. There was even a sizable area devoted to the studio owner's own collection of antiquated electronica: a working Vox AC-10 Twin, the Baldwin Electric Harpsichord originally used by The Beatles, a Hammond Novachord with over 140 vacuum tubes, and an original 1929 RCA *Forbidden Planet* Theremin — not to mention various Wurlitzers, Prophets, Mellotrons, and Moogs.

And somewhere, probably less than 500 miles away, a cruise missile was making its own electronic music as it screamed through the air towards us.

Alibi settled on to the couch behind the big board. She stretched out, leaning her head back on the arm rest at one end, raising her bare feet up on the arm rest at the other, a perfectly-eroticized parabola of down 'n' dirty rock 'n' roll. She was tall and thin and dark, with a crooked face and straight black hair that fell below her shoulders. She wore tight jeans and a t-shirt, no socks and no bra. Emaciated and sometimes boyish, yes, but there was *something* about her, something about her predatory energy that could be very, *very* sexy. It was this tension between beauty and beast, Thanatos and Eros, Biafra and Buchenwald, I suppose, that gave her voice whatever distinctiveness it possessed.

Chancre's guitar solo ended and you could feel the collective relief in the room. Even Art, generally unflappable, sighed as he cracked his knuckles over the knobs and dials. Miltown's fingers returned to his keyboard, maniacally tapping out his mysterious hacker's Morse; and Alibi's voice returned over the speakers, a croaking, gravelly contralto that reminded me of Marianne Faithfull after she'd died and been reanimated — the singing dead. I watched as Alibi, on the couch, sent both her hands down deep into her jeans and began to lip-sync the single's next verse:

Think of me as your own gay
Jesus, spread wide
on the sofa in your living room,
sorely tempted. A remote

control in one hand, rod of
iron in the
other — or has your harried little
cripple just been pre-empted?

We were in the Studio B control room, and it's where we'd been stuck for the past three weeks. Sound proof tiles covering walls and ceiling, Perplex glass wall between us and the main sound stage, tensor lamps and work spots, a Trident engineering console (34 channels of legendary A Range EQ and 92 inputs on mix), a producer's desk with an internet PC, a comfy couch, and hundreds of coffee cups, discarded cigarette butts, empty soda cans, and crumpled candy wrappers. The band had pretty much fallen apart a week ago, shortly after the US Government issued its first warning, and the trio looked ready to eat their young. Alibi had already broken the band's second commandment concerning incestuous fraternization, and began having sex with Chancre again, several times a day. (Miltown had stopped talking to Alibi after she had asked Chancre to drag that old futon from the back of his truck into the studio's only bathroom.) Yes, the band had survived the heroin addiction of its guitarist, as well as multiple charges of sexual assault, three consecutive HIV scares involving its lead singer, two charges of municipal-phreaking by its keyboardist, the conviction of its first producer on charges of child pornography, and a fatwa against the entire band after the release of their *Virgin Berth* follow-up EP called *Gee, Jihad* which included the tracks "Saddam Yankees" and "My Sharia," but nothing had prepared them for the pressure-cooker of having to deliver another #1 hit. Gone were the carefree days of shouting moronic and/or sexist lyrics to small groups of moronic and/or sexist fans, coaxing sexual favors from other band's groupies, and cock-teasing the marketing directors of whichever penny-ante record label had been stupid enough to sign them that week.

Me, I just tried to stay out of their way and take notes.

Meanwhile, the chorus of the new single kicked in, another zombified outburst by Alibi backed up by Chancre on bass and Miltown on vibes:

> *You know I love you — with your legs apart*
> *I don't care what I find or what you've got,*
> *I'll take it all, dear lord, and cross my heart*
> *this cannibal sex doll sucks à la carte*

Jesus. This was all getting to be too much for me. Three years ago, the "on-the-scene" critic for *Rolling Stone* said of Blister's second album: "Imagine if the Sex Pistols began doing gigs on cruise ships. Now imagine the cruise ship is the Titanic." You'd have thought that would have pretty much sunk the band, which was my intention, but I had underestimated Alibi Toutonghi, or at least misread the depth of her punk M.O.. When she read my review in *Rolling*

Stone, her reaction wasn't indignation, but elation. She'd finally found someone, or so she thought, who "got it." She called my editor that afternoon and said: "I want him *now*!" And three days later a band I had thought I had effectively excoriated, a property I had definitively condemned, was handed to me as my next assignment and my new home. And I've been writing vile and despicable things about them ever since. Their third album topped the charts and they promised that my scathing review of their next album would be included right in the CD liner notes.

Assuming, of course, Miltown could do anything about the ground-hugging 1,000-pound explosive warhead heading our way.

Chancre finally emerged from the bathroom. He looked, skeletal, glassy-eyed, and thoroughly dissipated. Like someone who's been suffering for weeks from massive dysentery diarrhea. Like Iggy Pop on a *really* bad day. He mumbled something unintelligible, his lips wriggling like a half-rotten halibut slapped over his mouth, and collapsed into the chair next to Miltown. He zipped up his fly and made a half-hearted attempt to tuck in his shirt, then he pulled a Lucky Strike cigarette from a pack on the desktop and lit up. He took a deep watery suck, then exhaled in a long smoky groan. Alibi could fuck the life out of any man, and Chancre was barely half-alive to start with. It gave me an idea. I scribbled a few lines.

"Ok, Ali. How's this." I picked up my notepad and began to read: "'Some people have compared Alibi's singing to a disease of the loins, but it's probably more accurate to characterize her vocal stylings as a disease of the lower intestine, marked by severe diarrhea, inflammation, and the passage of blood and mucus. A walking cloaca of infection, wayward bacteria, spirochetes, protozoa, and various parasites.'"

She smiled. "You're going to get me some *weird* dates, man."

Miltown paused at the keyboard. "Weirder, baby. You mean Weird*er*." It was the first thing he'd said to her in several days.

Chancre guffawed, sending out several puffs of cigarette smoke, his laughter as indiscriminate as his sexuality. A relentless heroin addict for nearly a decade, Chancre had lost whatever sense of humor he once possessed. However, like a blind man whose other senses are subsequently heightened, Chancre could *recognize* even the most questionable, the most light-weight attempts at wit, and he'd *always* react. It got to the point that most people who knew him would go out of their way not to say anything even remotely funny when he was around.

Miltown immediately regretted saying anything. He returned his hands to the keyboard, typed out a line or two, then sighed. "Fuck. I can't do any more. *You* give it a shot," he said, sliding the keyboard over to Chancre. Like a drunk trying to focus on an eye chart, Chancre's eyes widened, then narrowed, then widened and narrowed again. Then he began to type, hunting and pecking his way into the Bureau of Alcohol, Tobacco, and Firearms' targeting computers.

"I'd say we've got two minutes. On the outside," Miltown said.

"Thank God for small miracles." That was Alibi from the couch.

"Please! Can you all just keep it down!" Art snapped, looking up from the equalizer for the first time. "Or we'll *never* finish this song."

And Alibi sang over the loudspeaker:

In patermelon sin
the deeds undone
and done again as my life's undone.
in patermelon sin

Behind the word "sin," in the background of the recording, you could clearly hear a cell phone ringing.

"Aw, shit," Art said. "We're going to have to do this *all again*."

Chancre suddenly stood up.

"Dudes!" he shouted, waving his hands in the air. "I did it! I hacked the system. The screen says 'OK'! Look, it says 'OK'! I did it!"

Miltown leaned over. "You idiot! — that's '*Zero* K.' We're screwed!"

I sat in the corner and watched as Miltown began hitting Chancre with the keyboard.

It would only be a few seconds now, I wrote.

"Pop"

First and last lines from
In Watermelon Sugar by Richard Brautigan

If I were a band I'd want to be Blister.

This story was inspired by a summertime visit to the real-life Bomb Factory in Los Angeles, and by the consumption of nearly six pounds of chocolate-covered gummy bears, courtesy of Erik Gavriluk, the owner. (If you're curious, that's approximately 350 little brown gelatinous Poohs. A digestive adventure I do not recommend.)

Written between 10 March and 3 April 2003

Labiovelora

*As the streets that lead from the Strand to the Embankment are very
narrow, it is better not to walk down them arm-in-arm.*

Virginia Woolf, *The Voyage Out*

1.

I KEEP THE MISCEGENATION PATTERN tucked
way back in my vagina. It's a secret place for a secret
configuration, but it's not hidden as well as it could be.
Loose lips sink ships, after all, and the pattern occasionally
slips out if I'm not careful during sex. I'll be on my back,
hips wide open, lips wrapped around some anonymous
maypole, mindlessly humping my Little Miss Muffet up and
down, and before I can say "O God, Rob," the pattern
comes loose and drops, plop, just like that. Within a few
seconds it can snake its way right up the urethra of the
unsuspecting maypole and next thing you know it's
insinuated itself tightly around the vasculature of its
testicles.

What happens next is all too predictable. I come quickly
(*too quickly*, natch!), but the maypole undergoes a long
succession of terrific ejaculations, shaking and shimmying,
and I can feel pulse after pulse after pulse. For a second or
two, I feel all-aglow with undeserved self-satisfaction,

thinking I've given this maypole the greatest fuck of its life; it's stupid, I know; and I realize it's not me, not really, it's just the miscegenation pattern settling into a new — albeit temporary — home.

I don't know why the pattern doesn't just reattach to me when it comes loose. It's stupid that it doesn't. It should work that way. I don't know why it shoots straight into the maypole, but it always does, even though it can't survive there for long. For that matter, I don't really understand why it comes loose in the first place, except that I can't let myself get too distracted while I'm fucking. So, yes, sure, there are trade-offs in the whole arrangement. There are always trade-offs. As Thomasina Blackmoan says: *limning your profile is a course of illumination and shade*. Whatever the fuck that means.

Anyway, as soon as I realize the pattern's jumped ship, I pull myself off the maypole. There's a brief refractory period after its initial orgasm when there's nothing I can do to get the pattern back, so it's time to just sit back and relax for a bit. Not enough time to do anything useful, of course, like wash the dishes or paint my toenails; but just enough time to start feeling guilty for having lost the pattern in the first place. Except, it's not really lost. I know right where it is — and I'll get it back, soon enough.

Don't get the impression this happens a lot. I'm usually very careful, very focused while I fuck. I take my job seriously, even if I'm not all hyper-anal about it. It's only happened three times before (twice by the official count), so dropping the pattern a few times is really no big disaster, I swear.

At least, it never has been before….

2.

Alain Sapiens looks away. He can't believe what he's hearing. She's crazy. She's completely crazy. He's in love with a crazy woman.

He looks towards the counter and the barista pulling drinks; he looks out the window of the café into the dark street. He looks into the empty cup of coffee cradled between his hands. He looks everywhere but at her, even though he wants to look at her more than anything.

Sapiens closes his eyes. He listens to the slow hiss of the espresso machine. The clink and plonk of coffee mugs. The muted conversation from others in the café. He wonders again if any of his students are here, watching, observing, wondering what he's up to.

What *is* he up to?

He opens his eyes, but he avoids looking at her face. He lets his gaze linger on the taught muscles of her neck, and then over the gentle curve of her bare left shoulder. It's enough to make his middle-aged pulse race.

How old is she? Twenty-one? *Twenty?*

He lets his eyes wander over the strange tattoo that runs down her arm, the tattoo he recalls having traced earlier that morning with fingertip and tongue: the unusual swirls and dots, like something written in ancient Aramaic, a canticle in flesh of memory and longing....

He brings the empty cup of coffee to his lips. He takes a drink of air, frowns, returns the cup to the table. He lets his fingers dance around its rim. Sapiens, a professor of psychology at the Saint Anne Divinity College, knows crazy. He knows that he should worry about sitting here, with her, in public. He knows he should worry about the kind of woman who would spin tales like this, and tattoo herself like that.

He takes a deep breath. His hips yearning to move with her again. Sapiens looks back out the window. His brow furrows and he squints and he can see in his reflection the deep creases and stretched lines of his middle-aged face, and he can read the complex atlas of confusion and apprehension that emerges. Not a great place to visit, he thinks. Not a great place to live, either. So who is he to find fault? He knows the relevant entries in DSM-IV, the *Diagnostic and Statistical Manual of Mental Disorders*. He knows them chapter and verse. It's not like the only problems around this table are hers.

"This pattern," Sapiens says. "It's something you're supposed to protect? Some *secret power* thing?"

3.

I give the maypole a little more. It's a bit cat and mouse, I know, and, well, sue me. I can't resist messing with the old guy's head, at least a little. And I stop the crying act. I've taken that about as far as it will go. I do wonder for a moment whether I am doing the right thing, coming to a maypole for help at all. When your house is on fire, you don't call your neighbor's goldfish. But the circumstance surrounding my dropping the pattern this fourth time, the coincidence of my having just been with *this* particular maypole … it's destiny or karma or something.

Anyway, there's no point in dwelling on the what-ifs. I'm a can-do sort of girl. Try not, do; and all that sort of shit.

So I dive back in, tell him a little bit more about the pattern, keeping it simple. But it's hard to keep him focused. Like most discopes, he's just not too bright.

4.

Sapiens nods, uh-huhs, and hmms. Outside a police car races by, its roof light twirling red and blue. There's no siren, only the distant sound of tires racing over wet pavement. It's been raining on and off for hours now, and as he stares out the window the rain begins again. It's a funny-looking rain, spattering carelessly against the glass. There's something mucky about it, too, something sooty or petrochemical, and the streaks that form on the window leave a visible trail. It makes Sapiens' reflection look like it's crying.

God cried, Sapiens would lecture his students, *when the Third fell like tears from Heaven, a driving torrent that must have cast the angels to Earth in an unforgettable deluge.*

"I can't believe I'm here," he says in a whisper, still fixed on his own reflection. His lips feel a little dry, parched, but he is compelled to continue. He's an academic, after all. There is comfort, if not sense, in talking. "I can't believe I'm here with you," he says again, a little louder.

Giselle doesn't respond, but he can feel her gaze, her attention, as intense as the beam of a lighthouse. He feels both illuminated and blinded. It brings to mind John 8:7, and Jeremiah 13:23, but especially Acts 12:7:

Behold, the angel of the Lord came upon him, and a light shined in the prison....

Sapiens touches the glass, touches his distorted image. He has lived a life of ambiguity, of multiple realities existing simultaneously. He has worn himself out juggling science and religion, sex and the church, the psychopathology of mind and the incorruptibility of spirit. He can't do it anymore.

"Do you know Paul Verlaine?" he asks. From the corner of his eye, he can see Giselle shake her head and he realizes he has never wanted anyone so badly as he wants this woman — this girl — this *angel.*

Sapiens clears his throat, recites the first stanza of a poem he learned in his early twenties:

> *Le ciel est par-dessus le toit,*
> *Si bleu, si calme!*
> *Un arbre, par-dessus le toit,*
> *Berce sa palme.*

He stops. His accent is marginal, but he has put his heart into it. It's probably been fifteen years since he's recited poetry like this. And now, today, it's pouring out of him.

Sapiens mouths the second stanza to himself, silently, as

he stares into the street:

> *La cloche dans le ciel qu'on voit,*
> *Doucement tinte.*
> *Un oiseau sur l'arbre qu'on voit*
> *Chante sa plainte...*

Outside it starts to rain harder, patters against the glass. Across the street, a heavily bundled man pulls the hood of his parka over his head against the wet and cold.

5.

I straighten my top and shift a bit in my seat and I tell him more about the pattern. He's still having trouble concentrating, but what the fuck am I supposed to do about that? Every time I twerk a muscle, he breaks a sweat. Then next thing I know we're in the fucking dead poet's society or something.

The problem of course is that he's one of those bleating Catholic types, and deeply fucked-up when it comes to anything sexual. Even without the pattern in me, he can't keep his mind off a certain rocket docking in my spaceport.

Anyway, I do my best to sit still. And I make sure to leave out any disturbing references to the origin and history of his particular flock.

6.

"Do you really love me?" Sapiens asks. It's a crazy question, but he can't stop himself from asking it anyway. Earlier that day, back at his place, she *had* said she loved him, or something to that effect. Now he can't stop saying the most ludicrous things. He turns from the window, turns towards Giselle; but he looks down, still averts his eyes.

He knows he's pathetic. He knows he shouldn't be here. But he can't leave. He's a deer, caught in the headlights of her divinity, of her holiness. He *yearns* to hear her voice. He *yearns* to gaze into her eyes. His angel. His *savior*. While his penis, stiff inside his pants, twitches in absurd anticipation just *thinking* about her.

How old is she really? Eighteen? *Seventeen*? Oh God. Is this what it's like to be a drug addict? he wonders. Is this what it's like to be an alcoholic? This mad unquenchable *need...*? He's been lead around by his balls before, but never, *never*, like this. This *is* a religious experience, all right. The kind of religious experience that gets you thrown into jail, usually after a good stoning. You can have what you want, sure. But you can't want what you want. It's the oldest lesson of all, he knows.

He says, "I thought you weren't coming tonight. I thought you weren't going to come." His voice cracks. His eyes go a little misty. Lines from another poem come to mind, and these he whispers under his breath:

> *Soon my Angel came again;*
> *I was armed, she came in vain;*
> *For the time of youth was fled,*
> *And grey hairs were on my head.*

He waits for a response, but again she says nothing. He glances back out the window. A young couple walks past the café, their figures distorted by the wet glass. They hold one another, arms around hips, a ripple of togetherness, merging together, slipping apart, changing shape in the glass as they move. Another reminder of angels in our midst, he thinks; traveling incognito, shape-shifting....

The couple disappears around the corner. Sapien continues to stare after them, until he realizes that Giselle has turned her chair and he's now face-to-face with her reflection in the glass. He watches, mesmerized, as she runs a hand through her hair, then uses both her hands to gather a pony tail which she lets go.

Angels are always in disguise, Sapiens knows, veiling the fact that they are without size, that they exist on the scale of thought not matter. Sapiens recalls Jacob in Genesis, wrestling with his own angel in the wilderness. Yet Scripture tells us again and again that they are *not* glorified human beings. The word "angel," after all, comes from the Greek word *aggelos*, which means "messenger," a manifestation of intent. Angels appear as often as words or a gentle pressure of wind even if unnoticed, as they appear in imitation flesh and blood. And yet who does not persist in imagining the natural perfect state of angels is the form and figure of man. Or woman.

Sapiens clasps his hands together, as if in prayer, and squeezes; but he is not praying. He is suppressing an urge to reach across the table to touch her, to grab her, to pull her over, to kiss her, to taste her in his mouth again. He stares at his joined and interlaced fingers and he realizes they look grossly unfamiliar: gnarly and spotted and hairy and *old*. He squeezes harder and his knuckles crack, a tiny pop of mortality. How has he become so *old*? How is it he cannot recognize himself? Look at these hands! The hands of a sunken Lazarus, grafted to his body. They can't be *his* hands.

"Do you really love me?" he asks again, his voice stronger this time, and he looks straight into her face.

7.

Oh, man, I can't take it. I can't take it!

I have to look away. It's so ridiculous. *It's so embarrassing!* If I have to listen to this maypole for another second, I'm going to lose it. I can handle *love* when it's a mindless mantra in bed. I can handle *love* when it's tied up in a tangled scream of leg-splitting pleasure. I can even handle limited doses after the fact, lovey-dovey thank-you's under the breath — luckily the swift application of foot to back usually sends the maypole off the bed and on to the floor hard enough to close *that* tap. But *desperate* love, *earnest* love, *treacly* love, ugggggggg, makes me want to *fwow up*. Who can keep a straight face when someone pulls that kind of shit on you?

But I pull myself together. I don't have time to fool around. I take a deep breath and —

8.

Giselle smiles — she smiles! — and Sapiens can hardly breathe. His chest tightens. It's like he's having a heart attack. And in a way he is. The joy is unbearable. It's an explosion of light. He closes his eyes. He squeezes his lids tight — but Giselle is still there, burned in afterimage. She moves for him in the darkness, a sinuous angel in this sanctuary of imagination and memory. They wrestle, as they had earlier that day, skin to skin. Her skin blazes gold with a celestial purity, even as his own self-image is darker, greyer, cratered with history.

"You remind me of an angel," he says. "Like David — if David were an angel."

No. That's not right. Not like David. Not exactly. But he can't find the right words. He hasn't been able to find the right words for any of this. Perhaps there are no words.

He opens his eyes. He closes his mouth. Language is as confused as vision, as memory, as imagination.

9.

It's not hard getting the pattern back, you know, at least it shouldn't be. So in some ways — if you pardon the expression — I was in virgin territory. In the past, it's just been a matter of coaxing the pattern back into my vagina, which is where the pattern wants to be anyway, really. Having to *find* the maypole with the pattern was never an issue. In the past, after the pattern jumps and the maypole climaxes, it's just a matter of minutes before I can get to work wringing it out and bringing it home. I've just got to keep milking the bull until the pattern comes gushing back.

The pattern keeps the maypole nice and hard, and hungry, and the sex we've already had has usually fused a few of its neurons already so the maypole's your standard puppy dog by this point, all panty and starry-eyed and eager to please, sticking straight up the whole time, like I said, but now tracking me as I walk around the room, a little teetering flagpole pointing towards the great female magnetic north. Even in the worst of times, it's hard not to get a kick out of that, right?

10.

"So you've lost this pattern before?" Sapiens asks, desperately trying to focus. He's cupping her left hand between both of his.

She nods. "Two times. Well, three," she says. "That is, three times until tonight."

11.

The first time I lost the pattern — when I was fourteen and stupid (we won't go into it) — it took about an hour-and-a-half to get it back. I was a little panicky and had a hard time focusing. I was so distractible then! But it turned out OK in the end, despite having to spend four weeks in Reform as punishment. The second time I lost it, I was able to reclaim it in under fifteen minutes, so fast I never even had to cop to *that* accident, at least not publicly. But the last time — that is, the time *before* tonight — it took eight hours to bring the pattern home, and man did the shit hit the fan.

It wasn't my fault, really. I did everything by Hoyle. But I'll tell you this: you can get pretty sick of keeping the same maypole around for hours on end, and *all* you're doing is pumping and grinding, going at it, and going at it, and going at it, waiting for the pattern to come loose or shake loose or let go or whatever it does when it's time to come home to

Mommy. We'd take a few breaks from the really vigorous intercourse, when nature calls or I need a cold drink, but otherwise pattern-recovery's a full-time job. It has to be, even if — as was the case that third time — the maypole's cherry and raw, and everything's a blur of crying and coming and crying and coming. I remember when the maypole first started to squeal in pain and I wondered when the laws of biology (or physics!) would put a stop to things, but the maypole kept going and going, maniacally eager to pile drive until I told him it was OK to stop. Amazing what they'll put up with for a good lay, eh? Thank you, Mother Nature!

Dealing with my boredom or the maypole's agony, of course, is only a small part of the ordeal. It's not like the miscegenation pattern's your tonsils or something, something that doesn't really do anything, something you can live with or without, your choice. No, if that were the case it wouldn't be such a big deal to become a Vessel; it wouldn't be such a big deal to feed and care for and *protect* the pattern.

12.

"Until tonight?" he asks, not sure he's following her at first, not even sure he's really listening to what she's saying. "You lost the pattern tonight," he says. And suddenly he understands the implication of what she's saying. He loosens his grip on her hand.

"You were with someone else." It's a statement, not a question. It's not even an accusation. He's too stunned for that.

She leans back in her chair, enough so that their hands pull apart, enough for him to feel the tremor of loss, the crevasse, that could open between them at any moment. Sapiens leans forward, leans across the table, chasing her receding hands, but she's moved them back into her lap. He's stunned. Shocked. Broken.

Broken?

Christ. He doesn't know. He can't actually tell how he feels. He grabs hold of his coffee cup — it's empty and cold — but it's something, anything, to hold on to. His left hand starts to tremble.

She was with someone else?

13.

Do I give a shit about a maypole? No. Like I said before, I take my job seriously, and the job's not about maypoles. You need to understand that. As much as I like to play games (and I *do* like to play games), I'm not about to start slow-pitching the pattern. The pattern's *Numero Uno*. It's all that matters.

Here's the deal. It's *Bad News* if I drop my pants and the pattern goes south. But what can you do? It happens, and you cope. If it's stuck outside me for more than an hour or two, I suppose you could say that that becomes *Really Bad News*. After three hours, you're officially in *Deep Shit*, and after six hours — read my lips — it's *Shitsville*. You just don't *ever* want to go there.

But if the pattern's still AWOL when the *Labiovelora* rolls around — if it's still cruising up and down some maypole's urethra — or worse: cruising the neighborhood — well, you can throw in the towel. That scenario's something like *Shit Planet*. Everything's up for grabs. Thomasina Blackmoan would say, "To repattern is an invitation necropolitic." Which means, roughly translated, "You're just *so* fucked, and so is the horse you rode in on."

14.

As major metropolitan areas go, Providence is slow to rise. With the exception of the Portuguese bakeries that dot the eastern edge of the city like raisins in sweet bread, few people roll out of bed before 5:00 am, and vehicular traffic throughout College Hill is non-existent until well after 6:00, long after the crew teams from the local colleges have completed their morning regimen of running and rowing. Sapiens' day began, as usual, at the crack of dawn, shortly after 6:15, bringing with it equal amounts of loneliness and hopelessness, and the familiar tired faith and grim forbearance; the usual morning prattle of local news on his clock radio, the half-full dishwasher, and the half-empty bed. On this day, like most others, he was little more than a machine, participating in a mourning ritual absent joy or anticipation. Wake up. Sit up. Stand up. Brush teeth, brush hair. Pee. Pull on shorts, pull on sweatshirt, socks, sneakers....

Outside the sky was cloudless and blue, and the air cold and clear without a hint of the incipient precipitation that would drench the streets outside the café later that evening. Sapiens left his small, one-bedroom apartment, turned down Congdon Street, and ran. He ran, inhaling hard, exhaling harder, passing the southern boundary of Brown University on his left and Saint Anne's Chapel on his right. He ran, picking up speed as he started down the steep hill towards downtown, trailing clouds of white steam with each breath, well aware that the battle to stay in shape was another battle he was losing.

He passed the First Baptist Church half-way down the hill, then turned south-east, away from Waterplace Park, away from the urban convergence of the Moshassuck and Woonasquatucket rivers, the so-called revitalized center of Providence, a city that despite the best efforts of upscale marketers was still best known for H.P. Lovecraft and Buddy Cianci, rats in the walls and rats in public office. By the time he reached the promenade at the bottom of the hill, he noticed an uncomfortable tightness knotting the muscle of his left calf, and before he reached the first of the new Venetian-style footbridges that crossed the river that ran through the center of the city, he had to stop.

Sapiens bent over, hands on his knees. He must have looked as if he were going to collapse, heaving, gasping for breath. And for all he knew maybe this daily ritual *was* killing him, slowly, in degrees. Oh that bastard Nietzsche! That which doesn't kill us, makes us *weaker* and *weaker* and *weaker*.

An icy breeze sliced across his back, freezing the bare gap between shirt and shorts, and —

"You OK?"

It was a woman's voice, close by. He tried to wave her on — whether he was OK or not, he certainly didn't want any help — but she moved closer and *touched* him.

Not a *physical* touch. Only a shadow at first, falling over his arms and legs as she stepped closer, blocking the winter sun. The gentlest of pressure, this touch, this absence of light, and it should have chilled him, but instead, miraculously, *warmth* coursed through Sapiens' body. His chest relaxed. The knots in his legs unwound, vanished.

She touched his shoulder with her hand, and suddenly power was flowing into his arms, his legs. Air filled his lungs, and without thinking he stood, chest out, shoulders back. It really was as if, his batteries running low, someone had plugged him in. Sapiens laughed in surprise, and when the woman grinned in response, he took his first good look at her. She was medium height, with bright blue eyes, a button nose, and full red lips. Her auburn hair was razor cut in bangs with long waves that fell past her shoulders. She was slim but curvy, dressed in a one piece running suit, physically fit. Attractive, obviously, just not his type.

And yet….

His hips began to move, and not without volition. He laughed again, this time in embarrassment. Sapiens felt his pulse quicken. His eyes sharpen. His attention focus. Whoa. He wasn't just plugged in — *he was turned on*.

"You OK?" she asked again.

He didn't know what to say. He steadied himself against the river wall at his side.

You think you know everything, Sapien told himself later. You think that the intricate model you've created in your brain is a reasonable abstraction of reality. Then something comes along and shatters everything you assumed about your world — and yourself.

"Maybe you shouldn't be alone right now," she said, sliding her hand under his arm; and this third touch made his knees weak. He nodded as if in a dream. When he looked down, he saw he was sporting a massive erection, visibly tenting his jogging shorts. A hard-on! For *her*!

She led him away from the water, back towards College Hill, and he followed. She didn't seem worried about his health. She didn't seem worried about anything at all.

"Come with me," she whispered, and he was suddenly a fifteen year-old boy, about to discover what all the fuss was about.

15.

To be honest, I don't know what it means to be fucked. I don't know what will happen if the pattern stays out so far past its bedtime that it "repatterns." And I have no idea really what a "necropolitic invitation" might be. All I know is it's BAD. The kind of bad you *never* want to experience.

But I *can* tell you what happens before that time, what happens during those first few hours after I'm careless and the pattern slips from my ruby red lips.

First, my cell phone starts to ring.

I know who's calling. And I don't answer.

16.

She was with someone else.

Sapiens stares hard at the coffee cup before him. His grip around it remains tight. Being in her presence, here in the café, drives him mad. *Life is not a feast nor a spectacle*, Sapiens realizes, *but a predicament.* George Santayana had that right.

He forces himself to push the cup aside, brings his hands together. They're still gnarled, swollen, dappled with age. But he recognizes something else in the lock of hand in hand, in the interweaving of fingers. *This is the church*, he thinks, recalling a rhyme from childhood; and he raises each index finger so they touch at their tips: *and this is the steeple.*

Yes, he recognizes *this*. An abstraction for every decrepit structure he has ever built with his own hands. The wasteland of years teaching at Saint Anne's. The years wasted groveling for funding and promotion. The years pushing naïve students into unpromising theological careers. The years running between local parishes and social services, play-acting an agent of moral rectitude and positive change. Years spent hiding — from himself first, then others — feigning intimacy while keeping an emotional distance from faculty and students, from friends.

Everything he touches turns to stone. He's like the anti-Midas. Like Gorgon.

> *What are the roots that clutch, what branches grow*
> *Out of this stony rubbish?*

Sapiens flexes his fingers — they are stiff and swollen — and he feels the stubborn complaint of aging muscle.

When had he lost faith in the absolution of self-knowledge and self-confrontation? When had he lost faith, too, in the Gospel and the healing power of love? When had it happened? Was there an exact hour, a moment, when everything changed? Was his a single fall, or a long age of measured descent?

17.

Time stretches, everything slows, and sometime after that first phone call, sometime in the second hour, there'll be a knock on my door. I know who this is, too. And I don't answer it either. It's the same local "ex-officio," checking up, which is just so fucking distracting — not to mention discourteous — when I'm inside busy screwin' my little heart out, doing the *here kitty kitty* with some recalcitrant maypole, just to get the pattern back into its warm fragile safe. Like, *hello?*

People?

Maybe I'm busy doing something important here!?

There's another knock. Then:

"Hey, Gis'! You OK? Is everything OK? I was just in the neighborhood and I was just going to drop by and I just happen to notice the hemen's down to a dribble and…."

Gab gab gab. And all this through the fucking front door!

Man, there's nothing worse than these ex-officios, these ima'am pretenders, I tell you. Usually former Vessels hoping for a comeback, these women are like dirty old men or nosey neighbors, groupies masquerading as the near and dear, hoping to re-make a name for themselves by dogging the *hemen*, or just hoping to cop a feel of the pattern itself. When we're feeling particularly snotty, we call them *Rimmers*.

So I shout back through the door, my hips moving all the while: *Yes, yes, I've just got terrible cramps, ow, everything's fine, just really bad cramps, see?*

You understand, Vessels have been known to drop the pattern during a severe estrogen crash, or even running a high fever, so this little untruth (even if it doesn't actually fool *anyone*) usually gets the ex-off on the other side of the door to give up, at least for a little while….

18.

Giselle reaches across the table and wraps her hands around his. The steeple of the church he's formed from his fingers is pointing right at her. She gives his hands a tiny squeeze and he can't suppress the sudden surge of good-feeling that physical contact brings. The café grows noticeably brighter, warmer. He takes a deep breath.

He can't believe how much has changed in the last twelve hours. How much has changed *for him*. What matters, he suddenly realizes, is not the Santayana predicament, *per se*. It's paying attention to its message. And it's paying attention to the meaning of its messenger.

He looks into Giselle's eyes. They're so unbelievably beautiful. Intoxicating, of course, but also tender, kind, comforting, eager, enthusiastic, mysterious, magical….

It's ridiculous. There aren't enough words.

He returns her delicate squeeze with his own. He peels his hands apart, cleaving the steeple in two, razing the tiny structure. He keeps his eyes on Giselle. He takes hold of each of her hands. And even this simple reciprocity feels like a celestial circuit has closed. Her love pours into him.

Forget the church, he tells himself. It's never comforted him like this, never wanted him, really. In all the long years he spent there, it never understood him. He was an alien, outside the bounds of their understanding. And if they've *both* betrayed him, well, the *church* never made any effort to win him back. Giselle, though, had returned. She was here, now, and she was a miracle worker. Now the church will have to accept him, and now — with a clear conscious — he can say no, thank you.

"I'll help you get the pattern back," he says. "I'll help any way I can."

19.

Getting the pattern back should be easy. It should be the simplest thing in the world. But if I haven't got it back after *three hours*, I start to worry that maybe it's never gonna come home.

The impact is no longer local — everyone's starting to feel it, and it feels like shit. When the *hemen* slows, the jitters start, background noise at first, sure, but it just gets worse and worse, like caffeine withdrawal that sneaks up on you slowly until you realize you can't even hold a pen without doing the jitterbug. There's no covering up anymore. The whole thing goes official. The neighborhood watch goes into action, the *Exuded* are called in, and there'll be another phone call, shortly, a call I've got to take from a high-ranking slice, a *Vag Hegemoan*, speaking in *Tanakha*, the Only Tongue:

"*Vessel Giselle Cinnamoana he Miscegenatura,*" she says, using my full name in that icy tone that puts me smack in my place. "*Are you aware your flow has stopped?*"

It's a trick question of course because the only way I wouldn't know the *hemen* has stopped flowing is if I were dead, which is really the first point of the call: to find out if I'm dead or not. The rest is small talk.

"Vessel Giselle," she says, "what occasions our coupling so?"

I spill the beans and tell the truth, the whole truth, and nothing but the truth, because, well, because, you don't lie about something like this, not to a *Vag Heg* speaking in Only Tongue, not unless you're stupid.

"We have aroused several *Cloetura*, Vessel Giselle," she says at last, finally getting to the second point of her call, and every utterance sends a small puff of cold steam from the mouthpiece into the room. "We shall dispatch as necessitated."

And of course you don't just say *yes* — you say *yes, yes, thank you, thank you*; because what the hell else do you say when you get a call from the *Vag Hegemoan*?

So sure enough, within half-an-hour or so, six or seven Osakan *Cloetura* show up at my door, ready to assess the situation and "assist" — which if I'm lucky means they don't kick my ass.

Of course, if I don't answer the phone, I'm presumed dead, and it means the pattern has left Dodge and could be anywhere with only nine or ten hours to survive outside a living Vessel, or even less before the end of night. Either way, that's when all hell would break loose.

Hmm, that's a funny expression: "all hell breaks loose." Shows how like totally inculcated I am with discope culture. There is no such thing as Hell, after all. What there is, or so I'm told, is much *much* worse.

I don't mention this.

20.

Sapiens leans back. He's not listening anymore. He's made his decision. He'll do whatever she asks, so he's just killing time, waiting to know what's next, waiting for instruction in their new life together. It's a relief, actually. He's not anxious. If anything, he's eager. He's ready for anything, for everything. (Well, let's be honest: he's mostly ready for more sex.)

Giselle finally stops talking. That's a kind of relief, too. The less about "the pattern," the better, he thinks. The less he thinks about her classification in DSM-IV, the less cognitive dissonance.

Giselle takes another drink. She's been drinking a lot, he's noticed, ever since she arrived at the café. Drinking water, not coffee. Glass after glass of water. There's a large silver pitcher on the small table near the front of the café, along with plastic lids, napkins, and little glass jars of nutmeg and cinnamon. She's made three or four trips up there and back, refilling her glass each time. Sapiens watches her Adam's apple rise and fall as she finishes another glass. There's something mesmerizing about the gulping rhythm. It reminds him of that morning. The sun on his neck, the sway of her hips….

She was walking quickly, half a step ahead of him, and

his eyes had remained fixed on her bottom, on the form-fitting black lycra, swaying with an almost mechanical determination. If he'd been thinking clearly he might have wondered how she knew to get to his apartment, how she knew where to go. But it was enough to follow in her wake as she walked from the bottom of South Main Street back up College Hill. She held his hand and he trailed slightly behind her, a dog on a leash. When they reached his apartment, he was shaking with excitement. It took him three tries to get the key into his lock; and when he finally threw the deadbolt, the door flew open. They hurried through his living room, straight back to the bedroom, her strong hands all over him.

"Giselle," he whispered between gasps. "We should stop. You could be one of my students."

She put two delicate fingers over his lips. "Yes," she whispered. "I could be."

He put his hands on her hips and pulled her slowly back and forth, gently rocking her body against his, marveling at the mind-blowing shape of the female form. *Have I really never noticed this before?!?*

"What do you think?" she said. "Red head or brunette?"

He shook his head, not knowing what she meant. Language can be as alien as people, he thought, as he pulled her body firmly to his. She squirmed out of her jogging apparel, peeling off the black lycra. He fumbled out of his clothes and then found himself on his knees, his face so close to the furnace of her sex that he could feel waves of heat coming off her. This was it, he thought. It had to be. This was Rapture. *This* was the burning bush, and he was ready for her ten commandments.

He threw both arms around her and worked his way gradually back up her body. He has no memory of actually entering her, as if the memory itself is just too bright, self-erasing in self-defense. But he remembers coming again and again. He didn't even know this was humanly possible: five times overall, he thinks. He remembers her pink toes against his white sheets. Her remembers the way their hips fit together. He remembers the slightly bitter taste of the tattoo that ran up her left arm, a taste of almond liqueur. He remembers the afternoon sunlight rising over the hill of her thigh. He remembers the tumbler of *Pinot Noir* she poured over his head, and he remembers another twenty minutes of exorcising intercourse. He remembers her resting on his chest, he remembers staring at her nipples and thinking that they looked like dark mushroom stems. He remembers rolling back on top of her as she stroked his head and told him that he really needed to rest, and he told her he knew that, he knew he needed to rest, even as he mounted her for the sixth time. He remembers reading to her from Blake:

> *I heard an Angel singing*
> *When the day was springing*

And he remembers whispering into her ear, "My kingdom for your halidom!"

"Hey," she said, half-laughing, "you *really* need to take a break." She kissed him on his still-erect penis and rolled out of bed. She told him — as she dressed, as he reached for her — that she'd be back later, sometime that evening, and she suggested they meet at a small café up Thayer Street. He watched her gather her socks. He stroked her back with the pad of his big toe as she sat at the end of the bed and pulled on her sneakers. He watched her lace each shoe, and he watched his penis standing upright between them, a third person in the room, watching them both.

"Where are you going?" he asked. She blew him a kiss on the way out.

"W–Wait," he stuttered as she disappeared into the living room. "Don't go, not yet. Let me kiss your neck at least, let me kiss the tip of your breast, let me hold you, let me —"

He heard the front door open and close.

21.

The last time I lost the pattern — well, the time *before* last, actually, the time when it took me eight hours to get the damn thing back — I was really *really* lucky, even if it didn't seem that way at the time. At the time, I thought I had screwed everything up, and considering the way I spent those eight hours, it's no wonder I was feeling a little bleak. Who cares how much *worse* things could have gone — that is, if it had taken me just forty minutes longer and night had slipped into *kwh*!

But I'm jumping ahead of myself.

The first three hours went by, and I got that crappy call from the *Vag Heg*, with some not-so-veiled threats, and already most of the Autumn Gateway had collapsed and the winds had kicked up, and you'd have to be pretty stupid not to notice something was rotten in Rotterdam. In other words, you'd have to be a maypole or oubliette. The sky had darkened and the clouds had opened up with this nasty rain that reminded me of redneck spit, a half-hearted coughing up of droplets dark grey and brown. I recall taking a bio-break and looking out my window, and the rain spattering against the glass looked like splotches of watery dung. I held out my hand and I could see the subtle tremor. That was only the beginning, of course.

By the *fourth hour*, when the true damming begins and the *hemen* flow has all but stopped, it's not just jitters anymore. The discomfort radiates out, its impact flowing along the same path as the *hemen*, a complementary wave of distress and anxiety, producing headaches, thirst, and shivers in *Labiovelorans* from Trenton to Timbuktu.

This was when the *Cloetura* really went into action, bless their little hearts, moving into the bedroom and clearing everything away from around the bed, taking notes as I humped, like this was a test or something.

I suppose I could explain a little bit about the *Cloetura*.

Just so you understand exactly how creepy they are.

First, they're not like other *Labiovelorans*. You don't see them often outside the *kwh*. It's not because they're shy. It's because the *Vag Heg* & co. keep them on a short leash. They're pit bulls for the *Vag Heg*, I guess: short-tempered, mean-spirited, eager for violence. They're small, maybe six inches in height, golden brown, no visible arms and legs. Except for the teeth, you might mistake them for Twinkies.

22.

Sapiens heard the front door open and close.

He sank back against the bed. He tried not to move. He listened. Listened in vain for the sound of the front door re-opening. The sound of Giselle returning.

He stared at the ceiling. It looked pale yellow, like vinyl that has decayed over time. Do they make ceilings out of vinyl? Ten minutes passed. He glanced to the bedroom door to make sure she wasn't still there, watching him wait for her. More minutes passed. Every part of his body felt sore. His neck, his shoulders, his back, his arms and legs. His erection, which had seemed as if it could do nothing but point heavenward, like a celestial telescope, had fallen back to Earth. He started to cry. Maybe he needed air, he thought. Maybe he needed something to eat. Maybe he needed a drink.

He rolled off the bed, groped around the floor for his discarded clothing, then carried everything into the bathroom. He started the bath, twisting both taps open, the water a loud torrent as the tub filled. He dropped his underwear into the bath, followed by his running shorts and shirt. He watched them turn tiny circles, then slowly sag and sink. He stood by the door of the bathroom and flipped the light switch on and off. The sun was setting and the small room was filled with a bright orange glow. He couldn't tell if the light bulb was burnt out or not. He flipped the switch again. *Are my lights working?* he wondered. He stared at the bare bulb hanging in the bathroom. More time passed. He rubbed his eyes. *Is the light on?* He couldn't tell.

He returned to the bedroom, collapsed on the bed, listened as the tub continued to fill. He stared at the front door. He rolled over. Was he still crying? He couldn't tell that, either. It was amazing. He really couldn't tell if he was crying.

23.

By the *fifth hour*, anxiety starts looking like fright. Physical symptoms worsen, too. My mouth is desiccated and I'm dry-heaving tears. I'd cut my tits off for a tall glass of lemonade, or maybe even a glass of ice-cold pee. Meanwhile my head feels like it's being slowly crushed. Even the discopes start feeling the change.

It sucks but there's nothing to do about it, so I just continued to fuck, sitting atop the maypole, working him as hard as I could. Anything to end this.

Meanwhile, the *Cloetura* have encircled the bed, low to the floor, but floating just high enough for me to see their epicanthic eyes. You could tell they were getting tired of the whole ordeal, of just standing around watching me work. The head *Cloet* kept clucking her tongue against her teeth. They were itching to take some action. Ten years ago, when we'd had our last run-in, the fashion was to strut around naked, but tonight these *Cloetura* wore tight black skirts around their loaf-shaped bodies, and I couldn't stop worrying about the kinds of knives these little pastries of malice were concealing under those tiny outfits.

By the *sixth hour*, it's the Panic Channel, all panic all the time. The pattern's in serious trouble. We're *all* in trouble. Razors slicing through your skull. Every muscle is twitching, there's the stink of uric acid. But give me some credit — I was still going at it like Rosie the Riveter.

Outside, you could hear the occasional bang, followed by a low rumble of thunder, and when the ground shook, I'd look up, and the *Cloetura* would be wobbling like duckpins.

The *Cloetura* don't have arms, but they can fart out a small cloud of smoke that can curl around pokers or scissors or knives, if needed. The cloud was rank, like a dog's fart. I remember those little curls of flatulence, crossed like arms with clinical dispassion as I sat on top of the unlucky maypole, working my hips like clockwork, tick-tock, sweating, smelly, looking like shit, feeling like shit, pulling out a succession of increasingly painful ejaculations from the maypole in what quickly felt like a raw grind of diminishing returns. And with each failed effort to recover the pattern, the *Cloetura*'s eyes narrowed a little more, until they were just horizontal slits beneath their black bangs, flat-lining me. Pure Twinkie evil. One of them would put away her knife, fart another arm, and flip-open a cell phone to report to the *Vag Heg*. You could tell they were hoping for the OK to slit *both* our throats, disentangle the dying pattern from the maypole's scrotum, and race it to *Melora Antigone he Miscegenatura*, my greedy little understudy. (Don't ask: the less we talk about her the better.)

Most discopes don't even *remember* this period: it's like one gigantic mental hemorrhage for them, an enormous sanity-preserving blind spot, I guess. But the really bad stuff was *still* to come.

By the *seventh hour*, it was like someone had dropped a fistful of quarters into the bed, magic fingers gone wild. It was like I was riding a bucking bronco. Did the earth move? Fuck yes, but it wasn't me. Real-world temblors were coming every couple of minutes and I had to keep my legs wrapped tightly around the maypole just to keep coupled. The bed shook, the windows rattled, and dust puffed from beneath the floorboards.

Some *Labiovelorans* suffered from convulsions and burst blood vessels during this time, or so I've been told. I was too busy to notice.

I remember crying and cursing and watching the clock. I remember the *Cloetura* climbing on the bed, every one of them glaring at me. The fuckers. They stood there, not saying anything, hardly moving. When they started whispering amongst themselves like high school girls, I really got pissed. They were bloating up a bit, darkening to a deep crimson. Looking like swollen tampons. Tampons, I suddenly realized, with malice aforethought.

It was a *bad* night. I remember around the start of the *eighth hour* feeling totally hopeless, feeling like I was doomed, like we *all* were doomed. I was screaming obscenities at the top of my pretty li'l lungs, slapping the maypole's face — but nothing I could do brought the pattern back.

Outside, the rain came down harder, then stopped, then started again. I began to hallucinate, I think. I remember cream squirting out the top of the *Cloetura*, like clotted milk from the blow-hole of a golden pastry whale.

I was ready to call it quits. The *Labiovelora* was minutes away. The *Cloetura*, growing restive and twitchy, moved in closer still, hopping up on my back. Any moment, I knew, curved knives would emerge from under their short skirts. Underneath me I could feel the sick wetness that meant the maypole's penis had begun to bleed.

Talk about performance anxiety!

Thomasina Blackmoan he Miscegenatura, my mentor, a great lady who'd you'd think couldn't even piss in anything other than Only Tongue, once surprised me by speaking in discopic English. I had whispered something stupid in class, something about thinking outside the squeeze box, and she had pulled me aside afterwards, after everyone had left, pushed me on to her exercise couch and slipped a joint between my lips. I puffed for a couple of minutes, and she just stared at me. Finally, she said: *Kid, don't ever fuck with the miscegenation pattern. Not unless you want skeletons in your shoes.*

I never heard her say another word in English. It was an

encounter I'll never forget. Too bad I didn't learn from it.

24.

Sapiens looks up. The name sounds familiar. What's she talking about now? The archbishop of the school's seminary is named Reverend Thomas Black. Could she possibly know him? Unlikely.

Black used to suggest to Sapiens, after a drink or two, that life is little more than a shaggy dog story, and it was a rare point of concordance between Sapiens and a colleague. Sapiens had been cautioned twice by Dr. Soren Beaselle, the dean of Saint Anne's, and later officially reprimanded, for sharing this same particular impression with his students, in his darker moments. Yet they had mostly misunderstood him anyway, often laughing, mistaking the light for the dark, thinking he meant life is a *practical joke*, with a punch line. Maybe it had to do with the egocentricity of youth, this misperception, or their blinkered theological indoctrination. Or maybe he was never so self-centered: maybe there was, for him, no personal in persecution: maybe his background in the sciences shielded him from their absurd innocence. Or maybe it was really Bad News, all around.

He wants to share this with Giselle, but he keeps his mouth closed. Something makes him think of Jacob again.

> *And Jacob called the name of the place Peniel.*
> *And Jacob was left alone.*

Peniel. Sapiens wonders where Peniel might be today.

"I had a friend," Sapiens says, meeting Giselle's eyes. "A friend named Thomas Black."

25.

I guess it's not fair to say I saved the sorry world from its sorry fate since I was partially responsible for fucking it up in the first place, but I finally got the pattern back that night. I got it back before we all lemming'd, before the *Labiovelora* came and I found "skeletons in my shoes." Like duh! Wouldn't be here telling you this otherwise, right?

So how did I do it? How did I get it back?

Fuck if I know! I just kept working my hips and praying. I have no idea why it took so long, or even why the pattern decided to come home when it did, except that in less than an hour we'd have crossed into the *Labiovelora* and who knows what the fuck would've happened then. So maybe the pattern got scared. Or maybe it was just toying with me the whole time. Who knows, and who cares.

All I know is that those first moments immediately after I got the pattern back were pretty great, full of calm and clarity. I remember feeling the pattern settle back into my belly, I remember watching the last few tendrils disappear up inside me with a dreamy slurp, and I remember my sideways grin beaming brightly again.

I showered and dressed and the *Cloetura* left the apartment. (A little reluctantly, I thought! They're a bunch of spiteful vessel wannabees, if you ask my opinion.)

The killer thirst was gone, but I drank three or four full cups of water anyway. Then I gave the strung-out maypole a kiss goodnight and a pat on the head. I remember looking into its lap before I left, and I remember how its penis was all shriveled and floppy. Limp, and caked with dried blood, a wrinkled little tangle of beef jerky. I'd been told by others that it would stay that way forever; and I wondered if the maypole, when he awoke, would feel relief or not.

But the miscegenation pattern was back in place, the maypole was off my chest, the *Cloetura* had high-tailed it back to Osaka or Wakayama or wherever they'd come from, and after a tiny post-coital tongue-lashing from the *Vag Heg*, I was free at last.

It didn't take long once inside me for the dam to break and for the *hemen* to resume its indispensable flow, beat after beat. The winds settled down, the gluey rain stopped, color returned to my cheeks, and I was once again your humble narrator, your happy-go-lucky templar knight with a furry thatch instead of a sword, neatly-shorn and sworn to secrecy, left to my own iconoclastic nomadic wanderings. I quit the apartment and raced down the stairs, eager to get back into the night and meet the *kwh* head on. By the time I had made it to the end of the block, I could feel the priming of my pump, and I was warm and wet and happy. The pattern was, too. Case closed. Party time!

26.

"Giselle, this stuff about the pattern. It's a little hard to…well, follow. I mean, well, I'm forty-four and — " Sapiens stops. He doesn't really have the energy or the will for this kind of discussion, but he needs to say *something*. "Maybe we should go back to my place and…?"

Giselle leans over the table. "Look, I was lucky last time. *You* were lucky. Patterns have been dropped before, sometimes even lost for good." She pushes her hand through her hair — it falls back over her right eye, an auburn waterfall of purity and light. All he wants to do is run his fingers through it.

"When a pattern dies, it takes a piece of the world with it. Understand? There have been die-outs. Big die-outs. Do you know what that means?"

Sapiens nods dully, but he has no idea what she's talking about.

"Even if the pattern isn't lost, if it's not back in place before the *Labiovelora*, bad things can happen."

"Bad things," Sapiens says dreamily. "Like what?"

"Who the fuck knows! But my teachers point to the Big Events. Like back in the Paleozoic, in the Permian Period. A pattern goes AWOL and wham! — ninety-percent die-out. Suddenly the reptiles rule the Earth."

"Right."

"One-hundred million years later there's another accident, and it's mass extinction of the dinosaurs. Ring a bell? Someone loses a pattern and BAM! — the mammals take over." Giselle leans back in her chair, spreads her arms wide. It reminds Sapiens of himself, lording it over a group of students in one of his seminars.

"But the dinosaurs," he says a little vaguely, a small frown on his lips; "I thought that was a giant meteor."

"Well, you thought wrong."

Something else comes to mind: "Hold on. A hundred million years ago no one was even around to lose the pattern."

Giselle shakes her head, looks at him like he's an idiot.

"Did you know there used to be *domesticated* sheep. Like dogs. But smarter. More flocky. Then, just over two thousand years ago — POOF! — they weren't. They were just *gone*."

"Someone lost a pattern…?"

Giselle nods.

"Sheep? Flocks of smart sheep? Jesus." Sapiens shakes his head slightly, and he can't help himself: his eyes roll. It's unintentional, nearly autonomic. He regrets it immediately.

Giselle snorts and crosses her arms. "Well, it was a different sort of pattern back then. Not like *mine*," she snaps. "Mine is *much* more important."

27.

The patterns weave and wire the *tetragramaton*. Thirty-six patterns in all, twelve each for day, night, and *Labiovelora* (or "*kwh*"). Each pattern touches the seasons: the axis of Winter, Spring, Summer, and Fall; the inabsissa of the Rain, Frost, Snow, and Ice; the inordinate of Heat, Cold, Temperance, and Folly.

The time of our birth is tattooed on our left forearms, time corrected by the Equation of Time. I was born in Frost and Folly in the Summer of August, in the year 1974. I was born at six in the *Labiovelora*. I was given the miscegenation pattern when I became a woman. I was eight years old.

I was taught to feed the pattern with my hips, and to protect the pattern from injury, theft, and misuse. I inverted the second time I bled and thus began my venery through the two-legs of day and night, relishing the hunt among the oubliettes and the maypoles, feeding, fucking, and keeping the *hemen* flowing. I keep the miscegenation pattern in my vagina, tucked far back where it can't be sniffed out by others that would do us harm. And I celebrate the impregnation cycle of the patterns on the day the miscegenation pattern inseminated me, each year on the surjection of January 4th in the *Labiovelora*, in Winter and Temperance beneath the barrier of Frost.

28.

Sapiens watches as Giselle traces an isosceles triangle in a thin layer of sugar which she has poured over the table between them. She points to one leg of the triangle, about three-quarters of the way to a vertice. "You are here," she says.

Sapiens nods. He has nothing to say.

"OK," he says.

But now Giselle is quiet. She looks up, tilts her head as if listening to a faraway sound. She doesn't move.

"So, what happened?" he asks at last. "You came in here crying. What happened tonight? What happened after you left me this afternoon?"

29.

I don't think much of the discopes. It's not that I don't

like them, or anything. After all, I spend two-legs of my life with them. It's just that they're all so *dim*, more like NPCs than real people. Like background characters in a computer game. I'm not supposed to say that, of course. It's considered impolite, even if it's the truth.

Anyway, I left the maypole I picked up this morning in his apartment near the university. I was getting hungry again, and this maypole was pretty much squeezed out. I needed to look ahead to the rest of my day. I gave him a peck on the cheek and skedaddled, cheerily telling him I'd meet him later that evening at a café right up the street so he'd let me go without too much of a fuss. I'm such a sweet little liar. Honesty's the best policy, sure, but it makes for a lousy Saturday night.

I grabbed a bite on the university's campus, and took limited pleasure in the bare-faced fuck-me eyes that followed my every footfall, the transfixed gazes of the Brown undergraduates — both maypoles *and* oubliettes — that tracked me as I paraded across the central "Green." I took a brief nap in the school's library, in a small room on the 4th floor filled with stacks of bound volumes of old newspapers. I considered picking up an undergraduate for the night, but decided I was ready to get off-campus. I did a little shopping on Thayer Street, ditching the workout clothes for something a little more after-hours, and I found a black leather cat suit in an antique clothing store, something straight out of "The Avengers." It covered my legs and torso but kept my arms and shoulders free. Some black boots and a thick wool sweater completed the ensemble. I worked my way back across campus and headed downtown towards the State Capitol. I was looking for more exotic fare, and there were several edgy clubs I'd scouted that fit the bill.

I soon found myself surrounded by three or four maypoles in a club called *Flute & Tine*, just west of the new Amtrak station. It was still early, so the place was quiet, not too crowded, filled with business types mostly. One of the maypoles catches my eye and I push the others out of the way and take its hand. The maypole's name is "Constance" or "Constantine" or "Constantinople" or some such — truth is this sort of information goes in one year and out the other. He's backlit by the bright neon of an animated beer display over the bar, which gives him a nervous kind of halo; and whenever he turns his head, his profile flickers around the edges, like someone's sprinkling pixie dust. Some of the other maypoles are starting a ruckus, so we move to a secluded booth near the back, but don't sit. Instead we play the tentative touching game. I carelessly tap him on the shoulder; he casually touches my hand to make a point. He's big, with rugged good looks, your typical urban cowboy, leather pants, denim shirt. A Marlboro Man with just a hint of Tinkerbell, I guess. I touch him gently on the cheek, tracing with fingernail one of the many grooves that line his face. He takes my hand.

"That's interesting," the maypole says, or something like that, gesturing at my left arm, trying to decipher the black scribbles that have been cut deep under my flesh. I shrug and run a hand over the soft denim of his shirt, eye-balling his black leather pants, trying to raise that pup tent by sheer oracular intensity. It works of course, and I feel the engine in his hips stir to life. I run a nail up the zipper of his pants. It makes a pleasant ticking sound against the metal teeth. Inside my belly I can hear the pattern growling, *feed me*, *feed me!*

"I like you," he says.

Like *duh*.

"But maybe when you tire of the pop-up book in my lap, you'll look into my eyes and read my mind."

It makes me laugh — a real laugh, it's so surprising. OK, maybe I was being rather obvious, but I'm always obvious. It's not usually a problem. The maypole tickles my tattoo, tracing the narrow serif *frost*. I smile as he rolls his hips against me, and we both go on automatic. There's some commotion near the door as we make our way out of the bar. Someone tries to grab my ass and someone else makes a play for my breast. My maypole pushes them both off and we hightail it, leaving a fight brewing in our wake.

"Your place or mine?" he asks, his thick arm wrapped around my tiny waist.

His, *of course*, so we head up to the Biltmore, a fancy-schmancy hotel where I've spent more than a few days and nights. He's all over me in the elevator, touching me, unbuttoning me. He's got a raised scar on his neck, from left ear to Adam's apple, and my fingers dance over its length. He has me half-undone before we get to his hotel room door, and my clothes go flying off as soon as we cross the threshold. I have to race to keep up with him as I unbuckle his belt and yank down his pants. We fall back on the bed and he touches me *there* and *there*. He says a few other amusing things, like how he likes the "golden arch" of my flat stomach, and he strokes me gently and places his hands on my thighs and says he likes my industrious hips, too, and he kisses me from tip of nose to dimple of chin and says over and over *I toll for thee, I toll for thee*....

The pattern ain't going home hungry tonight, obviously!

30.

"So I'm not the first guy you picked up out of the blue," Sapiens says. But before Giselle can respond, the café goes quiet, every conversation drops dead. Even the barista stops serving. Tiny ripples appear on the surface of the water in the glass in front of Giselle. Sapiens looks up. The table starts to shake.

"Holy shit!" someone yells. "Earthquake!"

31.

We screw and I get him to come twice, hard, in about

fifteen minutes. I can feel the pattern lapping it all up, enjoying our dance, pulsing brightly, and the *hemen* is flowing all around us. I can feel it spreading out through my hips and thighs, down my legs. It's high tide and the *hemen* is rolling out from my dark red luminescent vagina into the darkness of the hotel room to the darkness of the city and the darkness of the world beyond. The waves are slow and long. Holding on to the maypole, arms wrapped around his broad back, rolling my hips like some fundamental organic engine, I am carried blissfully by the *hemen*'s current. I stretch my hands way back towards the headboard as he slips his arms underneath each of my legs and raises them over my head and enters me a third time. I'm aroused but in total control, very focused, so I'm surprised when — just as my feet touch the headboard — I feel the sudden shift in gravity. It's the pattern changing position. My hips grow heavy, like they're made of lead or something, and I can feel the pattern popping loose.

I come — I'm also not expecting that — and all of a sudden the maypole pulls out of me — and damned if the pattern doesn't go with it. *What the fuck!*

I cancel the contortion act as the maypole rolls away from me and shudders and moans as the pattern hits home. He sits up, throws his head back, and begins to ejaculate out into space, again and again. We stay there together on the bed for about half-a-minute, the fucked and the fucked-up, and I watch not a little dumbfounded.

Shit, that was sloppy! And, man, am I pissed.

I give the maypole a rough push and he falls off the bed onto the floor, hips still jerking, totally unaware. I can see the ultraviolet pattern spreading throughout the maypole's testicles. I already have a bad feeling about this, that it's going to be a bad night, and I glance nervously at the standard-issue hotel clock on the side of the bed, wondering how long before the *Vag Hegemoan* and the *Cloetura* track me to *this* miserable hotel.

The maypole stops thrusting. He's finally finished ejaculating into the empty air, but the maypole's boner keeps a bead on me as I get up and start to pace back and forth. I give the boner a gentle slap for the hell of it, and it wobbles back and forth, before locking on me again.

Shit. I'm feeling more than pissed. I'm angry.

I duck into the bathroom and fill one of those cheap plastic hotel cups with water. You'd think they'd splurge for real glass in this swanky place, but no. I take a long drink. I give myself a once over in the mirror and step back into the bedroom.

The maypole's gone.

What the fuck, part deux!

I check under the desk, under the bed — but there's no under the bed, just a wooden frame that goes all the way to the floor. I check in the closet behind two sliding mirrors and I check the windows, which can't even open. This is not what's supposed to happen. *Where the hell has the maypole gone?*

Shit. No one ever expects disaster. No matter how much preparation you think you've made, there's always a grey area when you're in a crisis, a fucking twilight zone between what you plan for and what actually happens. I'd been trained all my life to take care of the pattern, to feed it, and to protect it. I know hundreds of ways to conceal the pattern, to camouflage it inside my vagina. I know how to keep the crabs away, as well as the petty filchers. I know what to do if the pattern is arrhythmic, what to do if it metastases, and even what to do if it has trouble sleeping at night. I know thirty-six ways to induce ejaculation (six of which work for oubliettes, too), and I know ten ways to permanently incapacitate a lover during coitus. I'm no amateur.

But I was never trained to deal with a sleep-walking maypole!

I grab my clothes. (Where's my underwear! I can't find my fucking underwear!) I grab my small bag. I exit stage left.

The hallway outside the hotel room is empty, just a long stretch of faded carpet. The ride down the elevator is excruciating. I find myself punching the lobby button over and over.

I hit the front desk first. I tell the red-haired oubliette behind the counter my husband's sleep-walking, but she's no idiot. She smiles and tells me she's not at liberty to release information about hotel guests. I hit the hotel bar next, but the maypole's not there either. Where would he go? Did he even have time to grab his clothes? I should have checked if his clothes were missing. But surely someone would have noticed a naked cowboy sleepwalking through the lobby!

I race out into the street and check with a line of cabbies. No one's seen anything of course. I speed-walk back towards the Amtrak station and the bar where I had picked up the maypole earlier. I'm not thinking too straight and I lose a shoe someplace on the way. I toss the other shoe when I notice the first one's gone, just before I reenter *Flute & Tine*. It lands next to another sandal lost in the gutter, as well as an abandoned tall black boot. Like somehow this is the Well of Lost Shoes, right here in front of this dive.

Inside the bar, I go straight for the bartender. There's a clock above him. It's after ten, Miller Standard Time.

Fuck fuck fuck. It's already been thirty minutes....

32.

The tremor ends, and the café returns to life. A few people in a panic grab coats and bags and leave. Others go right back to their mochas and medicis, to their books and their dates. Sapiens keeps his eyes on Giselle the whole time. She seems oblivious to the quake, or maybe annoyed by the interruption. Now she's back to the three sides of the triangle she's sketched in sugar on the table.

"Now pay attention," she says, and he tries his best. "This is the structural model for the three dimensional

Geometry of Time...."

Giselle slides her finger through the sugar, drawing a capital N next to one side of the triangle.

Sapiens nods, but his mind has already started to drift. He is thinking of Sigmund Freud. Freud had his own so-called structural model, composed of id, ego, and superego. Sapiens never really thought of the relationship among these elements as geometric, let alone triangular, but here, now, sitting across from the love of his life, his own angelic messenger, his personal Savior, it makes as much sense as anything.

Giselle continues forming letters in the sugar, one for each side of the triangle — N, K, and D. And Sapiens notes that from where he's sitting, the base of the triangle is facing him, making the figure a pyramid or an arrowhead. It's one of the oldest symbols of masculinity, he thinks. From Giselle's position, the imagery is reversed. She is nearest one of the triangle's vertices — the arrowhead is pointing straight at her. From her point of view the drawing might as well be the archetype for cup or grail: an ancient symbol for the divine feminine.

"This is the Golden Triangle," she says. "Time is tripartite, three-fold, and it moves around these three legs. D for Day, N for Night, and K for *Kwh*."

"How come no one's ever heard about this *Labiovelora?* This 'Kway' thing? Or is it a big secret."

"'*Kwh*' not 'kway.' No, not a secret. Not exactly."

"Can't you move things around while everyone else is asleep? Wouldn't people notice the change in the morning?"

Giselle shakes her head. "The *Labiovelora*, the *kwh*, it's not like that. You can't really change things. Things are already different."

"OK, sure." He sighs. "But how come *no one* knows about it? How can it be kept secret?"

"It's not, I told you. People know. *You* know. There are even web sites about it," she says.

"Oh, well. Jesus. Web sites."

Giselle turns to the window. The street's deserted. She reaches over and grabs Sapiens' wrist, turning his arm to check his watch.

Sapiens says, "You need to go, right."

"Yes." Giselle stands, grabs her sweater. "I've already wasted too much time. It's time to find this guy."

"To find the guy you slept with. The guy who's got your pattern."

"Yeah."

Sapiens fumbles his fingers together nervously. "Do you — " Sapiens pauses. He feels like a teenager, asking someone to a dance. "Do you want me to come with you?"

Giselle laughs, and for a moment Sapiens thinks it's the end of the world.

Then she shakes her head, smiles. "What did you think? I was going to let you get away?"

33.

If you had seen me when I first received the miscegenation pattern, when I was eight, you would have thought I looked a little bit old for my age. The reason's obvious, isn't it? *Triscopes*, those who are born during the *Labiovelora*, live on average a third longer than the discope drones stuck in day and night. For every calendar day that passes, a drone has lived just a day and a night, while a triscope has spent an additional twelve hours living in the *kwh*, the period between the end of one day and the start of the next, midnight's midnight, also called the *Labiovelora*.

"The distortion of time and the clock of space obscure their own image," *Marmos he Voekel* pronounces to every First Year in Reform, "and the resemblance of the Greater Heavens and the Earth are projected onto the three-space of day-night-*kwh*, which is its own distortion of the Greater

Heaven, just as the celestial projection onto the plane of the
two-space of day-night is a distortion. This obscures the
precise relationship between the Greater Heavens and the
Earth which…."

Blah blah blah.

I doubt you really care *why* it works. The *what* — when
night turns to *kwh* — is much more interesting.

The transition is subtle, like when dusk eases into night.
It's what Thomasina Blackmoan would call "penumbral
ambiguity." But if you know it's coming, it's pretty obvious.
First, the light changes. It doesn't change in intensity, but it
becomes richer, almost savory. Light in the day and night is
so *bleached*, so bland. But at *Kwh*break, it's like throwing open
the spice cabinet. Streets blossom in its flavorful radiance,
and you start to notice things that you would have missed
moments before — the thin film of oil called *arrow zawl* that
runs down the faces of tall buildings; the dark blue cracks
that limn the sidewalks like varicose veins; the bright green
moss called *jism* the fills the space where curb and gutter
meet. Traffic slows and then stops altogether, and the
discopes, already fading into the background, disappear
entirely into shadow, silent and inert, unfelt and soon
forgotten, the deepest of slumbers. The streets crowd with
pedestrians, bikes, and rickshaws, working their way in-
between stalled cars and buses. And by the time the *kwh* is
underway, there's a sheen of *arrow zawl* over everything. The
streets glisten and bikes swoosh, like after a spring rain. It's
the only time, I think, when the city feels truly alive.

34.

"Do you – do you want me to come with you?"

Giselle smiles, and his heart skips a beat. "What did you
think? I was going to let you get away?"

Sapiens jumps up, nearly overturning his chair. He can
hardly believe it. She wants him. She really wants *him*. My

God, he thinks, she need only speak, or smile at him again, and he might just fall to his knees, right there. Who cares what other people in the café might think. Who cares whether any of his students are there.

"Thank you," he says. "Thank you."

Giselle leans forward. "You're gay, right?"

35.

Let's cut to the chase, OK? You're not really interested in the fact that the *Labiovelora* is "synchronoptical." Or the fact that the miscegenation pattern is one of three imperative patterns called the *Troisillia*, right? It makes me feel smart, I guess, knowing all that crap, but you couldn't care less, right? And mostly it *is* crap. So let's just focus on the juicy stuff for now.

Like knowing the sexual orientation of some innominate maypole.

Or like knowing that I fuck at least twice a day, once during the morning and once at night. That I do it to keep the *hemen* flowing. And that when I keep my legs spread wide apart, I'm also keeping apart the legs of the triangle that represent day and night.

Or like knowing that the miscegenation pattern is dark red, smells like honey on toast, and has about a million tiny teeth that can tear through bone or boner. That it's a living thing and the main support of the Tripartition of the Geometry of Time. And that if it's lost, I can't fuck, the hemen stops flowing, the two legs of day and night slap together, and — well, it's the end of the world as we know it.

36.

Sapiens stands there and blinks. Seconds pass. *Months* pass. He blinks again. Giselle pulls on her heavy sweater.

He can't have heard her correctly. Gay?

"Gay?"

"Come on. We have to move," she says, taking his hand and tugging him gently. With her other hand she rubs her brow with her fist, like she's got a headache. "We've got less than four hours of night."

"I need to rest," Sapiens says suddenly; "that's what I need. You told me that. I need to go home and rest."

Giselle shakes her head: "Tomorrow. Now you need to come with me."

"Yes. Yes." He glances towards the back of the café....

"Why do you think I'm gay?" he asks, and this time Giselle rolls *her* eyes.

Oh God, he thinks. *Does* everyone *know?* Is he so transparent? Giselle hands him his coat. He blinks. Seconds pass. Months. *Years.* Then Giselle is at the door of the café, calling him. He moves past a table of locals, then a table of college students. He imagines Thomas Black at another table, and Soren Beaselle. *Do they all know?*

Tiny bells jingle over the front door of the café. She's leaving.

"Giselle, wait!"

He rushes after her. Outside, there are no people on the street, no cars. It must be after midnight. The rain has turned to a light drizzle, and Sapiens notices how it leaves a spattering of brown marks on the sidewalk, like tiny bits of shit.

"Wait! Giselle, we need to talk." He runs to catch up. "You're wrong. I'm not – I'm not gay. I mean..." He's out of breath. And he doesn't know what to say.

Giselle brushes her hand softly over his wet cheek. It smudges brown, like the sidewalk.

"I'm not gay," he says again, and Giselle responds by kissing him full on the mouth, her tongue slipping between his lips. She takes him by the hand.

"I know," she says, placing her other hand behind his back, pulling him close. She kisses him again and it's another round of fireworks. Sapiens feels the rapidly growing bar sinister, the erection impatient, struggling against the thin material separating *him* from *her*.

He struggles to complete the denial. "I'm not gay. I'm not. Really. You know. I'm really not…."

"No," she says. "No, you're not. Not *now*."

Giselle turns, and Sapiens, still stunned, follows as she leads him away. They turn south towards downtown and the waterfront, towards the point where the Providence and Seekonk rivers converge. Sapiens has more to say; he's sure he has more to say.

Doesn't he?

37.

The patterns are usually small, about the size of a fist. Some are smooth and some are pokey. Some are blue, some are gold, and some are the color of a mound of wet dirt in springtime. Some make you feel hungry when you get close to them, some make you laugh or cry. Some make you keep your distance. Some are fundamental — Air, Water, Earth, and Fire — and some are just for kicks. Some are traded — yes, there's a market for patterns — and some are held by one family, forever. Some are prized, some are desired, some are needed, and some are stolen. In the Reform Library you can read about the canton of every pattern, and see the hundreds of ways they have been categorized in the *Fundis her Nomenclature*, this big encyclopedia. You can read about the rational emotive patterns (the ones that make you laugh or cry), the situational routine patterns (the ones that make you hungry), the body form patterns, the hurt grade patterns, the cadastral patterns, the *Troisillia*. I suppose there are as many classifications as there are academics who study them, and there are a million patterns and a story for every one. It would take a Samantha Spade to sort it all out.

The miscegenation pattern is one of the *Troisillia*, so it's not traded, and it's hidden and protected. It's cadastral, but also situational. It's small and, in appearance, wholly organic. It is usually about the size of a quarter-dollar, but when it stretches out, its tentacles can reach several body lengths. Thousands of tiny hair-like stimulators lengthen and contract near the end of each tentacle, and the hairs are sharp enough to draw blood if you brush your hand across them the wrong way. They become teeth when the pattern's mad. When the pattern is close to soft tissue it turns a light pink and when it makes contact with the body of a Vessel, it flushes deep red, ultraviolet. It draws its breath from the pumping action of the hips of the Vessel. It's particularly well-designed in that it makes you out-of-control horny if you get too close to it, which means, I suppose, that even if I wasn't such a hot piece of *Labioveloran* ass, the Vessel for the miscegenation pattern would never fail to get a date.

38.

They race down Angell Street until they cross Congdon and Benefit, retracing in the dark the jogging route Sapiens follows every morning. They dip closer to the river, connecting with South Main, past several upscale bars and restaurants, the Rack and Lamb, Lisabeth's, and an old movie theatre called the Cable Car as it darkens its marquee. It's raining harder again, but maybe cleaner, and Sapiens' breath steams back into his face as he runs beside her, heart pounding. Mostly though, despite everything, he wonders if she will come back with him to his apartment when they finish whatever they are doing.

He notices for the first time that she is barefoot.

39.

The bartender of the *Flute & Tine* remembers me from earlier this evening. He doesn't look happy. He says I made a bit of a disturbance. He points to the remains of a large mirror on the wall behind him. He says it was *my* fight. I ignore him, but I understand. The pattern doesn't care how it gets fed and when a maypole gets close to me it doesn't matter its "sexual orientation." The flag flies up the pole — the Big Salute — *My Cuntry 'Tis of Thee* — and I am grievously desired, regardless. *Let mortal tongues awake,* and *let all that breathe partake!* Of course, some resentment and jealousy among nearby maypoles is not uncommon; and if I had known I'd be coming back here again so soon, I never would have gone fishing here in the first place.

Without the pattern tucked up in my vagina, the effect I'm having on the remaining clientele is less marked, but there's enough of the miscegenation's aura that I'm still getting looks up and down the bar. Some are looking just 'cause I'm female, an outlier in a gay bar. But I can smell the other kind of looks, too: the hungry looks. But now's not the time.

I come right to the point and the bartender is eager enough to get me out of there that he answers all my questions. Sure, he remembers the guy I left with, but tells me he's no regular. A VIP of some sort: he came in with several monied friends and was the hottest ticket all evening.

Until you showed up, he adds ruefully.

I ask if the maypole came back later, after we'd left, but the bartender shakes his head. He's also not much help on where he might have gone after abandoning me at the hotel. But he does suggest another bar, closer to the water, a little sleazier than he thinks I'm accustomed. Some of the maypole's VIP friends talked about heading over there. The bartender reels off two or three other establishments in that same neighborhood that might suit just as well. I know them all.

"You like this sort of thing?" he asks, just as I turn to leave.

"What do you mean?"

"Fucking with men."

I decline to answer. The pattern's aura's obviously not having much effect on him. I leave the bar and grab one of several cabs waiting up the street. I give the driver the first address, near the water's edge, and we pull away. It takes less than a minute to zip through the tiny cluster of skyscrapers that Providence pathetically calls "Downtown," and soon we're at our destination near the water's edge. The cabby's an Indian-looking maypole, and he's surprisingly politic when we arrive. He suggests I might prefer a *different* kind of bar. But I can already tell this is the right place. I can smell my baby. I even imagine I can see the faint ultraviolet glow of the pattern, spilling out of the tiny windows that run around the bar's cinderblock exterior.

I ask the driver about the other clubs the bartender mentioned, and after a moment's hesitation he points farther out along the water, towards a long narrow wharf. He asks me again whether I know what I'm doing.

I pay the driver and get out. The cabby waits a moment and then pulls away, slowly. I get the feeling he'll circle the block a few times, but I don't care.

I move across the street, trying to be inconspicuous as I watch an eager stream of maypoles come and go. It is a *seriously* seedy dive, alright, no doubt about it, and I begin to worry about going in. Not from fear for my own security, you understand; but because I can't think of a way I can get close to my maypole without alerting him first. I have no idea what state he'll be in and the last thing I want to do is to scare him off, to get him running again.

I'm toying with some theories, you see. Trying to explain the sleepwalking. But nothing makes much sense. The best I come up with is that maybe it all has to do with the fact that the maypole's homosexual. After all, I've never dropped the pattern with a homosexual before. Which means — well, I still can't connect the dots.

I stand outside the bar for another minute or two, strategizing. Just waiting until he appears won't work. He may not even still be there for all I know. But I can't fathom a way to sneak into the bar, at least not discreetly. Even without the pattern tucked up inside me sending out its own sexual SOS — the offer that can't be refused — even without that, I'm still too patterned up, I'm still way too hot, and I'll be noticed. And if the maypole doesn't want to come with me, forcing him will be next to impossible.

I realize I need help.

I give a half-second's thought to calling the *Vag Heg*, and even less thought to contacting the *Cloetura*. Either way, I'd be nailed for sure. Even calling one of my peers would be trouble. And messing up this badly — well, they'd sew my lips up but good this time.

No, if I'm going to get help, it'll have to be through some unofficial channels. Only problem is that I don't know any unofficial channels....

Then it occurs to me. Of course! That maypole from earlier in the day. That closeted college professor I picked up jogging along the waterfront, not too far from here, in fact. He'd be easy enough to recruit, and I'm pretty certain I can use *him* to infiltrate all these clubs....

I glance skyward. Shit. It must be nearly eleven and I'm already feeling cold and clammy, and *thirsty*. Thirsty enough to drink the Narragansett Bay. My time is running out.

I take a step away from the bar, look around, get my bearings. I told the maypole I'd meet him at ten, at that café near his place. But who knows if he's still there, waiting for me to show up. — Oh, fuck that, I tell myself. Show a little spine! *Of course he's still there!* His little pecker is probably poking out of his pants like a prairie dog.

I take a deep breath and start the run back up College Hill.

There's a thunderclap in the distance, and a few seconds later it starts to pour. It's a heavy dirty rain, all too familiar, and there's not a drop of refreshment in it.

40.

Sapiens is dazed and out-of-breath when Giselle gives him a light push. He starts across the street towards Moby's Dick, the dirty-looking dance bar off the wharf at the southern end of the Providence River, right near the point where it converges with the Seekonk. The pattern's been on the move apparently. It's the fifth club they've visited in several hours. He crosses the street anyway, one hand over his head in a useless effort to shield himself from the return of the fecal drizzle. He feels somnambulant, propelled by a dream logic he can't resist as he approaches the bar's entrance — two doublewide doors painted with tap-dancing whales in monkey suits. Somewhere far in the back of his consciousness he wonders what Freud would make of this particular imagery, while beneath his feet the ground begins to thump. It might be the heavy bass of the music, he thinks. But then again it might not.

Sapiens pulls open the right-hand door and enters the bar. His first thought is he's walked into the scene of a traffic accident inside a fog bank. Thick white clouds obscure everything, and the only things he can see are flashing red-and-blue lights. Only when his moves deeper into the bar does he notice shadowy figures moving through the fog — and then deeper still, the fog lifts and he sees just how many men are packed into the space. The music is deafening. The floor is pulsing with the beat. There's the sudden and heavy scent of cigarettes and beer, and sweat. There's hostility, too. A kind of sexual anger. He can feel it flowing around him, a current that's pushing and pulling him, interacting with the music. Maybe it's the effect of Giselle's lost pattern, or maybe it's just that sort of bar. It's hard to hear, to see, to think, but at least Giselle's instructions to him had been simple. Find out if the pattern snatcher is inside, pass him the note, then come back and report. *Fast.*

Sapiens approaches the bar, clutching the small piece of paper in his hand. The note is from him, at least it's supposed to be, but Sapiens hasn't read it. He assumes it's an invitation. A lure. And he's a kind of Cyrano. He passes several well-dressed men and can feel their eyes roving over his body. It's not a bad feeling. Not at all.

Despite the detailed description she gave him, Sapiens doubts he'll be able to pick anyone out in the midst of this musty throng. It's too dark, too smoky, too anonymous. He circles the main floor twice, but still doesn't see anyone that fits Giselle's description of the pattern snatcher. The closer he gets to the large circular bar in the center of the club, the stickier the floor becomes. He flags a bartender working busily within its perimeter. He shouts to be heard over the music. He asks if there is another room somewhere. The bartender gives him a smirk — part friendly, part knowing — and then a thumbs-up. Sapiens returns the thumbs up, but the bartender shakes his head and leans closer.

"Upstairs!"

The bartender jerks his thumb towards the back of the bar, all friendliness gone, and Sapiens moves away, working his way through the crowd, casually scanning faces and bodies. For the first time in many hours, he's not feeling overwhelmed by Giselle's tug on his groin. But if he's awakening from his trance, it's soon replaced with another. *All that we see or seem*, he knows, *is but a dream within a dream....*

He squeezes past a long line of men, smoking, drinking, half-dancing, checks out each as he walks past, and then he finds the narrow staircase. There's a sign on the wall — in the shape of an arrow or an erect penis — pointing upstairs, and a legend beneath it that says "To The Crow's Nest." There are even more men here, one or two per step, and he has to squeeze his way to the top.

The Crow's Nest is small and somehow even more

crowded than downstairs. It's impossible to move without touching — shoulder to shoulder, hand to hip, ass to ass. Black lights mounted into fixtures high on the walls illuminate the room, and every scrap of exposed white clothing fluoresces. It makes the space feel both brighter and darker than the traffic accident downstairs. Sapiens pushes through a small group of college-aged drinkers, and they all stop what they're doing to ogle him as he goes by. He ogles them in return.

In the center of the Crow's Nest are several backless couches pushed together, or maybe it's one big bed. A dozen men are sprawled out, a tangled mass of shadow and black light glow, touching, kissing. There's another tremor then, another tiny earthquake, but the only reaction is a kind of fraternal jubilance, a few brief drunken cheers. Sapiens keeps moving. He notices the sexual anger he felt downstairs is gone; there's a different current up here, and it's drawing him towards the back of the Crow's Nest. He pushes past another knot of men and before he realizes what's happening, Sapiens' knees go weak. He stumbles towards the wall for support. The room is getting brighter. There's something back there. Someone he can't *see* yet, but he can *feel*. Sapiens drops the note from Giselle; he lets his hand slide into his pants and down to his groin. He grabs hold of his swollen penis.

Sweet Jesus Christ! How could she not tell me!

He pushes off the wall with his free hand, staggering forward. There's a tight cluster of men near the back. They're shielding something, someone, he's sure. He pushes forward, wipes the back of his hand across his brow, wipes away a thin sheen of sweat. It's a locker room back here; the heat, the smell of masculinity, is overwhelming. Sapiens pushes aside the last man blocking his way, and it feels as if he's opened a furnace door. There's a blast of intense heat, pressing him back. And there's bright light, yellow and silver and gold. He throws an arm over his eyes, to shield himself from light and heat, and half-turns. But he can still see him, standing right there, a living flame, a human flame, fire burning in the shape of a man. Sapiens gasps. He has never seen anyone — or anything — so beautiful.

He shall be as the light of the morning when the sun riseth, even a morning without clouds! The day spring from on high that hath visited us!

Sapiens sinks to his knees. He places his head against the Christ's radiant thigh.

41.

There are no maypoles in the *Labiovelora*, at least none that I know of; only women, like myself. It's because none are born there. Maypoles are our breeding partners, as hard as that is to imagine, so the act of reproduction occurs only during the day and night. To reproduce, a triscope must be impregnated by several maypoles. And only if the resultant birth takes place in the *Labiovelora* is the consequence another triscope. Otherwise, if the birth happens during the day or night, it's just another humping drone — a pole or hole, an ejaculator or oubliette, a "male" or "female" — thrown back into the day and night, like a small fish tossed back into the sea.

The holes — *du estra nepenthe* in Only Tongue — copulate a lot, keeping the maypoles — *du testur extensis* — mildly distracted. But the value of any hole is limited to producing more drones. Discopes can never give birth in the *Labiovelora*, and so that's all they can do: produce drones. The spermatozoa that's shot into them by maypoles might as well as be shot into the air. It's no different than mutual masturbation.

When I become pregnant, when I turn from being a *Vessel he Patterna* to a *Vessel he Conceptura*, the miscegenation pattern will pass to another triscope host (and hopefully not my fucking understudy). But I am careful not to become pregnant until the season is right; I am careful to regulate my spermatozoa intake since I have never used any sort of contraceptive.

42.

"You came with her?" the pattern snatcher says, and despite the pounding of the music from the bar below, or maybe the pounding of Sapiens' heart, the snatcher's voice cuts through *everything*.

Sapiens nods.

The snatcher grins. "Stand. Stand up," he says and Sapiens stands, trembling. The snatcher holds out his hand, but not for Sapiens. Instead, the sea of bodies in the Crow's Nest parts at his gesture, and he starts towards the stairs. "Let's go find the little bitch."

The devotees stand aside as Sapiens follows right behind him, keeping close, close enough to remain bathed in his light, his heat. Sapiens follows the snatcher downstairs and straight out of the bar.

43.

When the maypole emerges from the bar I can see immediately he's got that other maypole with him — Mr. Tall, Dark, and Criminal — the jerk that snatched the pattern — the fucked-up sleepwalking maypole possibly named Constantine. My initial feeling is immense relief. I'd just about given up on my bait-boy's returning, but now, just in the Old Nick of time, I figure my problem's solved. Not only have I found the pattern-snatching maypole, but he's coming straight to me. Now it's just a matter of getting him someplace private and quickly fucking his brains out.

I start across the street, stepping off the curb, and I can see that the pattern snatcher Constantine is less a sleepwalker than a sleep*runner*. I suppose it explains in part how he was able to get away from the hotel so quickly. He's running towards me, moving fast now and all I can think is, *Well thank fucking god*. I want to get this over with, and he sees me and he's already hot to trot. Perfect.

It's only after his hand reaches into his inner pocket that I notice the other maypole — the one I used as bait — is waving at me, both hands high over his head, looking frantic like he's trying to warn me off. And he is, I suppose, because a gun is coming out of the snatcher's jacket and he's pointing it at me. A gun!

It takes a second to believe what I'm seeing. I couldn't be more surprised if it were a five-pound salmon in a tutu. I see the first flash from the muzzle at the exact instant a new thought occurs to me. A thought that I now realize — rather pointlessly — is way overdue:

Maybe this maypole isn't a sleepwalker at all.

Maybe it wasn't some unconscious snatch on his part. Maybe this maypole has actually — deliberately — *stolen the pattern*.

Something grazes my left arm and I feel an explosion of pain. This is bad.

Don't fuck with the miscegenation pattern? Man, I have fucked with it royally.

44.

Without thinking Sapiens leaps forward and lands on the pattern snatcher's back. Maybe it's the fact that he can see Giselle again, at the end of the wharf across the street, and he can feel her gentle tug on his penis, and his loyalty returns. Or maybe it's because he wants this man — this Christ, this fiery embodiment of David — so badly he can't risk letting him get any closer to Giselle's siren call. Or maybe he just can't stand guns.

The second shot goes wild as they both fall to the ground. Giselle is on top of them before he knows what's happening. Now she's pulling on Sapiens' arm, rolling him off the pattern snatcher's limp body. She's fumbling with something.

"What time is it?" she snarls, and it takes him a moment to realize what she's asking. She's trying to steady his arm, trying to read the dial on his watch.

"After four," he says as she drops his arm. Giselle says something that he doesn't catch, then she turns and runs.

"Giselle!" he calls after her. He struggles back to his feet. He's not in great shape, but he can run. He knows he can run. He starts after her. He doesn't feel the shot that punches through his body, but the whole world rolls, like he's on a ship, and he finds himself running head first into the pavement. Something warm and wet is pooling around his ear — it actually feels nice — but he can't move. His vision is fixed on the edge of the curb in front of him. Out of the corner of his eyes, he can make out a few stars in the sky. Someone jumps over him.

45.

I fucking run. I run hard. I'm breaking a sweat. I have no idea what's going on, but I'm not so stupid to think I should just hang around and wait to be shot again. My arm is hurting and I keep touching the place where I think I was hit as I race down Water Street. I find an alley running parallel to Tockwotton Avenue and when I get a chance I cut towards the Seekonk River. The grounds really shaking now, and it's not so easy to run. But if I can make it to India Point Park, I think, I'll be safe. I keep examining my hand — the one that keeps probing the place I think I got shot — but the hand keeps coming back peachy keen not red so it can't be that bad. If I'm bleeding, I'm not bleeding much.

I keep sight of heaven as I run. My head is about to pop — the *hemen*'s been stopped way too long — but if the maypole's watch is right, the *kwh* is already starting. I can at least lose the pattern snatcher — the pattern *thief* — in the

Labiovelora. He can't follow me there.

I reach India Point Park and find a shadowed place where I can lay low. I'm hunkered behind some small sculpture, Roger Williams and his dog it looks like, and I'm tucked partway into the brush, crouching, leaning up against the statue's concrete pedestal, a few feet from a park bench. There's a maypole sleeping on the bench, some indigent, snoring. He's got one arm wrapped around a giant, partially eaten loaf of Portuguese sweet bread. I can smell its fruity aroma from where I'm hiding. It mixes nicely with the park's own smell of old beer and piss.

I'm breathing hard, but the city is quiet. I'm not far from the I95 overpass, but I can't hear a single car — and when I look at the sky, I can see it's changing. The orange glow from the lights downtown are fading. The clouds overhead are thinning. The stars are moving. The streets are growing brighter, brighter with the oily sheen of *arrow zawl* and the flavorful light of *kwh*break.

Something snaps; a branch somewhere to my right. How clichéd, I think. It's the sleepwalker of course. Except, I have to remind myself, he's no sleepwalker. He's something else, a thief, a lunatic, a lunatic thief? Whatever. He's about ten yards away and moving straight for me. He must have seen me hide.

I check the sky again. The transformation is almost complete. I check the bum on the bench. He's already fading, sinking into shadow. I see a cone of *kwh*light sweeping over the north end of the park, like a searchlight. Even from here I can smell its distinct flavor of sage and charcoal. The cone is expanding, and any second now the entire park will have passed into the *kwh*.

I let out a sigh of relief. I'm going to be OK. Any second the lunatic thief is just gonna slip away, too, like every other discope, and I'll be safe....

Safe. Well, that's fucking relative, isn't it. Don't forget I've lost the pattern. It's been out of my body for over six hours and the *Labiovelora's* begun. Who the fuck knows what *that* will do. This could be another die-out.

I stand up, brush myself off. The *kwh* has begun. The bum is gone; he's vanished into the deepest slumber of all; and the park bench is empty. So the world spins, its flavors are released, and the sky is filled with the silver light of the *Labiovelora.* Now I —

Fuck! Before I realize what's happening, I'm knocked off my feet. The pattern thief's hit me beneath my shoulders, hard in the center of my back, and I am thrown forward by the full weight of his body. I hit the ground hard, half on the sidewalk, half on the grass. He rolls on top of me, and I can feel the miscegenation pattern hot inside him. I feel its tug — from my heart all the way to my clitoris. I can tell it wants to come home. Or maybe I just tell myself that.

But hold on. What the fuck is happening? It doesn't *matter* how fast he is. The maypole can't be here. He can't be pinning me like this. We're in the *Labiovelora*! I want to call "time out!" — to pause this game — to stop everything and ask what the fuck he thinks he's doing here in the *Labiovelora*, but that's when he socks me hard in the face.

I open my eyes sometime later — I don't know what time it is except that I know that it's still the *Labiovelora* — I can smell the cherry-flavored light of mid-day — and I'm spread-eagled on a bed staring at a ceiling. Everything feels slippery, as if the walls, the floor, the bed are all floating on ball-bearings or something. The room's not big. Maybe we're in a cheap motel or flop house. I notice there are ugly little cartoon birds and rainbow stickers all over the walls, children's stickers, so maybe I'm in some kid's room. Constantine — surely not his real name, but the only one I have for now — appears over me, missionary style, naked from cowboy chisels to twinkle toes. He leans towards me, brings his face close to mine, and I wonder if he's here to fuck. I try to sit up, but I can't. I'm tied down. I lift my head and look down the length of his naked body. I notice two sets of narrow golden wings on either side of the inner thigh, tickling me as they flutter madly.

He slides away and sinks out of sight and I feel something nibbling at my toe and at first it's not unpleasant — apart from the general circumstance, of course. Then it starts to hurt — *a lot* — and I can't believe it. He's eating me!

The Raze of Lucretious, *Hemiptera homunculus*, is a triscopic insect that has mouthparts adapted for piercing and sucking, and two pairs of narrow arrow-shaped wings, belonging to an order that includes the non-anthropoidal stinkbugs, bedbugs, and other true bugs. I don't know much about them; at least not more than you hear casually in the *kwh*. I thought they were pretty much extinct, but I was beginning to think maybe this maypole wasn't a maypole at all. The Raze were cock-sniffing holes, and you could really only tell them apart from the other oubliettes by finding the two pairs of wings they had instead of lips around the bugs's proto-vagina. The Raze were mostly a nuisance bug, homophagists, interested in sucking the trace amounts of *hemen* found in maypoles after sex with a *Labioveloran*, and as such were of little consequence. They weren't much worse than mosquitoes. But the Raze were gynecomorphous. I hadn't heard of the Raze ever looking like a maypole before. And this bug (if that's what it was) hadn't just battened on to a maypole to snag a taste of *hemen*. It seemed to have gone out of its way to grab the miscegenation pattern itself, the regulator of *hemen*, and run. Maybe this creature isn't just a dumb bug? Maybe it didn't find me by accident? Maybe it's something else entirely?

All good questions — *just fucking late to the party!*

I look up into the face of this thing, and I have to admit, it's not a bad-looking bug. It smiles at me — a big showy smile — and for a second I forget about the pain in my foot, probably due to the sudden stirring in my loins. The pattern's working its magic, I can tell, just not on my behalf. I wonder again whether the bug wants to make love to me, and the idea isn't totally repellent. The bug moves back down my body and I feel a certain thrill of anticipation as his hot breath moves between my breasts and over my belly. I scream when the creature starts to chew on another toe.

I don't know what's binding my arms, but I'm not about to let this fucking insect eat me. So I just sit up, straight up, and deal with the consequences. I hear something ripping to my left and right, I feel something cutting through my skin, and I know I've messed up my wrists, but it doesn't matter. This thing has the pattern *and I want it back*.

I tighten my abdominals and roll forward on top of him, and we're over the foot of the bed and on the floor fast, wrestling, pressing belly to belly. I feel a blur of arousal — mine and his — and he's already hard, so I count on nature taking its course. I'm still partially yoked to the bed, I realize. One of my ankles is still tied to something up there. I scream my fucking wildest scream and pull my leg free. I hear something rip around my foot, but I don't have time to worry about that either. I use both my legs to roll him over. He slides into me, and I can feel his autopilot kick in, and he starts humping. His face is pressed into the space between my neck and my shoulder and I can feel his mandible breaking through my skin. It hurts but not too bad. I must be getting used to his chewing me — either that or I'm being anesthetized by some nasty bug juice in his mouth.

In less than a minute, he climaxes, and the miscegenation pattern flows easily and quickly back into my body. Ha!

The bug roars as the pattern leaves him — *acmegenesis voce* — a sound that I guess is part climax and part rage, and then he falls deathly silent. I pull myself off him and get as far away as I can. I'm on fire all over — everything hurts — but at least I'm not worried about the pattern now. The bug can only get it back if I lose it, and I'm not about to drop it again.

The bug's eyes are closed, he's passed out, maybe even dead, and I plot my escape. Then I want to slap my head. I'm such an idiot! This isn't a kid's room at all. The walls are covered with pictures of birds, yeah, but I see now that the birds are surrounded by thousands of tiny black dots, little bugs, maybe ants, maybe something else. The cartoon birds are being overwhelmed by thousands of tiny cartoon insects. Along the wainscoting are more birds, pictures I'd missed when up on the bed, more birds drawn in crayon or chalk, and thousands of bugs swarming over their birdy bodies. It's like a giant kindergarten cave painting, depicting some heroic struggle of bug vs. bird. Fuck. *Where am I?* You think you know everything. You think that the piddling system you've created in your brain is a reasonable take on reality. Then something comes along and shatters everything.

I stand slowly, unsteady on my feet. I'm finding it hard to balance, but I don't look down. I don't want to see what's there. Or rather what's *not* there. I keep my eyes on the big bug — the pattern thief, the so-called maypole — collapsed against a giant ant mount near the far corner of the room. There are several other mounts around, some nearly as tall as I am. I'm in some sort of rent-control formicary. Some sort of bug's-nest apartment, hidden in the *Labiovelora*.

The big bug's not dead of course. He lifts his head. His eyes open. Looks at me. He moves *fast*, so fast I don't see what happens. All I know is that we both go flying and smack into something hard. I thought we were done with this kind of shit. I hear various body parts *thunk* against wall, floor. I invert and we're both engulfed by my vagina.

Everything's warm and quiet. In the distance I can hear my own blood pumping, and the soft sound of the pattern, back in the Sanctuary, singing. Constantine's supine on the gravelly irritate that lines the path to the pattern's Sanctuary. He's semi-conscious, confused by the transition. The passage here is narrow and the air is thick and heavy and humid. The walls are glistening, dark red with ultra-violet tracery. There are several pieces of wire around both my ankles, still cutting into the flesh. I see now that I'm missing three toes on my left foot.

I disentangle the wire. It stings. The bug's eyes are rolled up into its head. I bind his wrists and ankles, but the wire's a little short for a good knot. I pull it as tight as I can, then turn and hobble down the excavate, my fucked-up feet squelching across the soft ground towards the pattern's Sanctuary and my vessel's own pulsing darkness.

I'm more than halfway to the Sanctuary when I hear the bug in the tunnel behind me. It's no surprise, I guess. I didn't really expect the wire to hold him for long. I decide to wait for him here, outside the Sanctuary.

When the bug catches up, I can see his wrists have deep red grooves where the wire had held him, and there is blood all over his hands. The rest of his naked body is very pale, almost white, and thinner than it was a few moments ago. He's slightly stooped, like a praying mantis, and his face is dripping with some kind of silvery mucus. He doesn't look like an urban cowboy anymore. He takes a few steps closer, encroaching on the perimeter of my personal space. He opens his mouth, tries to say something — but nothing comes out except several burps of stinky air. He could use breath mints and more than a little time in the sun. We give each other the evil eye, but I think his is more evil than mine. He takes another step closer and I shudder. I've never had a man this deep inside me.

"*Arco ordo adam norstroma!*" he shouts. He's got no problem vocalizing this time. At first I think he's speaking *Tanakha*, the Only Tongue. But he's not. I don't know what the hell he's speaking. "*Hetaera hexaemeron hysteron proteron!*"

He holds out both his hands as if he's showing me how bloody they are, how much I've hurt him. He shakes his head slowly and I notice that he has no eyelids.

He brings his hands together, like he's about to pray. He surprises me by talking discopic English again: "*Please*," he says, speaking slowly, his voice soft and suppliant. "We *beg* you. We plead. We *bleed*."

He takes another step forward, as if to move past me, to head into the Sanctuary. I cut him off, and we're in each other's face again. He's not going to get any farther inside me.

I meet the insect's eyes, but I can tell his attention's really elsewhere. I know the outer horizon of the Sanctuary is just a little farther up the passage. It's called the *Panthera Daemoan he Sur*, and I can hear the sphincter which forms its entrance heaving with the slow and sonorous sound of the miscegenation pattern itself.

The bug retreats a half-step, then raises both shoulders and shrugs. He's smiling and I sigh. Maybe it's stalemate.

Then his penis starts to grow.

For a few seconds I'm mesmerized as it begins to lengthen and thicken. It's as pasty as the rest of his body and dewy with sweat; the tiny wings on the inside of his thighs resume their flutter. I spread my legs and spill a molten syrup all over the floor. It glistens fiery silver and orange as it pools around my feet, the viscosity of honey, rippling the air. Milk begins to drip from my nipples, as well, but this is not my doing. His penis is still growing; but it's not becoming erect, I realize; it's just engorging, growing thicker and longer and *heavier*, drooping slowly to the ground. When it touches the thick membrane of my tunnel, a tremor ripples out in all directions, a long wave that I feel roll under my bare feet. His penis starts to twist and turn back and forth, a pale serpent, alternately slapping and wiping its head against my endometrium.

I know what this thing is now. I know what it's called,

and it's around my hips before I can do anything about it. *Scin!* The Serpent has me in its grasp. The Raze's mandibles crank back out of its mouth as I'm pulled closer. My nipples are so rock hard they ache and I am spraying my milk wildly, much of it over the maypole's body. With each squirt the creature squeals and alters shape, throwing off one disguise after another, morphing from maypole to bug to snake — and to something else entirely.

I am growing woozy, vague. It's all been a charade, a masquerade. How could I have known! But I've got to hold on to the memory of those who carried the Destroyer into the temple.

I must be screaming now. Someone's screaming now. It must be me. I feel the orgasm explode between my legs and the shockwaves roll over my body. The walls ripple and I fall backwards towards the entrance to the Sanctuary.

The miscegenation pattern flees the Vessel. It rushes past me, its sharp tentacles whip over my face. I lose consciousness in a cathedral whiteness. My last thoughts are not for the Sanctuary, though my duty to it has been irrevocably compromised; nor to the pattern, though I have failed it miserably, too; nor to the maypoles or oubliettes — they will probably be spared awareness of the coming change. Neither to the Raze of Lucretious, nor to the other unwitting carriers who have lost as much as we have without knowing it. But to all my sister *Labiovelorans*, who have suffered so much on my account, and whose suffering may have only just begun....

When I awaken I am inside the *Panthera Daemoan he Sur*, laying half across the thick muscle of the entranceway. I'm mostly surprised: I'm not dead yet. I can hear my blood flowing around me, even though the distant singing has stopped, and the passage here is cold and silent and dry. I am still naked and my body is smeared with the milky ejaculate of the Destroyer and my own breast milk. I stand.

My legs feel weak and I wobble. I lean against the irregular-shaped wall at my side. After several minutes, I start back through the tunnels, to retrace the passageway to the surface.

The walk is long and difficult. Some paths have constricted or collapsed, and I have to double-back more than once to find another way. I stop several times to rest. I stop once to drink from a small stoup near my ovary, but the basin is desiccated. My head is pounding and I am so thirsty I think I may pass out. I make a wrong turn. I retrace my steps. Nothing looks quite right. I don't recognize myself anymore. I wonder if I will find my way back to the mouth of the temple, and part its giant doors like lips, or if I will wander my own hidden labyrinth until I die of thirst, or starvation, or trip and fall into the dimness of an unseen endometrial crevasse.

"Quick! Quick! Quick!" I shout, constricting the back of my mouth and snapping my lips closed and open. I listen for the familiar echo but there is none. I may not be dead yet, but I'm not doing well.

I know the miscegenation pattern has left me for good. The Sanctuary is withered and dry. Nothing of it remains. Nothing but a few vestigial memories of *hemen*, radiating outward. Is the pattern itself dead? I don't know. And I don't know if this is all my fault, really. But it doesn't matter. Everything's fucked. I have a feeling a lot of holes and poles will die. Maybe a lot of us, too.

But if the pattern's still alive, there's still a chance to set things right, I suppose. So I'm going to get it back, Destroyer be damned. I'm going to get it back whether it's hidden inside monster or Raze, maypole or man.

I finally reach the opening of the temple.

I can make out the lips at the entrance, high above me, but I don't invert, at least not yet. I start the long hard climb upward, not sure what I'll find when I get back outside. I should probably be very scared. I should probably turn tail and hide.

Fortunately, I'm not that sort of girl.

46.

Eta ordo adam andame! Arco ordo adam norstroma!
Ah las anova adam, ordo adam nostroma!

0.

So it is now written:

The **Ecaser Lord** stepped out of the alley and strode into the empty street, dressed in the silver and gold raiment of Christ II of Pisa, casting a bright golden glow over the diminished buildings and cars.

The **Ecaser Lord** reached out the five fingers on each of his five hands and touched the new Geometry of Time: the spin of the Earth and the Golden Pentagram of *dje*, *hor*, *ess*, *veh*, and *vol*.

Above him, the hands of the steel clock that hung over the entrance to the Industrial Trust Company building in downtown Providence were frozen at twelve minutes past the hour of six in the morning.

The **Ecaser Lord** made the Sign of Water in the air, and crossed into a small city park where he sat awaiting the others: representatives of the *Djessens*, the *Horsay*, the *Essens*, the *Vehmen*, and the *Vol*. With each passing minute the sky grew darker in measurable degree, from west to east, as if an immense pall were being pulled slowly across the heavens. There would be no more sunrise that morning, nor another day, nor night that follows, nor *kwh*.

The **Ecaser Lord** smiled as this last brief dawn gave way to the impending shadow of *dje*. Across his eyes passed a

procession of objects, black and indistinct, the figures of
people picking up their books, their cards, their balls of
wool, their work-baskets, and passing him one after another
on their way to bed.

"Labiovelora"

Epigraph and last line from
The Voyage Out by Virginia Woolf

When I read Woolf's first and last lines for just the second time, this entire story, start to finish, came to me, and it was then a race to get as much of it down as quickly and accurately as possible. Re-reading the first and last lines now, I really have no idea where the hell it all came from. The fact that it was Woolf must've influenced me, as well as the title, *The Voyage Out*. But why? And what's it all about? I guess the short answer to the second question is "No matter how much you think you know, there's always someone who knows a little bit more." It's nearly always true, and it's something we nearly always conveniently forget.

Excerpt from "Macbeth" by William Shakespeare
Excerpt from "The Waste Land" by T. S. Elliot
Excerpt from "A Dream within a Dream" by E. A. Poe

Written between 7 August 2003 and 27 December 2004

Enough

THE BOY WITH FAIR HAIR lowered himself down the last few feet of rock and began to pick his way toward the lagoon. He passed two more bodies — both shot in the head — before he reached the densely-vegetated cove one-half mile to the north. He paused then, listening for sounds of pursuit; and when none were forthcoming, he rolled his pack off his back and tossed it into the hidden boat. He climbed into the stern of the rickety long-tail and sat on the narrow wooden seat, facing backwards, taking a few deep breaths before starting the engine. He used his shirt sleeve to wipe the sweat from his face, then craning neck and body, he steered the boat from the lagoon into the open water of the lake. There were two empty canvas bags tucked under the seat — perhaps old rice sacks — and keeping a hand on the throttle he draped one bag over his head and shoulders. It was an uncomfortable disguise, scratchy and hot under the late-afternoon sun, but the last thing he wanted was to be mistaken for the Caucasian man who had crossed these tropical waters — and killed — earlier that day.

He slipped his free hand into his pocket, fishing for the ID badges he had taken from those former employees of the Transnational Orbit Corporation. His memory couldn't shake the image of their sprawling bodies, or their dark faces pressed into red mud; nor his imagination the sound in the early morning of artificial thunder, ballyragging and cruel. Word of their murder would spread through the small Thai municipality from which Orbit drew its non-technical workers. And even though all five were carrying pistols,

271

which meant they were hired guns, not one of them carried a holster, which meant they were amateurs. No expectation of risk associated with their employ for the remote peninsula laboratory would mitigate their arbitrary deaths, not among their families, nor their friends. Someone had considered them expendable, if he considered them at all.

Maarten pulled open the throttle and the boat jumped, picking up speed. He eased the bow east, putting the setting sun at his half-turned back, and aimed for the shallow and brackish inlet that would carry him out of the largest natural lake in Southeast Asia, known to locals as *Thale Noi*, the Inland Sea, and into *Thale Nok*, the Gulf of Thailand.

The first hotel came into view forty minutes later, perhaps a mile farther to the south along the gulf coast. Soon the string of gently glowing pearls was laid out before him: the Rajamangala Empress, Hanoa Resort and Casino, Royale Thai, Pan-Asia Hilton. Even at dusk, the water before these hotels was active with holiday-makers, mostly *farang* like himself, white and European, in small sail and paddle-boats, dinghies, as well as yachts. It was hard not to be impressed by the Songkhla Peninsula: dark blue water, distant hills sinking into shadow, and the glittering lights from the historic town and sea port where the lake connected with the open sea of the Gulf. A single large square-rigged ship, running skysail and moonraker, passed slowly between Maarten and the shore.

Maarten let the canvas sack slip off his shoulders as he turned the rented boat towards another large hotel, the Songkhla Longun. The wind changed, and Maarten's shirt began to luff in the dull breeze. He slowed as he approached the hotel's marina, then cut the engine entirely as he passed the *Algul Siento*, a sleek white cruiser tethered to the outermost slip. For a moment, he forgot about the dead bodies near the lagoon. He kept his eyes forward, but his hand began to tremble as he marked the soft glow of yellow light from the lower cabin and the movement of shadows within. The middle-aged skipper of the boat, a light-skinned Thai in an eggshell captain's jacket, was working outside near the bow, getting the trim cruiser ready to pull out again. Maarten looked away, trying to act casual, disinterested, pre-occupied, invisible; but he was unable to contain the nervous grin that was spreading across his face.

He's here, he thought.

"I was getting worried."

He threw his pack on the bed and turned to Nora. Pale skin and large eyes, crew-cut flaxen hair, the girl looked a little bit like a lemur. But a smart lemur.

"More death," he said, pulling her into his arms. He kissed her on the cheek, and then dipped his face into the nape of her neck for a full draught, but she pulled away. He worked off his clothes — they stank of sweat and swamp — and he tried to kiss her full on the mouth, but this time she pushed him back against the bed. He began to sneeze.

"Fucking air conditioning."

Nora laughed and undressed, then lay down beside him; they faced one another, legs intertwined, silent. They fit together well, he thought, like two pieces of a jigsaw puzzle. A puzzle of which they were only a small part. He pulled Nora closer, her body warm in the air-conditioned room. She licked the cold sweat from his forehead. He sneezed again, but had nowhere to wipe his nose. He got up and headed for the bathroom.

"I hate travel," he said, and Nora laughed again. When he returned, he tossed the five ID cards on the bed, then sat beside her. She sorted through them only briefly, buried her head in her hands and cried.

"He's definitely here," he said, and he reached for the phone on the stand beside the bed. The receiver was the old-fashioned kind, heavy and black. It felt good in his hand. Nora looked up. She'd stopped crying, and Maarten nodded. "The boat's back. You were right."

She didn't say anything, she didn't move, but her eyes narrowed. With his other hand Maarten grabbed the tattered notebook off the counter and turned to its first page. When he started to dial, Nora moved closer and started to play with his wet hair.

"He won't stay long," she said.

"No. They're prepping the boat to head back out. If he's going back to the labs, we won't have much time." He placed the old-style receiver to his ear. This was the first of the final phone calls, the last chance to bring together as many of the remaining pieces of the puzzle as he could.

Nora rolled off the wet bed and began to pace, naked, back and forth. She padded over to the honor bar, cracked the cap on another tiny bottle of Sang Som whisky, a local blend of industrial ethanol created in a chemical factory in Nakhon Pathom. She turned to Maarten as her somnambulant tongue began to explore the lip of the bottle. She was thinking, her eyes far off. "He won't go back to the labs. He'll sail farther north, to the offices. We'll catch him when he returns, in the morning," she said.

Maarten nodded. There was no point arguing. Nora was always right. She took a long slow pull of whisky.

"He's here," Maarten said again, only this time into the receiver, speaking to Binh Milai Nghiem, a woman from Vietnam. She had checked into Room 1968 of the Songkhla Longun earlier that day. Maarten didn't speak Vietnamese any more than he spoke Russian or Thai, but he counted on the polyglotism of others, and he wasn't often disappointed.

"We're meeting tomorrow morning," he said to Binh, and the thin Vietnamese voice on the other end of the line suddenly filled with fury. Fury was a language he did understand. Maarten consulted the notebook and his notes, or rather the notes that Nora had collected. Binh had lost her father when the old man stepped between a rogue corrections officer and his target in Nha Trang, back in South Vietnam. The steel knife that had been thrown from across the open market had split her father's cranium. Six others were injured as the so-called "corrections officer" raced among the food stalls, upsetting with equal disinterest vegetable carts and lives.

Maarten slid his finger to the next name and number on the list. He dialed Akemi Lemai Mitsui in Room 1939. She worked in a small ryokan outside Kyoto. Her sister had been killed in Tokyo by a "drunken tourist" driving a speeding Toyota 2000 GT. Cars spun out as the driver raced through a busy intersection, and the Toyota clipped the motor scooter upon which Akemi's sister was riding, sending it through a window of a crowded Tokyo *sushi-ya*. "Be at the pool by oh-seven-hundred," he said to Henri Granson, a middle-aged banker from Switzerland. He was in Room 1476, facing the pool. Both his son and daughter-in-law were killed above Lausanne when they were forced off an alpine road by a certain "psychiatric outpatient" driving a Ferrari 355 GTS. "Everything's ready," he said to Marthe Resnais, a French teenager in Room 1957. She lost both parents when a Yamaha XJ500 motorcycle collided with the main gate of a department store in Paris, between the Opéra and the Gare St-Lazare. The bike's fuel tank exploded after the driver — a certain "Algerian anarchist" — jumped free. Her parents were burned beyond recognition. Albert Evrecy, a surgeon at the American Hospital of Paris, lost his daughter an hour earlier, when the same motorcycle bounced down all 4,352 steps of Montmartre in the north of Paris. His daughter cracked her head on a concrete pedestal as she jumped out of its way. He was in Room 1944. "It's now or never," he said to Damien Holt, a businessman from Florida. His mother had been killed when a motorboat driven by a certain "drug runner" jumped shore and plowed through an outdoor wedding party before dropping back into the causeway on the far side. Damien was currently delayed by bad weather in Chicago. "I don't want to hear excuses," Maarten said, massaging his temple with his free hand. He hated playing the heavy. "No one's going to wait for you." There was an explosion of American expletives, and Maarten hung up.

Nora came to sit beside him. She was holding another treasure from the honor bar, an unopened bottle of Stolichnaya. He smiled and she held it out to him, and Maarten admired the gold cursive script of the label over the simple drawing of the Hotel Moskva. He took the bottle from her and unscrewed the cap. It came open easily, too easily, and he wondered how many times the vodka had been cut by the hotel staff, not that he really cared. He put the bottle to his lips. He didn't like making these calls; he didn't like talking to the others, or re-reading Nora's notes. But he liked being here with her, he liked the feeling of having purpose, and he longed for closure. He took a drink, savoring the spicy after-burn on his tongue. It didn't matter whether the vodka was watered-down knock-off Cambodian, or straight from Russia. With love and longing and hate and fear he finished one drink after another.

Farmer, maid, student, surgeon, businessman….

He closed his eyes. The list was longer than that, he knew. So many innocent victims — and so many left behind. *Grieving friends, lovers, next-of-kin.* And why? For what reason? He took another drink and felt the familiar rage building inside him as he imagined the names on his list. Death by *corrections officer, drunken tourist, drug runner, Algerian anarchist.* He shook his head. Taken separately, he knew, each incident seemed credible, if unlikely. But together they weaved a vast web of treachery, a web with a single lethal spider at its center. *This* he had learned from Nora.

"Just because you're paranoid" she had said shortly after they had met, "doesn't mean they're not after you." It was one of a thousand rotten chestnuts she shared along with the misery, day and night, back in those dark days after the incident that had brought them together, after their own devastating loss. But Maarten didn't mind. Anything that sidetracked him from his own bereavement was welcome those days, even as she rambled increasingly and incoherently about the Mossad and MI6, calling on Her Majesty's Secret Service, or maybe the *Deuxième Bureau*, even the CIA. With her legs over his shoulders, it didn't really matter where her mind was.

Now Nora lay back on the bed, naked on top of the sheets. There were goose pimples on her arms and legs, thanks to the air conditioning, and she shivered slightly. He leaned over and captured her hard nipple between his lips. He tasted hotel soap and roses, and determination and loathing and payback, but no desire — not for him anyway, not anymore. He sank back on the bed beside her.

"Tomorrow morning," he whispered, and she sighed and draped an arm over his chest.

Time passed and Nora sat up, snagged the remote, and turned on the television. The TV was small and the reception was crappy, but Maarten was happy for the distraction. He sat up, too, and finished the Stolichnaya, while CNN International replayed the latest images of civil war in Iran. He watched an American-made tank firing towards a small clay building, a school. There was a bright explosion, then dust as tiny figures raced around the twisted remains of a jungle gym.

After a while, Nora stretched across the bed, across Maarten, to reach the phone. Maybe she'd been waiting for him to resume calling the names on their list, or maybe she just decided it was her turn. She opened the black notebook on Maarten's chest, and dialed Akando Lakota's mobile. He was in the Bangkok airport, negotiating flights. Akando's boyfriend had been beheaded in San Francisco when a fire truck — driven by a "disgruntled employee" — went out of control down Nob Hill. The ladder swung free, clipping anything that couldn't duck out of its way. She told Akando about the morning rendezvous. Nora also called Shira Lemos, an Israeli woman who had lost her son when the exclusive resort where he worked as senior sous-chef (a resort called Piz Gloria in the Swiss Alps) was attacked by certain "anarcho terrorists" in 1967. The resort was obliterated, blown right off the top of the mountain. Shira had arrived in Songkhla that afternoon and was checked into a room just down the hall. "Tomorrow morning," Nora said, "by the pool."

Maarten took another trip to the bathroom. Nora cracked a large bottle of San Pellegrino and joined him there, pouring the fizzy water into the small sink, emptying the bottle. She held it out to Maarten who just shrugged. She flipped the bottle over, held it by the neck, and raised it over her head like a club. Back in the bedroom, she pulled the two suitcases from under the bed. She unlatched each and began to check through their contents before adding the empty bottle. Meanwhile Maarten made several courtesy calls to families in Jamaica, Istanbul, and Chechnya. He felt bad for them, and for the others who simply did not have the means to travel at the drop of a hat. Nora called Sardinia and Iceland. Maarten placed calls to the Bahamas, Kuwait, and back home in the Netherlands. Someone (perhaps Maarten, if he were lucky) would call them all one more time, he said, if everything went well. They talked to waiters, painters, retirees, and taxi drivers. Anyone who had lost someone who had been in the wrong place at the wrong time, who had become collateral damage — or worse, comic relief — at the hands of a certain well-traveled *provocateur*.

Nora zipped both suitcases closed, then slid them back underneath the bed.

"*Konichiwa*," "*al salaam a'alaykum*," "*hola*," Maarten said, clutching the wrinkled cheat sheet in his hands. His accent wasn't great, but the message was clear enough. Without even a common language, they shared an uncommon bond.

"*Il est ici.*"

Shortly before three-thirty in the morning, Nora rolled on top of Maarten, and they held each other. If you couldn't have sex in common with someone else, Maarten thought, half-asleep and still more than a little drunk from the cheap vodka, at least you could have death. He slipped back to sleep and dreamt about making love to Nora, wrapping his arms around her waif-like body, thrusting and grinning, cranking out one *petite mort* after another. *Live and let die*, he whispered into her ear. Nora held tight and came quietly, never one big orgasm, one big O, but always a pair, two tiny double-Os, one after another.

He settled his head against her ribs when they were done, feeling the hard bone beneath his cheek, riding the rise and fall of each breath, listening to the beat of her heart. He opened his eyes and wondered for a moment if it had *all* been a dream; but he couldn't tell.

He closed his eyes again and imagined her heart, like his, black and hot, a chunk of burning coal under incredible pressure. He watched it burn through the eons, and imagined the time, not far from now, when the fire in their chests would at last ignite. After all the pressure and heat, there would be release. Maarten imagined explosive brilliance. Its light, he knew, would illuminate *everything*. And their hearts would change from simple coal to diamond hardness, and they would discover a new path. Yes, that's what diamonds are for — everlasting light, peace, *a way out*.

They slept like this, dreaming fitfully, until five, when the travel alarm began chirping. They showered together without speaking, and the alarm was still chirping when they returned. Maarten spread the plastic IDs he had recovered from the Orbit security guards over the bed. The local authorities — such as they were — would either have informed the families by now, or not. It wasn't his problem, and it was probably a risk, but he still pulled out the local phone book in the desk by the bed. He telephoned the two families whose numbers he could find. He couldn't understand a word they spoke, but made them each an offer, an offer he had made to many others over many years. Maybe they understood, maybe they didn't.

Nora changed into a black one-piece swimsuit. He kneeled in front of her and hugged her and kissed her lycra belly. He changed into his bathing suit, pulling up the black and blue shorts with thin racing stripes of red and gold, fingering the material, tightening the drawstring. She covered herself in a wrap and he pulled on a thin terrycloth robe with the words *Songkhla Longun* embroidered in large cursive letters on its back.

Maarten's family had been killed in Amsterdam, just blocks from where he lived. A tour bus exploded along the Stadthouderskade, near the Rijksmuseum, and Maarten escaped with only minor burns on his arms and legs. His parents were killed instantly, both decapitated by flying debris. His sister lost an arm and a leg to shrapnel, and then died three days later from her burns.

He met Nora in Intensive Care. Her fiancé had been injured in the same "accident." (A broken fuel line, they were told, met an open flame, thanks to a careless — and unidentified — "Scottish repairman.") They didn't speak, but spent hours sitting beside one another on the red Formica bench in the Garhadt Wing of the New Amsterdam Hospital, waiting for the worst news imaginable from the large swinging doors at the far end of the hall. They sat surrounded by others who drifted in and out of their own despair, whispering, sobbing, pacing, hour after hour, waiting for nurse, hospitalist, specialist, doctor. No one could fault any of them. When on the third day — just moments after Maarten had received his own terrible news — Nora was told her fiancé had died, she simply pressed her head lightly against his shoulder.

Eventually Maarten stopped crying: everyone does. And when Nora finally spoke, it was to say she wouldn't leave the hospital, not until they caught the man who had killed her fiancé. Maarten looked at her as if she were crazy. Who was she talking about? The operator of the tour bus? The Scottish repairman? The manufacturer of the defective fuel line? Maarten had a better idea. He took Nora's hand. "Let's get drunk," he said. She demurred, but they left the hospital together anyway. She reiterated the necessity of finding the man who had killed her fiancé in the first bar, and the second, and then again later in his apartment, and in his bed. She couldn't stop talking, and with each passing hour, her story grew. She talked about calling the cops, about conditions and conspiracies, the company, the circus, the *secret world*. Maarten alternately ignored and humored her. All things considered, it seemed the best approach. Then, six days after the accident, Maarten — really mostly interested in getting her to shut up — really thinking he was just calling her bluff — or, rather, not really thinking at all — said *why wait?* Why wait for the cops to find whoever was responsible, why not just find him ourselves? Why not just find the bastard and *kill him* ourselves?

Nora fell quiet, for the first time in days. It was a relief, really. And Maarten thought he'd hit the jackpot: now there'd be sex *and* silence. But then she started to glow. Her eyes opened wide, filled with an intense and sudden clarity. Maarten didn't quite get it at the time — and if it had been anyone else, nothing would have happened — but another bluff had been called.

That afternoon, Nora made several phone calls, weaving in and out of the paranoid narrative she'd perfected over the past week, each call slightly more hysterical than the last. Then she dragged him from bed, forced him to dress, and took him downtown to meet — "Seriously?" he asked — her stepfather, whom she claimed was a liaison officer in the mayor's office who worked with the internal security service of the KPLD, the *Korps Landelijke Politiediensten*.

They arrived shortly after dusk. No sooner had they entered his cavernous office in the Blunkpedt Tower in the old government center, Maarten could tell Nora's stepfather had as little enthusiasm for this get-together as he had. There were few words exchanged during the twenty minutes they all sat together, with Nora providing most of the talking and all of the emotion. Nora's stepfather was tall and gaunt, both sinister and spectral in the shadowy light of the office. He sat with his hands templed before him throughout the meeting, his face betraying only a cool tolerance, and Maarten couldn't shake the feeling that he was sitting across from a relative of Vladimir Putin, or Vlad the Impaler. A lot of energy was expended avoiding each other's eyes. When towards the end of their twenty minutes together, Nora's stepfather stood and — his face still a mask — thanked them both for coming in, Maarten heaved a sigh of relief. He was ready to get out of there, and eager to climb back into bed with his frisky, if somewhat damaged, girlfriend.

Maarten grabbed his jacket and stood. He extended his hand to Nora's stepfather, but the older man ignored it, and instead slowly pushed a plain manila folder across the desk.

It was a deliberate action, precise and with intent, but Maarten had no idea what it meant. He was about to ask, but Nora — clearly more savvy in this matter, as in others — simply reached out and flipped the folder open without leaving her seat. Her stepfather, saying nothing, moved towards the large window facing west, turning his back, seemingly transfixed on the distant rush-hour traffic. Nora began flipping pages, and Maarten sat back down.

There was, of course, no "Scottish repairman." No accident, either. Nora slid the open folder in front of Maarten. With a trembling hand, he turned page after page. Even with large blocks of redacted text, it was a revelation. It was a cover-up. A dozen cover-ups. A hundred! Page after page of "unpremeditated death," of "casualties in confidence," of "case closed" and "for secret services rendered." It was all there, the documented aftershocks of geopolitical skullduggery, and the falsified history to conceal responsibility.

Maarten continued to flip pages, and Nora stabbed her finger at name after name. "Corrections officer," "drunken tourist," "psychiatric outpatient," "diamond dealer." Cover stories for the crimes of David Somerset, Sir Hilary Bray, Peter Franks, Commander Bond, Burt Saxby, Robert Sterling, Colonel Luis Toro.... *So many names!*

Maarten closed the folder, overwhelmed and suddenly exhausted. But Nora wasn't done with him yet. She took his hand and forced his fingers over the small label that ran along the outside edge of the manila folder. It took him a moment to understand what she was showing him, but when this second revelation came it was at least as brutal as the first. So many different names, yes. But for all of them a single designation. A single number.

A single agent.

When Nora stood, her stepfather turned from the window. His face was dark, distant, but now also vaguely sad. Perhaps, Maarten remembered thinking, this was the first time manipulation, destabilization, assassination, and the raw exercise of power had struck so close to home.

"This will get you started," he said.

In his hand was a tiny slip of paper. Nora took it from him without a word, and together she and Maarten left the old government center.

Maarten quit his job. He didn't have a plan, but he'd always been good at action. He sold his parents' apartment and his own, and consolidated his inheritance. Soon he and Nora began to travel. Tracing each strand of the web. Finding some of those who had been caught. Working their way towards its center....

They finished dressing. Nora asked how she looked. Maarten said she looked fine. They kissed out of habit, and then Maarten picked up the first suitcase.

They walked through the lobby at ten minutes after six in the morning. It was deserted of guests. The few hotel workers — behind the front desk, or polishing the marble tile floor — paid them no mind. They walked towards the pool and then beyond to the edge of the marina. The sun was rising, still low over the water.

"The cruiser's gone," she said.

He nodded. The *Algul Siento* was not yet back in its slip. "Good."

Keeping the dock in sight, they returned to the pool. Akemi Mitsui, Henri Granson, and Marthe Resnais were there, waiting for them. They looked uncomfortable, standing together but not speaking. Granson was dressed like a tourist, in shorts and a brightly-colored shirt, but both Akemi and Marthe were wearing whatever clothes they had traveled in the day before. Those arriving on the early flights from Bangkok appeared next. Then those from privately-chartered planes and boats. Maarten greeted each new arrival with a handshake, and Nora placed several towels at a table with an umbrella and then ordered breakfast. They were an odd bunch, no doubt about it, thrown together by coincidence, happenstance; making everything up as they went along. Hotel guests arriving for their morning swim did their best to ignore the incongruous group — now numbering fourteen — but the hotel staff took notice.

Maarten ordered drinks for everyone. The waiter asked if they were all guests of the hotel, and Maarten lied and said yes. When the drinks began to arrive, he pressed a hefty tip into the hands of the waiter. Maarten didn't think it would change much, and he didn't think it would matter. At eight-fifteen, the hotel's concierge dropped by. More money was disbursed. Shortly afterwards, Nora went back to their room and returned with the second suitcase. As the morning grew hotter, the few with bathing suits took turns swimming.

Just after nine, Nora tapped him on the arm. "*He's coming,*" she whispered, pointing out into the Gulf. She could barely contain her excitement.

"It's time," Maarten said, calling everyone over. Despite the palm trees and the balmy weather, it felt like Christmas. Nora unlatched both suitcases and began passing out the pocket knives and sharp pencils, the broom handle, the tightly-rolled socks, the water bottle and cricket bat. Maarten balled his hands into fists. He turned away to give them time to pull themselves together; and waited, allowing his eyes to rest on the trim cruiser in the distance.

Orbis non sufficit.

"Enough"

First and last lines from
Lord of the Flies by William Golding

I always wanted to write a story about the extensive (and all but ignored) "collateral damage" in the James Bond series. Think about all those people whose lives he's upset, directly or indirectly, all the unintended victims of his casual violence who suffer and yet, within the frame of the series, are unimportant and unrecognized. This is their sadly pathetic (as it must be) revenge. Mine, too.

Written between 21 July 2004 to 22 April 2006

List of First/Last Lines

What follows are the first/last lines used in this collection. In nearly every case, the lines came from the relatively random act of grabbing a book off the bookshelf, and just running with whatever I got. In a few cases I rejected what chance offered, and usually for one of two reasons: the lines were too familiar (for example, "It was a bright cold day in April, and the clocks were striking thirteen"[1] — impossible to leave the source behind) or the lines left too little to the imagination (For example, "One summer afternoon Mrs. Oedipa Maas came home from a Tupperware party whose hostess had put perhaps too much kirsch in the fondue to find that she, Oedipa, had been named executor of the estate of one Pierce Inverarity, a California real estate mogul who had once lost two million dollars in his spare time but still had assets numerous and tangled enough to make the job of sorting it all out more than honorary"[2] — see?).

I worked on these stories one at a time, and only when I finished a story, would I grab a new pair of lines to start the next. Sometimes the stories came right away; other times, I'd stare and stare, put the lines down, take a walk, drink a dog, eat a beer, and come back just to stare some more.

I wrote about thirty stories during the three or four years I was experimenting with literary taxidermy. Some of them certainly deserve to be forgotten; others were interesting,

---

[1] *Nineteen Eighty-Four* by George Orwell.

[2] *The Crying of Lot 49* by Thomas Pynchon.

but never felt finished — maybe I'll revisit them someday.

But some of the stories haunt me. I'm not saying they're any good — not in the grand scheme of things. But they're the ones that stuck with me, more than a decade later. They're the ones I've shared in *The Gymnasium*, and these are the opening/closing lines that sparked their creation:

Introduction

We slept in what had once been the gymnasium.

Are there any questions?

> — MARGARET ATWOOD, *THE HANDMAID'S TALE*

"Beatrice Dalle"

The scent and smoke and sweat of a casino are nauseating at three in the morning.

"Yes, dammit, I said 'was.' The bitch is dead now."

> — IAN FLEMING, *CASINO ROYALE*

"Rum Alley"

A very little boy stood upon a heap of gravel for the honor of Rum Alley.

"Oh, yes, I'll fergive her! I'll fergive her!"

> — STEPHEN CRANE, "MAGGIE"

"The Engagement Party"

I saw him on a sleepless night when I was walking desperately to save my soul and my vision.

Whither *he* has gone, I do not know; but I have gone home to the pure New England lanes up which fragrant sea-winds sweep at evening.

> — H.P. LOVECRAFT, "HE"

"Quiver"

There was nobody to see him off, of course, why would there be, and now the rain was coming down again.

He let the clutch out fast and pulled away from the lights, leaving the woman leaning on her windowsill, not thinking anything, just breathing, dreaming.

— RUPERT THOMSON, *SOFT*

"*Sabotaje*"

There was a wall.

His hands were empty, as they had always been.

— URSULA K. LeGUIN, *THE DISPOSSESSED*

"Trump l'Oeil"

God doesn't play nice.

Hail the Führer!

— MARK MALAMUD, *THE RECTANGULAR RUINS*

"The Tyrant of Arcadia"

Before entering the supreme council room, Gabriel Baines sent his Mans-made simulacrum clacking ahead to see if by chance it might be attacked.

But of what he could not quite yet tell.

— PHILIP K. DICK, *CLANS OF THE ALPHANE MOON*

"Boardwalk"

"I really do think, Mr. Carnelian, that we should at least *try* them raw, don't you?"

They kissed.

— MICHAEL MOORCOCK, *THE END OF ALL SONGS*

"*Beta vulgaris*"

The beet is the most intense of the vegetables.

Indigo. Indigoing. Indigone.

— TOM ROBBINS, *JITTERBUG PERFUME*

"The Intruder"

The woman might have been sixty or sixty-five.

It was in such circumstances that Agnes longed to buy a forget-me-not, a single forget-me-not stem; she longed to hold it before her eyes as a last, scarcely visible trace of beauty.

— MILAN KUNDERA, *IMMORTALITY*

"Proof"

"There are dragons in the twins' vegetable garden."

Then she went up to Charles Wallace.

— MADELEINE L'ENGLE, *A WIND IN THE DOOR*

"A Terrible Memory"

I told her there's a reason it's worn around your neck, but she only laughed.

Perfect memory, like any good sadist, cannot resist the urge to wound.

— TREMOR MARSDEN, *NOT ON MY WATCH*

"Creator, Destroyer"

It is wonderful with what warm enthusiasm well-kept people who have never been alone in all their life can congratulate you on the joys of solitude.

And that is a moment of dark time, that is one of strange million-visaged time's dark faces.

— THOMAS WOLFE, "NO DOOR"

"Housemade"

I have a dreadful long-term memory.

And this baby, made in India, will always remind me that India, to some extent, made me.

— SARAH MACDONALD, *HOLY COW*

"Warm Fragile Safe"

While the present century was in its teens, and on one sunshiny morning in June, there drove up to the great iron gate of Miss Pinkerton's academy for young ladies, on Chiswick Mall, a large family coach, with two fat horses in blazing harness, driven by a fat coachman in a three-cornered hat and wig, at the rate of four miles an hour.

Which of us has his desire? or, having it, is satisfied? — come, children, let us shut up the box and the puppets, for our play is played out.

— WILLIAM MAKEPEACE THACKERY, *VANITY FAIR*

"Not in Our Stars"

I first saw the light in the city of Boston in the year 1857.

Fortunate is he who, with a case as desperate as mine, finds a judge so merciful.

— EDWARD BELLAMY, *LOOKING BACKWARD*

"Pop"

In watermelon sugar the deeds were done and done again as my life is done in watermelon sugar.

It would only be a few seconds now, I wrote.

— RICHARD BRAUTIGAN, *IN WATERMELON SUGAR*

"Labiovelora"

As the streets that lead from the Strand to the Embankment are very narrow, it is better not to walk down them arm-in-arm.

Across his eyes passed a procession of objects, black and indistinct, the figures of people picking up their books, their cards, their balls of wool, their work-baskets, and passing him one after another on their way to bed.

— VIRGINIA WOOLF, *THE VOYAGE OUT*

"Enough"

The boy with the fair hair lowered himself down the last few feet of rock and began to pick his way toward the lagoon.

He turned away to give them time to pull themselves together; and waited, allowing his eyes to rest on the trim cruiser in the distance.

— WILLIAM GOLDING, *LORD OF THE FLIES*

***

I enjoyed working on these stories. They were exciting and challenging in ways I hadn't expected when I read my very first opening line ("While the present century was in its teens, and on one sunshiny morning in June…") and began to stitch together that very first story ("Warm Fragile Safe").

If you find the idea of literary taxidermy intriguing, or think you might want to try your hand at it someday, keep reading….

You, Too, May Become a Taxidermist!

I started these stories as a simple writing exercise. An easy, fast way to challenge myself in-between other larger, longer projects. When I began, my curiosity was focused on where each pair of first and last lines (some of them with quite well-known trajectories) would take *me*. But that changed rather quickly.

Understand: I didn't write these stories alone. I don't mean they were collaborations (except, perhaps, indirectly, with the authors of the original lines), but that the idea behind literary taxidermy was always meant as an exercise for *writers*, plural. And that's how it worked, right from the start. I began with my friend Paul Van Zwalenburg (thank you, Paul!), then slowly added other participants, and we'd each take the same first and last lines, go off by ourselves, and then return a few days later with completed stories.

To be honest, I didn't expect much from the resulting effort. I assumed that given the same constraints, different writers would still come up with radically different stories. Sure, each story might have a character named "Agnes" (because she's mentioned in the first line), but beyond that? Well, it seemed obvious. There'd be *nothing* beyond that. The use of these first and last lines was no more than a random seed, individual writer's abilities and sensibilities would dominate the result, and the only interesting aspect (beyond my selfish curiosity about the path *I* took) would be to see just how wildly divergent the stories were. A little bit of *Wow, how did you get there?*, ha-ha, and then done.

I was wrong.

By the time we finished writing the first four stories, it became clear something *odd* was going on. Yes, the stories were all different, but certain *similarities* were cropping up in each of our narratives that didn't originate in the first and last lines — or at least, not obviously. So while it might make sense that all the stories framed by the first and last lines of *Casino Royale* would feature a casino, what would explain how those stories also featured ghosts? What was hidden within the first and last lines of *Lord of the Flies* to make conspiracies feature so prominently? You can *almost* understand how the first line of *A Wind in the Door* might produce stories for which "truth" is a theme, but why did every story framed by *The Dispossessed* feature clanking bottles of beer?

Were certain words in those opening/closing lines unconscious triggers? Was it subliminal suggestion — some sort of latent meaning hidden in a turn of phrase? Was it our own unrealized common circumstance, or knowledge of the source material? Authorial vapidity? Magic? I have no idea. But by the time the first dozen stories were complete, finding the unexpected (and often uncanny) commonalities across the stories was at least as interesting as what was in the stories themselves.

Which, long way around, brings us to the end of this book, and some thoughts for going forward.

First, as you've already realized, each story in this current collection has one or more absent siblings: new stories written by *other* authors with identical first and last lines. For *The Gymnasium*, I went for breadth over depth — nineteen stories written with nineteen different opening/closing lines, all by a single author. But those missing sibling stories are fascinating in comparison and in their own right, and I think it would be exciting to assemble an anthology composed entirely of stories with the same opening/closing lines, written by different authors.

Second, and to that end, I want to encourage you, the reader, to become the writer. Regulus Press has decided to host a competition to create a brand-new anthology of literary taxidermy. They're looking for writers, both amateur and professional, to fashion their own short stories from the opening/closing lines of several famous works of fiction. This is your chance to get your hands dirty and join the community of literary taxidermists.

For the latest on the competition (and to learn more about the possibilities of literary taxidermy), visit:

www.literarytaxidermy.com

I look forward to seeing what you come up with.

Mark Malamud
21 December 2017

28100848R00174

Printed in Great Britain
by Amazon